PENGUIN BOOKS

Murder on the Run

Medora Sale has a Ph.D. in medieval studies. A former
teacher of English, she is the author of *Murder in Focus*,
Murder in a Good Cause and *Sleep of the Innocent*, all
available from Penguin Books. She lives with her family
in Toronto.

MURDER ON THE RUN
Medora Sale

Penguin Books

PENGUIN BOOKS
Published by the Penguin Group
Penguin Books Canada Ltd, 10 Alcorn Avenue,
Toronto, Ontario, Canada M4V 1E4
Penguin Books Ltd, 27 Wrights Lane,
London W8 5TZ, England
Penguin Books USA Inc.,
375 Hudson Street, New York, New York 10014, U.S.A.
Penguin Books Australia Ltd, Ringwood, Victoria, Australia
Penguin Books (NZ) Ltd, 182-190 Wairau Road, Auckland 10,
New Zealand

Penguin Books Ltd, Registered Offices:
Harmondsworth, Middlesex, England

First published by Paperjacks, 1986

Published in Penguin Books, 1991

1 3 5 7 9 10 8 6 4 2

*Publisher's note: This book is a work of fiction. Names,
characters, places and incidents either are the product of the
author's imagination or are used fictitiously, and any
resemblance to actual persons living or dead, events, or locales
is entirely coincidental.*

Manufactured in Canada

Canadian Cataloguing in Publication Data
Sale, Medora
Murder on the run

ISBN 0-14-013882-X

I. Title.

PS8587.A35387M875 1991   C813'.54   C90-095720-4
PR9199.3.S165M875 1991

To Harry
sine quo nihil

Chapter One

The girl walked slowly along the street, her feet in heavy hiking boots dragging slightly with every step or two. Her hands were jammed in the pockets of her jeans; her chin was tucked into her sweater against the cold March wind. As she walked, she thought bitterly about the afternoon ahead of her. "It wasn't me," she muttered, kicking a small rock viciously out of her path. "I didn't make the agency go bankrupt." And just when she was getting somewhere. Everyone had been impressed with her artwork for the supermarket campaign, really impressed. Robert, of course, said that she should have been able to figure out by then that Smith and Hines was going under and that she should find another job before it was too late. So it was her fault, as usual. And it would be her fault if she didn't get this job, too. She considered going back to the apartment and looking over her portfolio one more time. Maybe there were too many pen-and-ink pieces in it. She could put in some zippier stuff — one of those really jazzy, sexy, geometric oil pastels, perhaps. She'd go home right now. No. There were four hours to get through before the interview and she needed to keep moving. Her pace picked up slightly as she pondered the technical problem of assembling her portfolio for maximum effect. But what if she didn't get this job, either? She couldn't go on living off Robert and listening to him sneer about people who slept in every day. Okay, she said to herself, if I don't get this one, I'll just go out and get a job. Any job. Polish up the typing, or whatever, and wait until things pick up. The effect of making the decision was magical. She took a deep breath of relief, straightened her shoulders, lifted her chin out of her sweater, and tossed her brown hair out of her eyes as she strode along.

Directly ahead of her a pleasant-looking, obviously baffled young man was blocking her way. He was leaning on the open door of his vehicle, a battered road map clutched in his hand. "Excuse me, Miss," he said, smiling politely, "but would you happen to know where Hawthorne Crescent is? I don't seem to be able to find it here." She stopped and looked at him, then bent her head over the map, her eyes squinting against the bright sun. The blow to her temple was so swift and hard that she felt nothing at all.

Less than two hours later Detective Inspector John Sanders found himself standing uneasily in the corridors of Toronto General Hospital. He had sent his working mate, Sergeant Ed Dubinsky, to find out what was new and to collect whatever the hospital had of interest. Compared to most of the world, Sanders was a tall man, and even lounging against the wall, he dwarfed the nurses and orderlies who rushed back and forth in front of him. In the midst of his calculations on the distance to the nearest coffee machine, Dubinsky loomed into view, filling the hall with his bulk, looking impassive as always. "Well?" Sanders asked irritably.

"Not much," said Dubinsky. "She's alive, out of surgery, unconscious, and probably won't make it."

"Can they tell what happened to her?"

"Pretty much. She appears to have been raped. There is" — he pulled out his notebook — "extensive injury to her face and to the cranium. That's the head bones," he added, by way of explanation.

"Yeah," said Sanders, "I know." A kaleidoscope of bloodied faces, smashed in and unrecognizable, rushed up from his memory, and his stomach lurched.

"Oh. Anyway, they've sealed up the evidence and sent it over to Forensic."

"Do we know who she is?"

"Not yet. Did you see her when she came in?" Sanders shook his head. "The bastard had sliced most of her clothes off; she had nothing on but hiking boots, half a sweater, and some scraps of jeans or something. She look-ed pretty terrible. Anyway, she didn't have any identifica-tion on her."

"Let's get out of here," Sanders said abruptly. "Where did they find her?"

"Rosedale Ravine, beside a path."

"Dammit," he said, rubbing his hand over his head. "I suppose we'd better have a look."

Five minutes later they were pulling into the city works department road at the bottom of the ravine. "Christ," he said to Dubinsky, as they walked from the car down the frozen footpath into the bitter wind, "who would feel like raping someone in this weather? Any why in hell do these women go for nature walks in the middle of deserted ravines? You'd think by now they'd have heard it was unhealthy."

"We don't know she was walking in the ravine. He could have done it somewhere else and dumped her here when he was through. The snow looks pretty undisturbed." They stood in silence and watched a small crew of men combing the area.

"Worthless exercise," said Sanders. "They won't find anything. Let's go. Nothing to do here until some results come in. And I need some coffee."

"Who found her?" asked Sanders, back at his desk, coffee in hand.

"Some kid from Leaside. Just a minute, I've got it all here." Dubinsky pulled out his notebook. "Yeah. Gavin Ellis, age nineteen, was running to work down this path about 10:30 this morning and noticed a dog growling and sniffing around something. Said he'd stopped to tie his shoe, otherwise he wouldn't have seen her or paid any attention to the dog. Those ravines are full of dogs."

"Did he do it?"

"Naw. Not unless he did it in one hell of a hurry. His mother said he left for work in his running clothes at 10:15. She noticed the time because he was already late. He isn't even much use as a witness, because he was plugged into one of those bloody radios as he ran, so he wouldn't have heard anything that wasn't pretty loud. Anyway, he ran over to Mount Pleasant and flagged down a patrol car at 10:35."

"Still, this Ellis may have interrupted him." Sanders twirled his pen around a couple of times, then started sketching outlines of bodies on the scratch pad in front of him. He added bushes behind one of them and drew in a tortuous path. "The others were dead when we found them."

"Pity he didn't interrupt him a little earlier, then."

Sanders was drawing in rocks and gravel on the path. "That bastard has been bloody lucky." He put down his pen. "He jumps strong healthy females in broad daylight. Not one of them screams or resists, as far as we can tell. They're all attacked in the open, and no one sees it. Jesus. What does he do? Hypnotize them? And where in hell were the patrols? Those ravines are supposed to be patrolled night and day." Dubinsky didn't bother to answer. Sanders dropped his head on his hands and stared at his sketch. "Well, let's look at the lot of them, and maybe something will connect this time." He pulled a thick file toward him and started to flip through it. "The first one — as far as we know, anyway. January 16th, a Monday. Serena Gundy Park. Barbara Elizabeth Lash, age twenty-seven, married, two kids, housewife. Left the kids at her mother's and went for a walk, trying to lose some weight after the holidays. Two o'clock in the afternoon, approximately. She was wearing" — he ran his finger down the page rapidly.

"What does that matter?"

"Who knows? Maybe this guy only attacks women wearing hiking boots or something like that." He skimmed through a couple of pages. "Nope. She was wearing wool slacks, a pea jacket, and snow boots, according to her mother. Just a few scraps of cloth, according to the first man on the scene. Nobody heard anything, saw anything. Found by a couple of kids playing in the ravine after school. I wonder if they still play there," he said, looking up. "Anyway, next victim. February 3rd, a Friday. High Park. Kirsten Johansson, age thirty-five, divorced, one child. A waitress. Lived with another woman who worked at the same restaurant. She had the afternoon off and went cross-country skiing. Roommate said she was probably wearing a heavy sweater, corduroy knickers, long red socks, and ski boots — as you might expect, since she was out skiing. Found by a man taking his dog for a run in the park at 5:00 P.M. Nobody heard or saw anything suspicious." Dubinsky yawned and scratched his ear. They had gone through this material each time something new had come in, and nothing in this recital excited him.

"Sandra Diane Miller, age eighteen, student. February 28th, a Tuesday. The old Belt Line park, south of Eglinton Avenue. That's hardly a remote area, you know. She was walking home from school. Lived at home with her family. Wearing gray tights, gray skirt, middy blouse — what's that?"

"She was in her school uniform, I think."

"Oh. Anyway, red ski jacket and snow boots. See, Dubinsky, they were all wearing boots. All we have to do is round up all the boot fetishists in town and ——"

Dubinsky pitched his coffee cup into the wastepaper basket. "It's winter, John. Every woman in the city is wearing boots. My wife is wearing boots. So is yours."

Sanders pushed the file aside and rubbed the back of his neck. "I feel godawful. I'm hung over; I got no sleep last night; I haven't had any breakfast; and I spent the morning propping up a wall in a lousy hospital. The papers are screaming for someone's head — mine seems the likeliest choice — and every female in the city is terrified and refusing to go outside without an escort. Except for the stupid ones who are getting themselves killed. Marie thinks we're doing nothing about it because nobody gives a damn what happens to women anyway because we all work so late every night and don't make enough money to buy a vacation retreat in Florida. Or something like that. I lost the drift of her argument around my fifth or sixth scotch. Anyway," he said, dragging himself back to the file on his desk, "Miller was found soon after by two boys also walking home from school; she was still alive, almost naked, sexually assaulted, with half her face a bloody pulp. But they didn't see anyone else. She died on the way to the hospital. So, what does that tell us?"

"It tells us that he raped them and he beat them to a pulp and sometimes cut their throats if they didn't seem

dead enough. You left that out," said Dubinsky impatiently. "And they're all under five foot five, so we're probably
looking for someone who is at least five foot six and
doesn't like tackling someone his own size or bigger. And
there weren't any signs of a struggle at any of the scenes, so
he probably attacked them somewhere else and dumped
them. For chrissake, John, until something comes in from
Forensic on this one, there isn't anything in that file we
haven't gone over a hundred times. Let's go get some
lunch."

Sanders stood up without comment and reached for his
coat. His thin face was set in lines of black depression.

Amanda Griffiths stood on the bridge looking down over
Mount Pleasant Road where it bisected the ravine. She had
walked her friend Jennifer up to the bus stop. After the
bus left with her safely on it, Amanda and Leslie Smith
would walk little Heather home to the enormous house
next door to Amanda's. Really, thought Amanda, everyone was getting ridiculously paranoid. She was sick of
moving around in a big group all the time — like a herd of
sheep, she thought, or a school of green-uniformed fish.
She liked that; she'd have to put it into her next letter to
her mother. Her eye was caught by the two bright yellow
police cruisers parked by the side of the path leading down
into the ravine. This is too much, she thought. "Look,
Jenn. The ravine's full of cops. Johnson must have seen
the rapist again and called them out." Jennifer groaned
dramatically. Every day they got endless lectures on the
subject of traveling safely and avoiding supsicious-looking
characters, but Jennifer's tirade on the subject was cut
short by the arrival of her bus.

Amanda waved good-bye to Jennifer as she got on,
then, two minutes later, to Leslie as she ran up the stairs to
her front door. She and Heather plodded silently the short
distance to Forest Crescent; she conscientiously watched

until Heather had safely slammed her front door shut behind her; then she turned and trudged up the walk to Aunt Kate's. She hoped — without much expectation that her hopes would be realized — that Aunt Kate would be in. Somehow the house seemed very lonely on this bright and bitterly cold Thursday afternoon. She was supposed to be happy. It was the first day of the March break, and school had ended at noon. A whole afternoon with nothing to do, at least for Amanda. Leslie and Jennifer were going home to pack for Florida and the West Indies, respectively. It seemed to Amanda that she was the only girl in the entire school who wasn't fleeing south for the holidays this afternoon. She and little Heather next door, whose mother was a real estate agent and couldn't afford to miss the spring house-buying season. But who wants to spend the holidays amusing a ten-year-old? Even a nice one?

She walked slowly upstairs and through her bedroom to her study, dropped the knapsack full of books and notes on her desk, shrugged her coat off onto the floor, and headed back into the bedroom to get out of her uniform. She was shaken by a wave of homesickness. Tears spilled out of the corners of her eyes as she slowly began to crawl into her cords and warm sweater. It was very nice of Aunt Kate to let Amanda come and live with her while her parents went off to the States; it would have been silly to change school systems for just two years, and her aunt's offer saved her from being enrolled as a boarder. After fifteen years of being an only child, she didn't think that she would care for the communal existence, no matter how jolly it could be. But it was very unfair of her parents to be unavailable for the March break, or at least for the first week of it. Just as her spirits were sinking into the depths of self-pity, the front door crashed open.

"Amanda! Are you home? Let's go out and have

lunch!'' Aunt Kate's carrying tones galvanized her into movement. She grabbed her jacket and, taking them two at a time, leapt down the stairs.

"I don't know, Aunt Kate," said Amanda somberly as she spooned the last of her butterscotch sundae into her mouth. "It's just so awful around the school right now that I get really depressed."

"But I thought you were doing well there, with lots of friends and all that sort of thing. Aren't you? Oh dear, I'm really not very good at dealing with the crises of adolescence, I'm afraid. You'll have to forgive me. Put it down to lack of experience, and the general inelasticity of middle age." Kate looked inquisitively at her pretty niece, and then put down her cup with a small spasm of guilt. She had been too preoccupied with her own life; she should have been keeping closer track of the poor girl. "Now, if you were a Malaysian girl faced with an unsuitable choice of husband, I'd know what to say ——''

Amanda giggled. Aunt Kate's scholarly view of life always cheered her up. She looked at every problem as though it had occurred on one of her archeological expeditions and took it seriously, unlike most adults who assumed that what was wrong with you was merely some temporary hormonal imbalance. "No, Aunt Kate, it's not your fault at all. It's just that the atmosphere has been so grim lately. Ever since that girl at AGS was attacked on her way home from school — right in the middle of Forest Hill — everyone is jumpy. If you're under five foot four, like me, the whole world thinks you'll never make it home from school alive. It's depressing. And the new physics teacher is just awful. I had a whole hour of physics yesterday, and I don't think I'll be able to stand her until June. Physics used to be my best subject," she said mournfully. "I don't see why

Mrs. Resnick had to pick this year to have a baby. Conway is so mean, and yells all the time. She spends more time having fits than she does teaching.''

"She's *Mrs.* Conway, isn't she?"

"Mmm," said Amanda.

"She looked terribly familiar when I saw her at Parents' Night. I'm sure I've met her before. Didn't your dad have a Conway working for him on his last project?"

Amanda shook her head. "Dad has so many graduate students — I never knew any of their names except for the ones who used to babysit me when I was little."

"I'm sure I ran into her at one or two of those parties your dad gave for his crew. I remember that awful voice — whiny and aggrieved."

"That's her." Amanda pushed her dish aside. "I must have been hungry. I feel better now. And I like the school, really I do. It's a lot better than my old school out in Mississauga, especially since it's so close to downtown. Maybe I'll go shopping now — if you think I can walk down Yonge Street by myself."

Kate grinned at the challenge, unfolding her almost six-foot frame out of the booth. "I expect so. But why don't you walk over to the university about 4:30 or so and meet me in my office. We can celebrate the end of school with an early movie and then dinner. You're making me nervous now. I don't think you should be walking through Rosedale by yourself going home."

"Oh, Aunt Kate. Not you, too." And Amanda shrugged into her jacket, flipping her brown hair over the collar with a grimace at her aunt.

Sanders sat at his desk and drew little stick figures on a pad of paper. It was almost time to go home from a day that he might as well not have shown up for. He had arrived late and had had to chase after Dubinsky, catching up with him at the scene long after most of the routine work had been parceled out and half completed. Dubinsky had said

nothing — then — but some day it would come out in little jibes and digs at his not-so-superior superior officer.
And now Sanders should be running around, trying to find
out the victim's identity, what the preliminary findings had
been, whether this was the work of the same man, and just
what they had to go on from here. Instead he was sitting at
his desk waiting for the hours to tick by, pushing pieces of
paper around and pretending to be writing reports. Not
that he wanted to go home. The last thing he wanted to do
was to face Marie. Maybe he'd switch around and work
Friday, Saturday and Sunday. He looked up at the faint
sound of Dubinsky's cat-like tread. His partner raised one
enormous hand in greeting and dropped a sheaf of papers
on Sander's desk.

"Not much so far. Did you get the note from upstairs?"
Sanders shook his head. "I didn't think so. Anyway, they
want a mobile unit set up down there and the adjacent
neighbourhoods combed for anyone who might know
anything. Now."

"For chrissake! Do they realize how many 'adjacent
neighborhoods' there are to that ravine? How many men
are they giving us to do this? One?"

"As many as we like, they say. We're supposed to look
as though we're doing something useful to calm down the
citizens. Even if the activity itself doesn't do much good."
Dubinsky shrugged and pulled out his notebook. "Well,
this is what we've got. Number one: the lab found some
gold-colored fiber — a synthetic of some sort — imbedded in the girl's sweater. They'll give us more later, but it
looks like carpeting, they think."

"Sure. And when we find out who she is, it'll turn out
she had a gold rug and liked lying on the floor to watch
T.V. Any word on her identity?"

"Not yet. We might get something after the evening
news goes on."

"There's not much more we can do then. You go on
home. I'll see about setting up that mobile unit. I'll look

after it this weekend. It's time I got off my ass and started working." As Dubinsky picked up his coat, Sanders was reaching for the phone, his face blank and impassive.

It was ten o'clock on Friday morning before Dubinsky walked into the crowded, chaotic office and pulled out his chair at the pair of facing desks that he shared with Sanders. As far as he could tell, Sanders hadn't moved since the previous night. "You been home yet?" he asked casually.

"You're damn right I've been home," Sanders replied. "Have you ever considered how much time we waste driving home at night? And coming back in the morning? Do you ever think how nice it would be just not going home?"

Dubinsky gave him a guarded look. "No — no, I never do."

"I guess you wouldn't," he said. Why would he? thought Sanders. He isn't married to a painted doll who trapped him with honeyed, reluctant submission and then turned into a screaming shrew who paid out her favors one by one in return for concessions, until they didn't seem worth bargaining for any more. Sally was fierce, hard-working, and conscientious; she led Dubinsky a merry chase sometimes, but she was a real person. "You know, there's an apartment on a sublet ten blocks from here . . . but what the hell," Sanders said, clearing his mind for the time being. "The unit is ready to go. I have two shifts of four guys each. Where in hell have you been?"

"I just came back from interviewing a Robert Donaldson who works for an ad agency — he's an artist of some sort, I guess. His girlfriend — live-in type — called him yesterday morning at work to say that she had a job interview at two and was going to pass the time until then taking a nice long walk. When she wasn't home by six, he guessed that she'd bombed it and hadn't felt like coming home right then. That's happened before, he said. But she's never stayed out all night before, and after calling all her friends he called us. Anyway, he identified her — sort of. The hair and the body type are right. He's kind of shaken. We just got back from the hospital.''

"Could he have done it?''

"Maybe. He said he was at work all day, putting together a presentation. Easily checked. Do you want me to look into it?''

"Since you're going to be sitting around here doing nothing, sure. By the way, who was she?''

Dubinsky looked down at his notebook. "Mary Ellen Parsons, age twenty-three, commercial artist, currently unemployed. And the boyfriend's apartment has that smooth gray carpeting you get in offices. I checked.''

By Saturday at noon Sanders knocked on the twenty-fourth door of an imposing street close to the ravine. Beside him stood a taciturn young constable, hastily recruited from other duties to make up the special force demanded by the public, the papers, and therefore, the politicians. They had started Friday afternoon, and so far, the results had been less than worthwhile. Each fruitless hour spent reminded Sanders of the equally fruitless efforts made on each previous occasion, and only served to depress him further. Sanders knocked again. Finally he heard slow footsteps, and the door was partially opened, revealing a bright-eyed elderly lady and a large and sober-looking black Labrador retriever.

"Excuse me, ma'am'', said Sanders, for the twenty-fourth time that day. "We are police officers'' — he held out his identification, which she looked at long and carefully before raising her suspicious eyes. "We are investigating an attack on a young woman just a few blocks away from here, and we would like to know if you saw or heard anything at all unusual or suspicious-looking on Thursday — this last Thursday, the eighth.''

"Thursday, eh? Well, I don't know if it was on Thursday, but I saw something last week that disturbed me a great deal." Sanders looked up sharply at that. "I took Georgia here out for her walk at 6:00 A.M., the way I always do if I'm awake — and I usually am — and that's when I saw it."

"What did you see, ma'am?"

"One of those girls who deliver the papers around here in the morning, it was. It's a terrible thing, you know. It's dark out when they take those papers around, except during the summer. Can't you do something to stop them from hiring girls to do that?"

"I'm afraid we can't, ma'am," said Sanders, with barely concealed impatience. "If you let boys do it, you have to let girls do it, too. You know, equality."

"Piffle," said the old lady. "Anyway, as Georgia and I were coming along South Drive, there was one of those vans following the girl delivering the papers, moving very slowly just behind her. I tell you I was very worried."

"It was probably the manager for the district, ma'am — they often drive around to make sure everything is all right."

"No, it wasn't, young man. Because Georgia and I went right over and looked in the window at him, and stared at his license plate as well, and he speeded up and drove away. I tell you, he was one of those rapists, and you people should do something about him."

Sanders smiled, weary of the endless politeness this sort of duty required. That was what happened — nobody had anything useful to say, but every crank wanted to tell him what was wrong with the city, the police, the neighborhood. "Well, the young woman who was injured wasn't delivering papers, ma'am. She was probably attacked later in the morning as well. But I'll pass your comment along to the officers who patrol this area at that time in the morning. Thank you for your help." He kept smiling until the door closed in his face, and he turned away. He wondered if "neighborhoods adjacent to the ravine" could be construed as a description of Eleanor's house. It did back onto a ravine, although it wasn't quite the same one. Knocking on Eleanor's door was a tempting thought. Except that he'd still have this sour-faced kid stumping along behind him. It wasn't Sander's fault that the kid's weekend leave had been canceled and his love-life thrown for a loop. That'll teach him, he thought vindictively.

Five days later Sanders was sitting in the mobile unit, cursing its limited space and general lack of creature comforts. There wasn't even a bloody restaurant where you could get a lousy cup of coffee closer than fifteen minutes' brisk walk away. And what did they have? Nothing. Zero. Zilch. At least fifty suspicious-looking characters had been reported, most of them quiet, albeit odd-looking, neighbors, a few of them aged rummies who had staggered in from busier streets and neighborhoods, or up from the haven of the ravine where they spent their nights. None of them seemed likely to have had the strength or the desire to strip, rape, beat, and slice up a girl, even a smallish one. He had painstakingly followed up on most of the leads, only to end up back at nothing. And meanwhile the female population of the city was getting edgier and edgier.

The medical report lay in front of him. Contrary to expectation, she was still alive, but only just. There had been traces of recent intercourse, which along with the patterns of bruising on her body were consistent with rape by someone with blood type O positive. Her skull had been battered by a rounded object, possibly about twenty centimeters in diameter. There was probably massive brain damage. Other than that, she had been a vigorous and healthy woman, which probably accounted for the fact that she was still alive. That, and an unusually sturdy bone structure in her head. She was injured shortly before being brought into the hospital, in the opinion of the first people who had seen her. That would seem to let out the boyfriend, thought Sanders, who was at work then. Besides, the grisly details were too much like those in the earlier deaths to make him a serious contender.

The single ray of hope lay in those gold synthetic fibers imbedded in the remains of her sweater. So far Forensic had been able to establish that it was carpeting, and of a type of fiber patented by a U.S. company and made in limited quantities under license in Canada. Some patient telephoning had found them three manufacturers that used that particular fiber — it was pricy for a synthetic and most of the domestic market for carpet that expensive was for pure wool. Sanders had discovered that commercial clients, however, liked its durable properties and its imperviousness to damage from large rug-cleaning machines, and so it found its way into expensive office broadloom. Only one manufacturer was willing to admit to producing that shade of gold, and Dubinsky, working in the comfort of their own office, with their own telephone and coffee supply, was getting lists of people to whom it had been supplied. Impatient for an answer, Sanders called for the third time that morning.

"For chrissake, Dubinsky, what in hell is going on down there? Haven't you got anything yet?"

"Hold on," said Dubinsky, muttering as he reached for some papers on his desk. "It's almost impossible to get hold of anyone in those bloody offices who knows anything until ten o'clock, and it took them forever to find who had the information, but here it is. All the gold was ordered by an interior designer, who says that he got it for a small mixed-use building on Davenport Road — an antique dealer on the ground floor, and some architects on the upper floors, plus, I think, an importing company. He'll give us the names of all the people as soon as he looks them up. There was some yardage left over, which he had been planning to put in another smaller office he was doing, but the client decided he didn't like it once he saw the color, so the manufacturer jobbed it off to one of the cut-rate retailers on Finch — Family Carpet, I think. They sell a lot of rugs. The chances that they'll know who bought this piece are pretty small, but I'll go out there and see what can be done.''

"Great," said Sanders. "Either she was raped in the middle of the day in an office building on Davenport and carried off, no doubt under the amazed eyes of various passers-by, to some vehicle and dumped in the ravine, or she was raped in the apartment of some thrifty nut who buys his rugs at a cut-rate outlet, or God knows what. Well, go out to the carpet place, and good luck." He hung up the receiver and stared around him at the cramped walls. One more day of this and they'd be able to dismantle it, and return, empty-handed, to the Dundas Street station house. Still, he thought, maybe we should send someone to go over those offices inch by inch, just in case.

Chapter Two

April Fools' Day and Jane Conway sat hunched over her desk and stared without seeing at the pile of Grade Nine lab reports in front of her. If only she could force herself to mark them, to get them done and out of the way. The childishly messy script and awkward diagrams of the one lying on the top of the pile depressed her. Perhaps if she put that one at the bottom and started with a slightly better-looking one? This was a stupid game to try to play with herself. She ran her fingers through her light brown hair with irritation to lift it off her face. God, how she hated Sundays! Dreary, drab, dull — the April sun poured in through her dirty windows and made her apartment look tawdry and poor. And she was tired, tired beyond belief, and felt wretched. The scene in Miss Johnson's office kept crowding into her mind, the scene when her last thin thread of security and respectability had been neatly sliced.

It had been classic. Friday afternoon, that's when they

always give you the bad news, so you can spend the weekend digging your fingernails into your palms in rage and despair on your own time, instead of theirs. It wasn't really that she liked teaching. She had hated that first year, and realized that most of the students disliked her, except for a few drooping masochists who licked her boots and fawned pathetically for the occasional smile or pat of approval. It was Doug, in his smugly practical way, who told her that if she hated it, she should quit at Christmas; but of course she hadn't. She had waited until her one-year contract hadn't been renewed, so that she could suffer through the maximum amount of humiliation over it all. Graduate school had seemed such a haven at that point. In her naiveté she had thought that no one could fire you from graduate school. They just don't call it that. Now what was she going to do? For years she had known that she would need a safe, conservative job to balance her private self, or. . . . Already she could feel herself being sucked into the dark chaos she sensed was all around her. Dammit! They had almost promised her when she had taken this crummy fill-in appointment — five months, and having to work with someone else's notes and ideas, with every student comparing you unfavorably with the person you were replacing — had promised that when the science department expanded next year, there would be a job for her. Now what was she going to do? But her mind refused to consider the future. When she tried to think about it, her mind shied away, dodged, turned to other things, refused to compute beyond tomorrow's teaching load.

The ringing of the phone snapped her out of her mood and set her heart racing. It had to be Paul. This call should have come days ago, but never mind. This would make up for it at long last. Her voice was crisp and cool, expertly concealing the chaos that ruled her soul. The coolness degenerated into malice as soon as she realized who was on the line. "Oh, Mike. Yes, what did you want?" A pause.

"That sounds dreary even as an alternative to marking lab reports. And that's what I'm doing." She held the phone away from her ear a moment. "I'm afraid it's not something you can do in company, and I really do have to get them done." Another pause. "No, I have no intention of making next week difficult because I didn't get things done today. You'll have to console yourself some other way. Try reading a book, or something. You might find it a fascinating experience." At that she delicately dropped the receiver back on its cradle.

This was useless. What time was it? Maybe she should go up to the gym and work out for a while. The calming concentration, the quiet narcissism of all those jocks, polite and pleasant, but never paying any real attention to the people around them — that was what she needed. To be accepted and ignored at the same time. A run would be too isolated; the emptiness of her apartment was already beginning to spook her. But she needed to work off some of her restlessness. She jumped up quickly and reached over into the corner for her gym bag. The sudden movement made her lurch for a second or two in dizziness, but she took a determined breath, set her jaw, grabbed her jacket, and headed for the door.

As Jane Conway's slightly battered old orange VW Beetle moved down the drive from the parking lot behind her apartment building, a nondescript figure in a discreetly commonplace gray Honda that was parked across the street started his engine and pulled out slowly behind her. A group of three girls chattered earnestly on the steps of a house up the street, and as the VW passed them they stared for a moment and broke into fits of giggling. Unaware of car or girls, Jane drove steadily until she came to a stop sign. She pulled over, stopped, and opened her car window. The gray Honda stopped behind her; its driver glanced about him, got out, and walked up to her open window, smiling broadly. She gave him a blankly frozen stare, bent her head to listen to what he had to say, put the car in gear, and carried on.

Sunday should be a good day here, she thought, as she hurried down the steps into the health club. People were usually doing other things on Sunday afternoon: cooking enormous dinners, or dallying with their lovers, or hiking in the countryside. Maybe she would have the women's locker room to herself, at least.

Damn. There was a tall redhead, looking slightly confused, standing in the middle of the room holding a gym bag. Jane glanced briefly at her, opened a locker, and started to strip off her sweater and jeans. "Excuse me," said the redhead. "Are these lockers assigned? This is my first time here and I don't quite ——"

"No," Jane snapped, jerking her workout clothes out of her bag in a gesture which she hoped would discourage further chat. She turned her back and started to dress, suddenly shy of displaying her body in front of a stranger. You'd think I was a self-conscious fourteen-year-old, she thought as she pulled up the pants and dropped the top over her head. Then anger edged out her despair. Why in hell can't I be left in peace! It gave her the impetus to stride out toward the weight apparatus as though all were normal, fixed, healthy, and even in her life. Outside the facility, time dozed on the quiet Sunday streets.

He sat sprawled in his armchair, in a suburban development far from the centre of town, his long legs spread out in front of him, his handsome face slightly flushed. He was staring at his wife, whose plaintive voice was mixing oddly with the sound that blared from the television set. "Turn the fucking thing off if you're going to say something, then." She pushed herself up from the couch and moved slowly over to the set. She turned down the sound, hesitated for a moment, and then clicked the TV off. He continued to stare at her.

"Anyway, that's what the doctor said. He's worried about the cramping and spotting and wants me to go to a specialist — a Dr. Rasmussen. He says he's very good. And probably I'll have to quit work since I have to stand up all day, and that may be what's causing it. The store doesn't have any jobs where you can sit down all day. You know that." He made no response. She took a deep breath and plunged on. "This specialist charges $250 over OHIP, but Dr. Smith says he can't handle complications like this as well as the specialist would." She took another deep breath and looked carefully at him, trying to judge his reaction.

Her words flowed around him, meaningless and ugly, bouncing off the wall and booming erratically into his ears — "quit work . . . $250 . . . specialist . . . complications." As he looked at her, her body seemed to balloon grotesquely in front of him. The small protuberance of her belly grew larger and larger, threatening to engulf her completely. Shaken, he looked at her face. It floated loosely, puffing out, twisting, turning into shapes of exquisite ugliness, throbbing in accompaniment to the urgency of her words.

"You're not even listening to me. This is important. I know we can't afford it, but he says I'll lose the baby. And I know it doesn't matter to you, but I won't let that happen. Will you listen to me!" Her voice rose to something between a wail and a shriek.

He clutched his hands cautiously together. The rage flowing through them made them burn and jump and he held them carefully on his lap so that their spasms would not be visible. Very calmly he said, "Of course I was, Ginny. And we'll just have to do what the old guy says. I mean, we don't have much choice, do we?"

"Oh, honey. I knew you'd be reasonable about it. I was just afraid that you'd be awfully worried about the money." Relief flooded through her, and she made a move across the room as if to kiss him. He got up hastily and headed for the stairs — down three steps, past the kitchen placed cutely at the front of the house, turn, down six steps to the family room, turn, and down five more to the garage dug safely in under the townhouse complex. Smells of dinner cooking drifted up and down the stairways as he passed along them. Almost every room in every unit was on a different level, yet only in the bathroom and the garage did he feel safe and private. He switched on the light and headed for the sole object in his world that was his alone. He unlocked the door and climbed in on the driver's side. He took large gulps of air to settle himself and reached for an enormous folded map lying casually on the passenger seat. The lights on the walls lit up the brightly colored array of streets, parkways, parks, and wildlands that make up greater Metropolitan Toronto.

Circled in black was the enormous townhouse development on the northwest edge of the suburbs where he lived with his Ginny. There was an X in the center — "my house". Scattered about the large green areas on the map were big red circles: one in the top right-hand corner, at Serena Gundy Park; one lower, toward the left, at High Park; one in the center of the map, not very high up, along a strip of green that used to be a railway line, called the Belt Line; and one to the southeast of that, around the Rosedale Ravine. Somewhere inside each circle was a clear, thick purple X. He looked doubtfully at the last one. Perhaps he hadn't earned it. It had been entered a little prematurely. He reached into the glove compartment and drew out a plastic pouch filled with felt-tip pens in a rainbow of colors; he picked out a red one and let it hover over the map, drawing invisible circles around now this green space, now that one. He seemed to settle on an area, traded the red pen for a yellow one, and made a small mark with it beside another patch of green on the map. That done, he looked critically at his addition, put away the pens, folded up the map, and sat and stared unseeing through the windshield at the raw two-by-fours and industrial-grade plywood that made up the walls of his haven.

Eleanor Scott sat in the pleasantly comfortable sitting room on the second floor of the principal's house, a glass of scotch and water in her hand, looking quizzically at her friend Rosalind. It was late Friday afternoon, the nadir of Rosalind's life. Her usually bright-eyed, somewhat malicious expression was beginning to look dangerous. Heaven help anyone, thought Eleanor, parent or student, who impinged on her existence right now. Even her exquisitely tailored silk blouse and pale linen suit were looking the worse for wear. It was odd that Roz had gone to the trouble to coax her over here on such a bad day.

"You're looking a bit frazzled, Roz," she commented cautiously. "You should come over to my place and get away from all this. It's nice and quiet — Heather's off with her daddy. And then when the roof caves in over the gym or the cops raid the residence, nobody would be able to find you."

"Thanks for the thought, El," she said wearily, "but I couldn't move an inch to save my soul. And besides, it's not that bad. I had a new phone installed up here with a bell that shuts off." She put her elegant, well-tanned legs up on a small needlepoint-covered stool and dropped her head back on the chair in an attitude of total collapse. "But you're basically right. If anything more happens, I think I'll quit, or have a nervous breakdown. That would brighten up their lives, wouldn't it?"

Eleanor tried to laugh at the strained effort at wit. "I don't see what could possibly be that bad right now, though. I would have thought that everyone would be calm and happy after two weeks of sun and sand." Roz raised her head and then an eyebrow in her friend's direction. "And you should be looking more rested than you do, considering. I thought you were spending the break in Tortola. With Maurice.''

"I did," she said, with a yawn. "Or at least eight days of it. But he had to get back early, and so I stupidly came back with him." Maurice was the one aspect of Rosalind Johnson's life that she managed to keep away from the constant surveillance conducted by six hundred intensely curious students. "Anyway, the break didn't help. Things are worse now than they were when I left. I'm not sure that I can stand it any more." She finished her drink and wandered over to the sideboard to get another, leaving her shoes half-way across the intervening area. "First of all, one of the girls is going to get murdered. I know it, and I can't convince them that it's a serious threat. They just give me that 'Oh God, here she goes again' look and switch off. And if one more teacher leaves in mid-year to have a baby I think I'll scream."

"Who is it this time?"

"Physics. You'd think there'd be a million of them out there looking for jobs, wouldn't you? Well, there aren't. There may not be many teaching jobs open, but there sure as hell aren't any physicists hanging around looking for half a year's work. The one I finally managed to get is an absolute disaster. She's a sadist, and she's always late. You don't know anyone who can teach physics, do you? And is in need of a job? I'd do it myself — it can't be that hard — but no one is stupid enough to take on this job from now until the end of June." Roz laughed ruefully over her glass. "And if something doesn't happen pretty soon to smooth everything over, I'll have to find another science head. Cassandra is going crazy." She sighed. "Oh, well. I could be worse off, I suppose. At least I don't have a rash of resignations to cope with — yet." At that she spilled some scotch on her pale pink silk blouse. "Damn," she said, dabbing ineffectually at it. "Look at me. Anyway, you're wondering why I called you over. I think it was partly because I felt like talking to someone who has nothing to do with educating the young, and partly to discuss business. Do you remember old Cufflinks?''

"Good Lord! Miss Links. You're not going to tell me that she's still alive! She must have been ninety when she was teaching me geometry.''

"Not quite. But she was over seventy when she retired fifteen years ago. Well, she died last year and left us her house.''

"My God! Why?'' Eleanor tried to imagine a circumstance in which she would consider leaving anything valuable to her present employers, Webb and McLeod, Real Estate, pleasant though they were. She couldn't.

"She didn't have much family, apparently, or at least, family that counted. I think there was an unpleasant nephew, or something like that, and she preferred to see us get the property. After all, she taught here for forty years. Anyway, the Board has decided that we don't really have much use for a house in North Toronto, and that, rather than rent it out any longer, we should put it on the market. Would you like to handle it for us? I told them you'd be able to look after it all without having to have your hand held constantly. That's what's killing us about the rental agents. They drive the business manager crazy with phone calls.''

"Aren't you a sweetheart! I could use some extra business right now. How about pouring me another drink, too, and telling me something about this house. Like the inflated price the Board thinks it's going to get for it.''

Roz shook her head as she headed for the scotch. "You can worry about the house later. Divert me with some interesting gossip now that I've spilled all the secrets and scandals of my existence to you. What's new in your life?'' She handed Eleanor a replenished glass.

"In that sense, nothing.'' Eleanor shrugged with an exaggerated grimace. "Absolutely nothing new or interesting at all. In fact, I've been forced to take up health and fitness in my spare time these days."

"My God, whatever for? That's something I preach at the girls, but I certainly wouldn't want my friends to go in for it. What are you doing? Let me warn you, if it's all that jazz dancing and stuff, I have a staff member who tried it and she's limping around in a brace."

"Uh-uh." Eleanor shook her head in vigorous denial. "I'm running two slow miles every day, and I've joined a health club. I'm working out on weight machines." She flexed a bicep in Roz's direction.

"Good Lord, Eleanor. What an idiot! I'd never have believed it of you," she said, lifting one neatly shaped eyebrow.

"Come on, Roz. I had to do something. I couldn't climb up to my apartment without panting. I was going to have to stop selling anything but bungalows in case I couldn't make it up the stairs."

"But weight-lifting! It sounds absolutely ghastly."

"It's really not as awful as it sounds. Lots of cute young male creatures there — you know, the very nice but serious types. The other women are pretty snarky, though. I said something quite innocuous to someone in the locker room the first day I was there and she bit my head off."

"Probably thought you were making a pass at her."

"Good God! I suppose you're right. Well, I'll just have to be very circumspect while changing, I guess. You should try it, though. Then when some kid gets lippy, you can pick her up and throw her out the window. I'm sure Maurice would love you with sleek, rippling muscles."

"What a disgusting thought," said Roz, stretching out one perfectly formed leg in front of her, and eying it critically. "And just where are you doing all this running? Not out there on the streets, I hope. At least, not all by yourself. I'd hate to have to find another real estate agent because your mangled corpse was found in a park somewhere. Seriously, you know, it isn't safe."

"Don't be silly," said Eleanor, with an involuntary shudder. "First of all, I don't run down in the ravine and places like that. I stick to the sidewalks out here. And I'm much too tall to tempt him — everybody knows he likes his women short."

"Well, maybe so," said Roz, shaking her head dubiously, "but that kid up at AGS was a pretty athletic type, agile, strong, and fast on her feet — a demon field-hockey player and it didn't do her any good. Of course, at that age, they really think they're immortal and they're not very cautious. But I do wish you'd be careful — otherwise I'm going to have to come out and keep you company, God forbid."

"You're overreacting, Roz," said Eleanor, reaching for her coat as she stood up. "Can you imagine anyone tackling me?" She murmured something about next week for the house as she gathered up her belongings and got out the door. She walked toward the parking lot in a less frolicsome mood, however, than she had assumed for her friend's benefit a few minutes before. In the fading twilight houses, trees, and bushes melded into a single threatening mass, out of which suddenly emerged a tall, broad-shouldered man. Eleanor found herself stiffening, and moved rapidly toward her car, her heart pounding. When he passed her, she realized that he was just a boy, doubtless come to whirl one of the girls away for a dizzy Friday evening. "El, you idiot," she muttered, as she tried to put the key into the lock with trembling fingers.

Chapter Three

He drove slowly through the narrow streets that made up the center section of the subdivision, accelerating steadily and smoothly to compensate for curves, slowing down and braking without any sudden movement or jerkiness. That was how cops drove, he thought with satisfaction, and professional chauffeurs in their long black limousines. No one noticed you if you drove like that, as long as you didn't go too slow. Those were the ones they looked at — the slow ones. And the fast ones. Never the ones whose vehicles moved with fluidity and grace. "Fluidity and grace" — he had had a teacher who used to say that all the time. Funny expression, but he liked the feel of it on his tongue. He realized with a start that he had been waiting for too long at the stop sign. That was very bad. Someone might notice him if he waited too long at a stop sign. Nervously he shifted his foot from brake to accelerator with a jerk and swore as the engine roared in response.

He accelerated onto Highway 401 but stayed in the collector lanes. Only two exits and he would be leaving again. Then the wheel lurched involuntarily in his hand as he caught sight of the bright yellow of a police cruiser in his side window. Damn! But they were after other suckers today, not him. Not him — they would have no reason to be after him. They passed, and he flicked on his right-turn indicator. Yonge Street was relatively uncluttered at ten o'clock on Monday morning, and he got to Lawrence Avenue faster than he had anticipated. His mouth was dry with fear; his hands slimy on the steering wheel. He slowed down as he came closer to the intersection, hoping that an amber light would force him to stop. Damn these timed lights. They dragged you downtown before you wanted to get there. Then it changed and he stamped hard on the brake. A mistake. He looked at his watch; it was only 10:20. He had planned to get there at 10:30. That was the time he had written down in his operations book in the glove compartment. Should he drive around for a while? There were too many dead ends and one-way streets around here to do that. He might get lost and then he would be late — and that could be dangerous. The roaring in his head distracted him. It took a honk from the cab behind to make him realize that the light had changed again. Shit! Another mistake. He pretended he was looking for an address on a piece of paper so that his hesitation would be perfectly understandable to anyone looking at him. No one was.

He made a fluid and graceful left turn into the tiny street by the park and followed its twisting route into a quietly solid and expensive neighborhood. The park was on his right. According to the map, it should disappear soon behind a line of houses and then reappear for a long stretch. A tallish woman in flat shoes and a pale spring coat walked confidently toward Yonge Street. With a single, competent flick of the eye he took in her height, her speed, and the number of houses around him. That would be poor strategy. His self-confidence returned. He congratulated himself on the dispassionate and cool manner in which he had been able to classify her as impossible. "Dispassionate." That was a wonderful word, too. He continued on, slowly, but not too slowly. "Dispassionately the enforcer surveyed the scene and coolly chose the most strategic opponent." Some day he would write a book.

Suddenly he realized that he had passed the built-up area and that there was nothing to his right but parkland shading off into ravine. His throat constricted in panic again, and the roaring started once more in his ears. Up ahead he saw a girl — a short girl with darkish hair, walking slowly along a path in the park — all alone. She was so obvious. Maybe she was a trap. If he were a cop, that would be what he'd do. But there wasn't any place for one to hide. So she *was* alone. Christ, were these bitches stupid. He brought the vehicle to a standstill very gently. With practised ease he slid rapidly over to the passenger side and glided out, leaving the door open; holding his map in his hand, visible to all, he composed his face into a puzzled frown.

"Excuse me, Miss," he said, in his pleasantest tone, with a grin that his social worker used to describe as "engaging" — he liked that term, and used to practice looking engaging in front of his bathroom mirror — "but could you ——" A sharp growl cut him off. He jumped back. A monstrous Doberman plunged out of the undergrowth on the edge of the ravine. Its face was contorted in rage, showing its long yellowish teeth. Christ! He hated dogs. Vicious, filthy creatures. They made him shiver in disgust and fear.

The girl laughed. "Sorry, but Caesar gets a bit over-eager about protecting me. If you don't come any closer, he won't do anything. You were saying?"

His mind cleared for a second. "Oh, I wondered if you

knew where" — he grasped for a name — "Hawthorne Crescent is? I seem to be a bit lost."

"Sorry," she smiled. "I don't know the neighborhood that well. I've never heard of it."

"That's okay," he mumbled, backing toward safety. "I'll just check my map again." He jumped back onto the passenger seat and slammed the door, almost faint with terror. As the girl and the dog moved down the street, though, anger began to flood in to replace the fear. The next time he'd look and listen more carefully. But he had failed here. A second failure, now. That last time he had panicked like some stupid kid and run — all because of a bloody old lady and another dog. Perhaps he should move back out to more remote areas again, until he had polished his technique sufficiently to be good enough for inside the city. The city took nerve, determination, and skill.

John Sanders was sitting in the back booth of a small and rather grubby restaurant with a cup of cold coffee in front of him. As he glanced irritably at his watch a small dark woman slipped into the seat across from him. She smiled, then turned and gestured at Jerry, the morose proprietor. "What's fattening, Jer?" she called. "Bring me a Danish if you have one."

"No more Danish, Dr. Braston. I got a honey bun if you want. No one else likes them."

"Great. Can you heat it up and put some butter on it?"

Sanders looked incredulously across the table. "Haven't you ever heard of cholesterol, Melissa?"

"Look, the people I've been cutting up recently could have lived on goose fat and brandy and it wouldn't have made any difference. They all seem to have been scraped up off the highway or bashed in the head by psychos. Besides, I didn't have any breakfast this morning. They called me in early. Don't nag, John. You remind me of my husband. Never marry a heart man; they spend all day nagging people and find it hard to turn it off when they get home.'' She took the hot, extremely buttery bun from Jerry and began to attack it with vigor.

''What did you want to see me about, anyway? I can guess that this isn't a pass, is it? No one seems to be turned on by the smell of formaldehyde these days — except my husband. I think he gets a secret thrill, imagining me down in the morgue. You know, a closet necrophiliac.''

Sanders grinned. ''Well, I got your reports ——''

''I should hope so,'' she snapped. ''Those damned things were done weeks ago. If you're trying to tell me you just read them, after I busted a gut to finish them, that's the last time I ever do a rush job for you, baby.''

''No, no,'' he said hastily. ''I read each one as soon as it came in. But they didn't help much, that's all.''

''What do you want from pathology? A description of the murderer imprinted on the retina or something? I gave you what was there — that's all there is.'' She finished her sticky bun and was trying to clean the sugar and grease from her strong, short-nailed hands.

''I'm not expecting miracles, but you've worked on all three of these, haven't you?''

Melissa nodded, her eyes bright with curiosity and interest.

Sanders looked intently at her. ''Well, isn't there anything you get from the marks or patterns that would tell us something about him? I thought maybe you might have noticed something that didn't seem to be the kind of thing you'd put in a report.''

Melissa shook her head. ''There aren't things like that in this sort of case. I mean, if I notice something, I put it in. There might be more information in those cadavers, tests we didn't run because they didn't seem pertinent ——''

''What do you mean?''

"I mean that I don't really look hard for slow arsenic poisoning or black widow spider bites when the cause of death is so clear."

"No, that wasn't what I was thinking about. I mean, what do we know about him from the way he bashed them around, and from those knife marks — I don't know. I suppose if I can't see a pattern that tells us anything useful, there's no reason why you should be expected to." He pushed aside his coffee cup and rubbed his hand over his forehead.

"Come on, John," she said cheerfully. "Don't look so depressed. I can tell you a few things, but they didn't come from cutting those girls up. I can tell you I wouldn't go for a long lonely walk on a weekday between the hours of 10:00 A.M. and 2:00 P.M., especially in the vicinity of a large park."

"All that tells me is that you're not as stupid as some women, obviously. But I knew that already."

Melissa ignored this. "He goes for girls who are rather short and have medium brown hair and are bouncy. All the cadavers were in excellent physical condition — except that they were dead, of course. It was hard to tell whether they were pretty or not. And he obviously doesn't have a job, or at least, a day job, but probably has a late model car in good condition. So I would be looking for a fairly good-looking guy with light to dark brown hair who got fired around Christmas and is driving an '83 or '84 medium-sized car in a rather nondescript color — light blue, gray, tan, something like that."

John looked at her with interest. He had come to some of the same conclusions as Melissa had, but wondered whether she had based hers on something other than instinct. "Why?"

"The murders started in January, so before that he worked during the day or didn't feel like killing women — the first seems likelier. And what kind of a man does a girl instinctively trust? One who's good looking but not too good looking, with honest brown hair. If he looked like a rapist — whatever that means — wouldn't you have had a lot of girls reporting attempts? I mean, he would have approached some females who ran or screamed or something. Unless you have had a lot of these?''

"None. This is the first time I can remember when we had a rapist who didn't have a few unsuccessful attempts to his credit. That's how we catch them, usually." Jerry slouched over with the coffee pot and refilled their cups, a look of pain in his eye as he considered the cost of the extra liquid.

"You see, the funny thing," she said, swishing the coffee around in her cup thoughtfully, "is why any woman is going to trust some strange man enough to let him within ten feet of her when there's been so much publicity about this. He's got to be presenting himself as someone who's absolutely safe."

"What do you mean?"

"Well. Take a kid who's really — what do they call it? — street-proofed, the kind who wouldn't go across the street with her Uncle Jimmy to see newborn puppies. You can still put her into situations where she's vulnerable. Say, she was just asked to sell Girl Guide cookies, so she goes up to every person she sees who looks as if he'd buy cookies — and she feels safe and in control. If one of those guys approached her, instead of her approaching him, she'd scream, but she'd go off cheerfully enough with some friendly looking type who promised to buy six boxes."

"And where does that get us? None of these ladies was selling cookies, Melissa."

"No, but maybe we're looking for someone a woman would approach without any fear. Maybe he's an off-duty cop still in his uniform who usually works nights, for instance. How does that grab you?"

Sanders looked at her in horror. "Jesus," he said softly, "I wish you hadn't said that. But there's no one that crazy on the force." As soon as he'd said it a succession of possible candidates tumbled through his brain. He shook his head. "Anyway, what sort of guy kills them over and over again? I mean, that's what he's doing, isn't it? I guess I really should be talking to a psychiatrist about this, not to you."

"Psychiatrist!" said Melissa dismissively. "You don't need to be a shrink to recognize when someone's that loony. I would suspect that he just is never quite sure that they're all that dead, myself. And, of course, he's got a point there, hasn't he? That one who's in the hospital still wasn't all that dead when he got finished with her."

"Okay then, answer me this one. When do we get our next corpse? When is he going to stop?"

"The next one? Pretty soon, I'd say," she responded cheerfully. "And I don't suppose he'll stop until he gets caught. But it's been a month now, hasn't it? That's the longest interval so far. So either he's through for some reason or there will be a new one any day now. Anyway, thanks for the coffee and the bun. I have to get back to Forensic. Lots of work to do. Ta, ta." With a lively grin she gathered up her things and dashed back across the road, leaving Sanders no wiser than before.

Monday afternoon Jane Conway walked down the big front steps of the school and shivered in the cool spring air. The fifteen-minute walk to her apartment was going to feel like a ten-mile forced march. It was already 4:30, and today she had counted on leaving early so that she could collapse for a while before having to consider doing anything. Fat chance. As she trudged up to MacNiece Street and turned toward the square yellow-brick building whose fourth floor she shared with five other apartments, the whole neighborhood began to look drearier and drearier.

The left-over dirt of winter made the pathetic attempts of the spring bulbs and the pale sun to cheer up the world even more depressing than gray skies and empty flower-beds would have been. Parked a few yards to the north of the building was a gray Honda. Jane slowed down and glanced in the window, then stopped and opened the door on the passenger side. She slipped in for a few minutes of apparently earnest conversation before jumping out, slamming the door, and moving on with quickened pace. Without a backward glance she entered the front door of her building and headed for the creaky elevator. The wait was endless, the ride ponderously slow, and just as she was fumbling in her purse for her keys the phone began to ring, persistently and maddeningly. It took forever to locate her key chain, an eternity to find the right key, eons to fit it into the lock and make it turn. Damnation. This time it had to be Paul. She grabbed the phone off the hook and gasped "Hello," certain that by now he would have hung up.

A familiar, flat, female Toronto voice replied, "Hi, Jane. How come it took you so long? You busy or something? I was just about to hang up. It's me, Marny. Remember me, kid?"

"Of course, Marny. Hi. No, I wasn't busy. I just came in, that's all. Had some trouble getting the door open. How are you? Is anything wrong?"

"Why should anything be wrong? Can't I call you without something being wrong?" She brayed with meaningless laughter.

"No. But the last time you called something was, remember?"

"Oh, that. Yeah. Well, thanks for your help. It all worked out okay, so everything's fine now. But no, nothing's wrong. It's just that we're having a party tomorrow night and we thought maybe you'd like to come. For old time's sake, you know. It's B.Y.O.B. but there'll be plenty, so you don't have to worry about that. And there'll be lots of food and mix. We decided today that what we all needed was a party. Things are really dead around the office — except Jenny just got a promotion. Did you know that Miriam's moving to Vancouver because Ken got transferred? So she's leaving, and Jenny got her job. Anyway, that gives us an excuse." Once again she exploded into laughter. Jane waited with the phone some distance from her ear for the racket to subside. "It'll be at my place, tomorrow night at 8:30." Then she paused, and asked casually, "Do you think you could get hold of some stuff by then? I mean, the guys would take care of it — we're not asking you to donate it or anything."

Jane said nothing for a long while. "Well, that's pretty short notice. I'm not even sure I can make it to the party. I'm working these days, teaching; you can't just stay up every night and hope no one notices you're half asleep."

"Come on, Jane. That's not like you. We all know about working. But you don't have to stay long. And do you think ——"

"Don't worry. I wouldn't stay long. Look, I'll see what I can do. If you don't hear from me before the party I'll be coming, okay? That's all I can promise."

"But you'll try, won't you?" The discordant voice pleaded in her ear. "All the guys will be there. I promised them you'd come."

"Yeah, sure. I'll try." With a slight twitch of distaste on her lips, she cut off the connection and began to dial. She waited, looked at her watch, and hung up. She took off her raincoat and put it carefully away in the closet, picked up her briefcase and spread the contents on her desk, then looked at her watch again. As she reached once more for the telephone, it pre-empted her by ringing under her hand. She picked it up rapidly.

"Hi. Oh, it's you." She paused slightly. "What do you want?" And paused again. "I don't give a shit if I sound as if I didn't want to hear from you. I've got all kinds of business to get through tonight on the phone. What do you want, Grant?'' She listened carefully, picked up a pencil, jotted a few abbreviations down on a pad by the phone, and nodded. "If I can, sure. Are you going to Marny's tomorrow night? Oh. Well, my car will be outside her place from around nine until maybe eleven." She shook her head impatiently. "I'll call you if there's a hitch. Now get off the phone, will you?''

Once more she dialed and waited, this time with more success. She spoke quickly and concisely, glancing at the jottings on her pad, nodded and hung up. She looked once more at her watch. Five o'clock. She should be able to get to Paul now without too much trouble from his secretary. She'd put Jane's call through without thinking on her way out the door. But she had to get through before that woman left. He'd never bother answering unless he was expecting a call. She dialed rapidly, jerkily. The phone rang: once, twice, three times. Damn! She'd gone. At six times, a breathless voice hissed into the receiver. Sorry. He was at a meeting. Would she like to leave a message?

You're damn right she'd like to leave a message, you stupid bitch. "Please. Ask him to call Jane Conway at home. As soon as possible." And she slammed the phone down, patches of nervous color burning in her cheeks.

At nine o'clock Jane slammed her books shut, scooped up all the papers on her desk, and shoved them into her briefcase. She poured herself a scotch and took out a small green three-ring binder. She flipped through to the end of the alphabet at the back of the book: Wilcox, Paul. There were three numbers neatly listed: Law office; Parliamentary office; home (unlisted, emergencies only!) She took a deep gulp of her drink and dialed.

The phone rang four times before a cool female voice answered. Yes, of course she would call Mr. Wilcox. In the long pause, Jane could hear waves of sound, bursts of laughter punctuating the low murmur of conversation. Her heart throbbed painfully, and her breath seemed to catch in her throat. Finally a hurried voice said, "Paul Wilcox here."

"Hi, Paul," she said steadily. "It's me. When you didn't call last week I thought maybe something had happened."

"Look, baby. I can't discuss it now. There's a huge crowd of people here — can't you hear them? This is an impossible phone to discuss anything from anyway. I'll call you tomorrow after work — no, not tomorrow, better make that Wednesday. I have your number. Now, for God's sake, get ——" Suddenly his voice changed to cool and oily. "Very sorry. I really don't have that information here. I'll have to call you tomorrow morning from my office. Yes, I do have your number. In the meantime, don't worry too much about it. I'm sure that we can resolve the situation without any trouble. I'll talk to you tomorrow. Good-bye."

A tall, composed-looking woman was walking slowly into the lushly paneled study, carrying a drink in each hand. "Here you are, love," she said. "I brought you your drink in case you were on the phone for hours. Who was that? She certainly picked a wonderful time to call."

He smiled affectionately at her as he took the glass. "Just a journalist lady who's offering some flattering free publicity in exchange for some pull in front of the Municipal Board. We must change this unlisted number. The whole world seems to be on to it. It must be posted up at all the newspaper offices by now. What do you think? Should we get a new number and a little peace and quiet?"

She shook her head firmly. "It would be simply too much trouble to get that new number to everyone. The kids would have a fit. As it is, they complain all the time about it."

He continued to smile sweetly. "As you wish, sweetheart. Although perhaps we should give this number to the children and get another unlisted number for ourselves. And the kids' number could go onto the answering service. They'd get a charge out of that, I think.''

She shook her head doubtfully and turned to go back to the party. ''No,'' she said finally, as they were leaving the room. ''You'll have to put up with these people bothering you. After all, you're not home that often, and I would find it a terrible nuisance to have to disrupt my own life to save you a bit of trouble.'' Her smile was sweet, distant, and final.

Jane stared at her reflection in the mirror critically. Her current state of exhaustion showed in the dark hollows under her eyes, and her face seemed puffy and formless, all the firm gauntness of cheek and chin that she worked so hard to maintain was slipping away no matter what she did. But carefully made up she didn't look too bad, really. She was just applying her eyeliner when the phone rang; the pencil jumped, making a blur in the clean outline. Damn. It was probably that idiot Mike again. She leaned around the corner from the bathroom and picked up the phone from beside the bed. ''Hi. Oh, it's you.'' Her voice became cautious. ''I wasn't really expecting you to call. Now? That's impossible. I have to turn up at Marny's party tonight. I said I'd be there half an hour ago.'' She looked at her watch. ''You can always talk to me there.'' There was a mildly explosive noise in the receiver. ''Well, I don't know how you want to spend your time. I know it's crowded there. Some other time, then.'' She flipped open her green notebook as she spoke. ''Okay. Tomorrow's not bad. But remember, I work, and I can't possibly get home before four at the earliest. No. This is a teaching job I have. You can't just walk out early and tell some secretary that you'll be back in an hour or so. Okay. I'll see you some time after four. 'Bye.'' After she had hung up, she smiled in satisfaction, picked up her raincoat and purse, and walked out of the apartment. She left the building by a back door and got into her old VW, parked along with eight other cars in the cramped lot.

Marny's party was proceeding normally; the noise level and the guests were getting higher in direct proportion to the level of consumption. Tobacco smoke enveloped the room, mixing with a trickle of greeny-sweet dope from several corners. Jane's cheeks were burning, and her head swam miserably from the smoke and heat. She stared at the rum and Coke she seemed to have acquired by some magic means and raised it to her lips. The smell of it sickened her, but she poured half of it down her throat anyway in a desperate attempt to cool herself off, then she put her hand on the wall to steady herself as waves of nausea whirled through her. She became vaguely aware of a presence beside her, holding her by the arm, and an urgent voice speaking in familiar accents. "Jane. Jane. Are you okay? You look terrible. Come out on the balcony and get some fresh air." She allowed herself to be led through the door.

A deep breath of cool air steadied her. "Thanks, Mike. It's all right. I just felt a little dizzy in there for a minute. It must have been the heat." She turned and half-smiled at him. "I wasn't expecting to see you here. What are you doing these days?" Now that the rum seemed to have decided to stay in her stomach, it was beginning to cheer her up. Even Mike looked pretty good.

He seized the mood before it could pass him by once again. "Oh, Janie. You know what I'm doing. I'm waiting for you, like I always said I would." He grabbed her hard by the upper arm, his voice hoarse and shaking with intensity. "Come back home with me. You'd be much happier. Dad says that he's ready to retire whenever I want to take over the business — whenever we can get married. I can't stand watching you be miserable. Please!"

By now the air had cleared her head and restored her reason. She looked at the sturdy young man opposite her, whose broad shoulders, wavy brown hair, dark brows, and earnest look had made him, about ten years before, the most desirable boy in her high school graduating class, and laughed. "Mike, I wish you'd think up something more original to say one of these days. Can you honestly see me running a hardware store with you, all cosy and domestic? Come off it." She turned and leaned on the railing of the balcony. "First of all, I'm still married — and I'm not sure when or if I'm planning to get a divorce. And then, if I did, I sure as hell wouldn't do it just so I could end up where I started from. I mean, what would be the point of that? Besides, maybe I plan on marrying someone — well — more, uh, interesting." He was leaning forward painfully to catch her words before the rush of the traffic below snatched them away. Then she turned back to face him. "You know, sweetheart," she said, suddenly inspired. "I'm going to tell you a secret. I'm not at all what you think I am. Come here!" The snarl startled him almost as much as her catching him behind the neck and dragging his face down to her. She whispered something in his ear; then she let him go and pushed him away.

He stared at her in blank incomprehension. Finally he shook his head and spoke, very slowly. "If I thought that was true, I'd push you off this balcony. My God, Jane, don't say things like that to me. I can't stand it. You're just trying to drive me crazy." His voice broke, and he tried to catch hold of her again.

"It could be true, you know. You'll never be sure now, will you? Think about that." She ducked out from under his arms and moved back into the crowded living room.

"Well, if it isn't the farm queen and her rustic swain," said a mocking voice as they entered. "Hi, Mike. How're you doing? Not so good, to judge by the look on your face. If I were you, I'd leave her alone. She isn't worth the agony." Mike glared at the speaker and elbowed his way rapidly through the crowd and out the door. "Oh, dear," he said. "Did I say something that upset him? I am so-o-o sorry."

"Hi, Grant. You are a real bastard, you know. But I think it was what *I* said that upset him." She smiled briefly. "I thought you weren't going to come to this thing. You change your mind about Marny's charms?"

"Not bloody likely. But I might have changed my mind about you. Did you ever think of that?" He grinned and tapped her lightly on the end of her nose. "Come over here and let's have a little chat." He put his arm around her shoulder and propelled her toward a chair in the slightly darkened dining L. She shivered a little at his touch.

"And what are we going to talk about?" she asked with a touch of wide-eyed innocence.

"Oh, business, and gossip, and what you're doing with yourself these days. Then I'll get you another drink." He crouched down beside her chair, and began to murmur softly but intently close by her.

Finally he stood up and looked at her with her head tilted questioningly to one side. "Well?" he asked. "What do you think?"

"It's a tempting proposition, but I'm not sure that it's feasible. I have my sources, you know, and I would have to check with them. They don't like too much freelance distribution around town."

"Of course," he said, expansively. "It wouldn't really be much different, but it sure should be more profitable."

"And riskier," she said coldly.

"Perhaps." The mocking good humor had left his manner at this point and he was staring at her impatiently. She tried to return his look with one of casual unconcern, but the nervousness he engendered in her made her eyes flicker away under his gaze. He radiated power, rank ambition, and a certain raw maleness that had always put her off balance. He was rather short, with dark, elegant good looks that projected equally well from the stage or in front of the camera; few theater people in Toronto appeared to make as handsome an income out of the profession as he did. There were several other actors at the party, but in this crowd of hopefuls, underpaid bit players, and under-employed stars, he wore his prosperity with arrogance. The eyes that sized up Jane Conway at that moment were as bright with ambition and greed as her own. They were both in from the country, these two climbers, and they understood and despised each other's origins. The silk shirt and close-fitting jeans of Grant Keswick, the actor, were a very thin veneer, disguising and civilizing the body of Jake Matushek, the nobody. She used to sneer at Grant's cultured voice and little fits of bravado until, in that last fight, Jake had re-emerged and had hit her with sufficient strength and force to terrify her. Then he had thrown her into a corner of the room, speechless with fright and indignation, and had called her a worthless whore before he walked out.

"Come on, baby," he said at last, his voice softening. "Let's not fight about it yet. You ask around and see what happens." He moved around to the back of her chair and leaned over her. "You're looking terrific tonight, sweet-heart. I don't know what you've done to yourself but it seems to suit you very well." He buried his head in the hair behind her ear as he let his arm drop slowly down over her breast. She let her head fall back, and for a few moments gave herself up to the pleasure of it all. But when he moved around and pulled her to her feet with sudden and urgent force, her compliance disappeared. "Don't, Grant," she hissed. She grabbed both his hands and pushed them off, shook herself so that her dress settled back into its cool lines, and said, "Thanks for the compliment. It's fun and all that, but I have bigger fish to fry these days. No room for scroungers."

"Oh, my God," he breathed. "For a minute there I almost forgot what a bloody little whore you are. Fortunately, I'm not obliged to buy it these days. I leave pigs like you to the slobs that have to pay. I think I'll go home and take a shower." He turned and walked steadily out of the room.

Jane stared after him for a moment, then sauntered out of the dining area. She headed over to a chesterfield in the corner, where an extravagant-looking blonde was seated on the arm, leaning over an exhausted-looking brunette. "Jenny, Milly," she murmured, dropping down beside them. "How are things? It's been a long time." They nodded. "You two still working?"

"Hmm," said the blonde. "From time to time. Things are a bit tight all over these days. But I'm eating. What's up with you?"

"Dreary job," said Jane. "And dreary people. I'm teaching. It pays the rent." She looked around her. "The same old types seem to be here. How can you bear it, week after week?"

"It's not that bad," said Milly, the languid brunette, with a yawn. "As long as you don't have to talk to anyone."

"Let's get the hell out of here," said Jane. "It's too hot and noisy and there's nothing going on."

"All right," said Jenny. "Where to?"

"Somewhere where there might be a bit of action. How about the After Hours?"

"Okay," said Milly. "But I heard that the last time Linda was down there she got pulled in, you know."

"Crap," said Jane. "Linda is too stupid to get out of the way of a slow-moving train. It's perfectly safe, and this place is deadly boring." She looked around her once again. "Anyone else like to come along?"

Chapter Four

Jane stared over the red, blonde, and brown heads of twenty-four sixteen-year-old girls, her own head throbbing unpleasantly. She listened to the rustling murmur grow from surreptitious whispering to barely muted high-pitched giggles.

"Quiet!" she said, her voice *pianissimo* but nasty. "One more sound and the entire lot of you stays after the bell. I am quite prepared to sit here until five o'clock, if it takes that long for you to learn to work in silence." Liar. This day had already lasted at least a week. "Does anyone have anything she might like to say before we all start working?" She heard her voice, sharp, sarcastic, and shrewish, echoing in her aching head, cutting through the nervous hush. Amanda Griffiths buried herself deeper in her physics problems. Rosemary Hemphill turned to comment on the situation to the girl next to her, changed her mind, and opened her physics text in an elaborate parody of industry. But a flicker of interest — her first that class — darted across the lumpish face of Cathy Holl-ingsby, who put up her hand and produced her contribution to science.

"Mrs. Conway, we saw you going into the After Hours last night — my dad and me. Do you got there a lot? We would have stopped and said hello, but we had to get home. My dad said that it was a pretty interesting place."

The hush was palpable now. Amanda's interest in problems became all-consuming. Rosemary, silent for once, stared in astonishment at Cathy. Only Cathy would be stupid enough to say something like that to Conway. She wasn't the kind of teacher you made personal remarks to, especially when she was in such a bitch of a mood.

Anger made Jane's queasy stomach lurch; blood pounded in her ears. "My life outside this classroom is entirely my own affair," she said, her voice cold with rage, "and someone with such a miniscule grasp of physics as yours could well spend more of her time on problems and less on gossip. Get to work." The words echoed and re-echoed inside her fuzzily hollow head. Oh God, let that bell ring now.

Jane rolled off the bed and padded across the dull gray carpet into the bathroom. "Hey, where are you off to?" said a lazy male voice. "You only just got home. Come back to bed, sweetheart. It's been a while, you know."

"I know," she said, splashing water around as she washed with vigor. "But I don't feel much like a cosy little chat now. I'm going running while it's still sunny out there. You can stay if you like."

"Is that a good idea?"

"Which? Staying? Or running?" Shivering in the cool afternoon, she reached for the running clothes on the back of the chair. Neat shorts, a red T-shirt with "Run for Life" on it, proclaiming that she had raced ten kilometers for cardiac research last spring, and a gray hooded sweat-shirt.

"Running," he said, propping himself up on one elbow as he watched her dress. "I wouldn't have thought it was very good for you — or very safe. Where are you running these days? The same routes?"

"More or less. Up the ravine to Moore Park and then around and back, usually. And what's wrong with it? You think I can't outrun some rapist? Or do you think I'll do myself an injury getting more exercise today? You over-estimate yourself, baby." She turned her back to him and reached for her well-worn Nikes — she really needed a new pair, she thought, looking at the worn heels — and then sat down and put them on with great care.

"Wait," he said, as she started her warm-ups. "We still haven't had that chat, you know. How about a drink somewhere tomorrow after work?"

"I'm not sure about tomorrow," she said jerkily, as she swung her torso around in deep bends. "I might have something on. Why don't you call me?" She leaned against the wall and started stretching her calves.

"Can I call you at work?" He got out of bed and began picking up his own clothes.

"No. That's impossible. Call me here at 4:30." She was leaning against the dresser, stretching her quadriceps. "I'm off now. I'll be back in half an hour or so." She moved toward the living room.

"You're going to pull a muscle if you don't watch it," he said, pulling up his trousers. "You don't warm up enough."

"Goddamit, stop trying to run my life. If Grete Waitz doesn't warm up, why should I?" she said, and flung herself out of the apartment.

Jane shivered as the cold wind hit her bare legs. In spite of what she had said, perhaps she would just drag herself a couple of miles — enough to clear the chalk dust from her lungs, the knots out of her neck and shoulders, the stale alcohol poisons from her bloodstream.

The hangover, the exhaustion, and the sleepless night all made those first steps agony, but imperceptibly the pain faded, her head cleared, her shoulders dropped, and she fell into an easy stride. By the time she had reached the first corner she realized that the heaviness in her legs had disappeared. A long run, that was what she needed, to get away from the whole confusing mess. At that, she veered sharply left past the bridge down to the running path in the ravine. She had a seductive and illusory sense of tremendous speed as she relaxed and let her feet fall down the hill. She hadn't been running as fast these days. It must be the lack of competition; ever since she had walked out on Doug she'd mostly run alone. You had to admit that he was a good running partner — lousy to live with, but great on his feet.

It was stupid to have let Marny talk her into going to the party; stupider to have let herself get into that fight with Grant; stupider still to have dragged Milly and Jenny off to that bar. And if that bloody kid and her precious dad go around talking about seeing her there. . . . What in hell was a kid doing outside a place like that at 11:30 at night? I wonder what the school will make of it? She grinned as she panted up the hill imagining the look on her department head's face. What the hell, she thought, as she crested the rise, I've lost the crummy job anyway. A beer, that's what I need, five miles and then a beer, a bath, a sandwich, and at least ten hours' sleep. Stuff the marking, the girls, and the whole bloody school. She floated down the hill.

Time and distance disappeared; without any clear memory of getting there she had reached the end of the trail and was circling around to travel back the way she had come. Grant's interesting business proposal teased at the edges of her brain, and she began to idly calculate how much money she could earn if she decided to throw her lot in with him. The noise of rush-hour traffic distracted her a moment, and she stumbled slightly; she hadn't realized she was that close to the spot where the path drew near to the road. Then music replaced the calculations in her head as she picked up her pace again, and almost drowned out the running footsteps that started up behind her. The footsteps drew closer as she rounded the corner by the wooded section, and she slowed to let the other runner pass. *I wish I had leg muscles like a man's. Tuna on dark rye and a beer.* The music in her head slowed down as she relaxed her pace, and the footsteps behind her grew louder and faster.

The first class of the morning had started fifteen minutes earlier. Cassandra Antonini was moving purposefully in the direction of the prep room when she heard a shriek and a burst of giggles coming through the open door of the physics lab, followed closely by a rapidly lurching Slinky toy. *Damn that woman. Doesn't she realize it's my ass in a sling if some kid electrocutes herself while she sleeps in again?* Cassandra was a biologist, happy surrounded by fish and plants and pickled frogs, but nervous with the peculiar equipment in the physics lab. She swooped down on the Slinky. A second later she steamed into the room, roaring the group into order:

"Sally, Heather, Carol, sit down. Everyone, open your textbooks. Let's see, Miranda, how far did the class get yesterday? Right. Carry on, finish reading chapter seven and make notes on it. Silently! Susanne, go down to the vice-principal's office and tell Mrs. Lorimer that Mrs. Conway has been delayed. Run! And I shall be next door, with the connecting door to this lab open. I expect absolute silence from all of you." Awestruck, the girls subsided into stillness.

Maggie Lorimer received the news from Susanne in stony

silence; then, reflecting that it wasn't really the poor child's fault that her teacher had not shown up for work that morning, she smiled as warmly as she could manage and thanked her for bringing the message, before sending her back to class. With a resigned sigh she reached for her list of teachers who were free this period and the next, jotted down some names and went in search of someone to hold the fort. On her way back she stuck her head in the principal's office and gave her the news.

"It's really too much, Roz." Maggie dropped down in one of the comfortable chairs in front of the desk and spread her hands in annoyance and frustration. "What am I supposed to do? This is the third or fourth time she's done this since she came. She's driving me crazy. And the people who have to cover her classes are not too pleased about it, either. There's going to be a general revolt, I think. They'll start hiding in broom closets."

"Relax, Maggie. Our troubles may be over. I interviewed an absolutely marvellous woman last night for the part-time science job next year. She's been in Europe for two years with her husband, just got back, was teaching for the Etobicoke Board before that, and everyone thinks she's super. I checked around last night about her. Don't worry. She's coming back this afternoon, and if Cassandra likes her, I think I'll offer her a job starting Monday and get rid of Jane Conway at once. There shouldn't be a problem, I hope." Thoughts of lawsuits sprang briefly into her mind. "She's only here as a supply on a per-diem basis."

"Sounds great. Does she know any physics?"

"Basically she's a chemist, but she did enough physics in university to cope. I asked her — rather slyly, I thought — if she would mind teaching physics should the occasion arise. So all we have to do is to convince her that she would like to start working on Monday instead of next September."

"Tell her it comes with the job — you know, 'oh, by the

way, you start next week.' " Maggie laughed and retreated in the direction of her office. "I'd better try to raise *la belle* Jane at home. If the pattern holds, she's probably still asleep."

Jane Conway's phone rang shrilly in the empty apartment twenty times before Maggie gave up. She slammed the receiver down and went next door to the general office. Above the ringing of phones and clatter of office machinery, she asked whether either of the two secretaries had taken a message from Jane. In the controlled chaos of early morning, it was just possible, although not likely, that they might not have had time to pass along a message.

Sylvia looked up from the list of absentees that she was annotating as she called homes to check on the girls who hadn't shown up yet that morning. "Not a word. You mean she hasn't come in again this morning? I could have used a couple of extra hours myself. Do you want me to call her?"

"No thanks, Sylvia. I tried her a minute ago and there was no answer. How long would it take her to get to work, do you think?"

Sylvia flicked open one of her folders, checked an address, and said, "Ten minutes? Fifteen, if she's really tired. She only lives over on MacNiece."

"Okay. We'll give her ten minutes or so. I wonder if she'll have the grace to tell us she's here, or if she'll just sneak up to her classroom and hope that no one noticed she hadn't turned up. I think I'll just drift by there and see. Here, give me some of those absentees, and I'll do them."

But fifteen minutes later, it was only a mildly irritated English teacher, marking essays, who was to be seen in Jane's class. "Damn!" said Maggie, back in the office. "Do you suppose something has happened to her?"

"If you mean Jane Conway," said Ruth, glancing up from her typewriter, "someone said that she looked terribly ill yesterday."

"Yesterday," said Maggie, ruminatively. "When was that? I can't keep the days straight any more." She sighed. "But you're right. She sat at lunch and stared at the lasagna as though it was laced with arsenic. She was absolutely pea-green. She lives alone, doesn't she?" Sylvia, who knew everything, nodded. "I suppose I'd better go over there and see if something has happened to her. Oh, God."

"Why don't you take Helen Cummings with you?" suggested Sylvia tactfully. "Joyce can hold the fort over at the infirmary until you two get back. Shall I give her a call?"

"What an absolutely brilliant idea. Then if there is anything really wrong, she can cope. She has a stronger stomach than I have." Maggie was not looking forward to this.

The two women stood staring at each other in frustration on the front steps of the square yellow building. They had been alternately ringing the bell marked "Superintendent" and pounding fiercely on the front door for at least ten minutes. "Maybe we should go around to the back and see if we can get in another door," suggested Maggie desperately. Then the door slowly opened, and a slightly tousled gray head poked around it.

"Here now. Who're you looking for? What are you making all that racket for? If they ain't in they ain't in." She started to shut the door. "Any more of that and I'll call the police."

"Just a minute," said Maggie. "Are you the superintendent?"

"No!" said the head. "Not exactly. Anyway, what do you want?" It drew back, preparing for flight.

"Well, maybe you should call the police. We're looking for Jane Conway, Apartment 403. We're from the school she works at, and she hasn't come in today. And she isn't answering her phone. She might be very ill in there."

The head slowly re-emerged. "Well — if you think she's

sick, maybe we'd better go up and look." She cautiously held the door open just wide enough for them to squeeze through. "Now, I don't usually go into the tenants' apartments, you know. There's a law about that. 'Quiet use and enjoyment', it's called — that's what they have. And that means the superintendent can't go in when she feels like it, unless there's a reason. But I guess this is a reason." As she talked, she toiled toward the elevator, a large bunch of keys in her hand. "Not that I seen anything suspicious, mind you," she said, as the elevator groaned up to the fourth floor under their combined weights, "so I don't know what you expect to find." She flipped through the keys on her ring, slowly picked out the right one, and inserted it into the lock. "There you are," she said, as she turned the key with a grimace and flung open the door. "She probably spent the night out, I'd say. Not that it matters to me what the tenants do, as long as they don't have wild parties and wreck the apartments." She pushed her way in first, waddling slightly as she moved. "See? Nothing wrong here," she said, looking around the neat living room. She opened the bedroom door slowly and peered inside. "There, you see? No one in there. Bed hasn't even been slept in, I'd say. These girls are all like that. I don't know why you worry — half the time they don't come home at all at night."

"Do you know if she went out last night and didn't come back?" asked Helen.

"How should I know? They all have their own keys. They only bother me if something goes wrong. But I see them sometimes in the morning coming in, still all dressed up." She waddled out of the bedroom. "None of my business, what they do."

"Would you mind if I looked in the bathroom?" asked Helen. "She might have fallen and hit her head in there."

"Go right ahead," said the super. "It's through the bedroom, there."

Helen opened the door, looked around briefly, and shook her head at Maggie. They walked slowly back into the living room. There was nothing in it that would give a hint to its owner's whereabouts — a briefcase was sitting next to the desk; on it there was a neat pile of student papers, probably waiting to be marked.

"Should we call the police?" asked Helen.

"I don't know," said Maggie. "We'd feel like awful fools if she's sitting in the physics lab right now."

But as the two women looked hesitantly for the telephone, Sergeant Dubinsky of Homicide was carefully removing leaves and brush from the cold and stiffened remains of the girl they were looking for. The unhappy couple who had stumbled across her stood uneasily nearby, their story told, with no reason to stay, but loathe to depart.

Chapter Five

Eleanor Scott slipped her Rabbit into the last free parking space in front of Kingsmede Hall and looked uncertainly around her. Something very peculiar was going on. Two police cruisers were pulled up in front of the main entrance, giving the school a decidedly ominous air. She walked around them and went slowly into the building, where she cautiously peered into the room marked "Principal". It contained only the principal's secretary, deep in conversation on the telephone. "Is she available?" Eleanor mouthed soundlessly.

Annabel looked up and shook her head. She covered the mouthpiece long enough to hiss: "If you want to wait, she might be able to see you — but you know how things are right now. It's pretty bad."

"I'll be in the staff room," she muttered, completely baffled, "if no one minds." Her explanation was lost in a renewed spate of earnest conversation on the phone. She slithered into the teachers' lounge, hoping to find a familiar face. The head of the science department waved to her from a corner where she was sitting, clutching a mug of tea and a black and green cookie. Eleanor breathed a sigh of relief as she headed for the large comfortable chair beside her.

"What in hell is going on, Cassandra?" whispered Eleanor as she sat down. "What are all those police cars doing here?"

"Omigod — you don't know. It's the most exciting thing that's happened since someone rang the fire alarm during the Christmas dance ten years ago. Actually, I shouldn't be talking about it so flippantly. It really is awful. One of our teachers — poor kid — was attacked by that guy down in the ravine."

"Attacked? Is she all right?"

"Hardly. He killed her." Cassandra shrugged as she delivered the line. "I'm sorry. This is awful, but it's been a terrible day. And she was just a supply — that's not a nice way to put it, is it? — I mean, no one really knew her very well. And she was kind of a nuisance when she was here, too. Very difficult to get along with and not very reliable. Still, that's no reason for someone to get killed." Cassandra looked a little more somber as she attacked another mint Oreo. "I really don't like this combination of flavors," she said. "But between teaching and all this hysteria I am absolutely starved."

"Was this the person who was filling in for Vicky?"

"Hmmm," said Cassandra, with her mouth full. "So she was my baby, so to speak. Roz is in there talking to a terribly cute policeman. I'm just sitting here waiting for my turn. I wonder why it is that the prospect of talking to the cops always makes you feel guilty? And as soon as I finish talking to him I have to interview her replacement. That's one nice thing — Roz was going to fire Jane today if this new one was available, and now she doesn't have to bother."

"You do have a gruesome turn of mind, Cassandra," said Eleanor, shivering. The staff-room door opened to interrupt her rebuke, however, and Annabel's beckoning finger drew them out of their chairs.

"There we go," said Cassandra cheerfully. "My turn to be grilled." She followed Eleanor toward the door.

She gave it a healthy tug, caught sight of the principal, and started to make her excuses. "Look, Roz, I'll come back some other ——" She stopped dead. Standing directly in front of her as the door opened wider was a tall, slightly mournful-looking man who had obviously been in mid-sentence with Roz Johnson. There was a moment of grim silence as they stared at each other, first self-conscious, then embarrassed. Eleanor recovered first, however, and automatically extended her hand to him. "John, how pleasant to . . . I mean, this is a surprise. I didn't expect to see you here." He just as automatically took her hand and shook it. Damn! That was exactly what she had done the first time she had met him, just as if he were a potential client with a large house he wanted to sell. She dropped his hand like a hot potato.

"What are you doing here?" he asked brusquely. "Sorry, I didn't mean to put it that way." He took her by the elbow and steered her away from Cassandra and Roz, who were looking on with considerable interest. "Look, I have to talk to the head of the science department and then get some photos of the dead woman. But then I'd like to talk to you. I mean, alone somewhere. Not about this. For God's sake, Eleanor, you know what I mean. Say something!" His voice was low, but tense with exasperation.

"I'll be in the parking lot after I talk to Roz. Same old Rabbit, over in the corner there. Don't be too long." She smiled uncertainly and walked back to the other two.

Twenty minutes later, and not much wiser, John Sanders walked out of the spare, utilitarian vice-principal's office which had been turned over to him for interviews.

He bumped into Dubinsky, who was coming in search of him out of the small seminar room where he had been talking to a motley assortment of hastily assembled staff members. "Braston called while you were locked up in there," he said, nodding across the hall. "She has the preliminary findings."

"Come back in here, then, and let's hear them," said Sanders. "Anything interesting?"

"Well, maybe," said Dubinsky, opening his notebook and flipping back a couple of pages. "See what you think. The cause of death was cerebral hemorrhage, probably occasioned by one or more heavy blows on the temple with a broad, flat instrument."

"A rock?"

"Not necessarily, apparently, although it could have been a broad, flat rock. She had been dead about ten to sixteen hours before she got to the morgue, which places her time of death at between 4:00 P.M. and 10:00 P.M. yesterday. Which fits in with her having been teaching until 3:30, at least." Sanders opened his mouth to comment but stopped himself as Dubinsky carried on. "There were traces of recent intercourse (blood type O positive), bruising on right knee, and what boils down to nasty scrapes on the left knee and left hip, containing a great deal of imbedded gravel, like the stuff found on the path close to where the body was found. Also on both elbows and forearms — scrapes, that is, and gravel. No bruising anywhere else."

"None?" said Sanders. "Thighs, belly, neck?"

"Nope. She was healthy, well muscled, in good condition. Nothing remarkable about her except that she was ten to twelve weeks pregnant."

"Pregnant? Any knife marks anywhere on the body that we didn't notice?"

"None. Braston pointed out that she could well have simply stumbled and fallen, except that she obviously landed on her left side, and it was the right side of her face that was injured. And that when people in good shape fall face forward and to the side, and land on their arms, they don't usually bash themselves in the head fatally. In her opinion. But she isn't entirely ruling out accidental death."

"That's interesting," said Sanders, scribbling down bits and pieces from the account onto the paper in front of him. "It doesn't really sound much like the others, does it? Of course, the Parsons woman didn't fit the pattern precisely either. Maybe he was interrupted again. Did Melissa think she had been raped?"

"She didn't have any opinion on the matter. She got a bit ratty about it when I tried to push her. Intercourse she is willing to testify to, which might or might not be forcible rape."

"Maybe she wasn't. If he did rape her, he's leaving more and more clothes on them. This one seemed to be mussed up but was probably still wearing everything she came out in."

"Yeah," said Dubinsky. "but look at what she was wearing. He didn't have to take much off, did he? She's practically inviting him, dressed like that."

"Have you checked whether the gravel on the body comes from that section of the footpath?" Sanders suddenly looked at his watch. It was getting late, and there was a limit to the amount of time that Eleanor would be willing to wait. Dubinsky shook his head. "Then get on to that, and I'll go over what we have from here, and talk to that building superintendent. No need for you to hang around any longer."

"Sure," said Dubinsky, picking up his raincoat and heading for the door. "Have fun with the super."

Sanders scooped up the papers lying on the desk and strode quickly out toward the main door. As he passed the principal's office, Annabel popped out with two glossy eight-by-ten black and white prints. "These were taken for the yearbook, and they're the only pictures we have with her in them, but Miss Johnson said that you're welcome to them. We really don't need them back."

He took the prints with a vague smile and headed rapidly out to the parking lot. Eleanor was sitting in her car, flipping aimlessly through a copy of *Vogue* when he opened the door and slid in beside her. She jumped. "Oof! You scared me. I wasn't expecting you to show up so soon. I must be getting a bit edgy." She smiled tentatively at him. "You're looking pretty good, John." She paused a minute. "Well, actually, you don't, now that I look at you. Ghastly is more like it. Have you been sick?"

"No, I'm fine," he said abruptly. "Look, I can't talk to you in a school parking lot. The last time I tried that I must have been sixteen. Let's get out of here."

"Sure." Eleanor extracted her keys from her purse and started the car. "Where do you want to go?"

The answer to that one leapt into his mind with ferocious speed. He knew exactly where he wanted to go, and also knew that it would be impossible. They were so close to Eleanor's huge, uncluttered apartment, with its low, sloping ceiling and its glass doors that led out onto a deck that overlooked garden and ravine. But that would not be a good idea right now. "Let's get a drink somewhere quiet. Some place close, since I have to interview an apartment super over on MacNiece."

"Why don't you see him first, then, since it's just around the corner from my place? Then we can walk over to Yonge and Bloor. Would you like a ride to MacNiece? It's on my way. What did you do with your car?" She had looked around for an understated Toronto unmarked police car and had seen only the usual varied collection of teachers' and shinier parents' cars.

"I came with Dubinsky and sent him away again with it. Subconsciously I must have assumed that you would offer me a ride." He grinned and put the pictures in his hand down on his knee as he twisted to do up the seat belt.

"What are these?" asked Eleanor, picking them up. "Not pictures of the girl who was killed, are they?" She looked more closely at the one on top. "You know, I think I've met one in this group — in a funny kind of way. She lifts weights over at the health club I've joined. Snarky as hell. That one, with the longish hair." Eleanor pointed to the picture of Jane Conway standing with the rest of the science department in a huddle on the front steps.

"That one?" said Sanders. "Are you sure?" He took the pictures and pulled the second shot out to show her. "Do you recognize her in this group?"

"Sure. That one — same longish hair, same face, but you can see the snarky expression even better." She paused a second. "I guess she's the one, isn't she?"

He brushed aside the question. "She lifted weights? Recently? When did you see her there last? And what in hell were you doing in a health club where women lift weights?"

Eleanor put the car in gear and quietly left the parking lot. "Which question do you want me to answer first? Anyway, it had to be recently, because I just started two weeks ago, and that was when I saw her. I asked her a simple question, and she bit my head off. I was terribly embarrassed. And I was there because I've taken up health and fitness — for self-protection and the general fun of it." By this time the Rabbit had accomplished the very brief journey over to MacNiece Avenue. "Which house do you want?"

"Number thirty-seven. It's the apartment building," he said. "Right over there."

"If you give me a call — upstairs, my phone — I'll meet you in front of the house. Do you want the number?"

"I have it," he said, a little too emphatically, as he

clambered out of the car. "And I won't be long, unless she knows a great deal more than I think she does."

"I take it that the lady wasn't very well informed," Eleanor said lightly after the waitress had put their beers down and left.

"Not very well at all," said Sanders. "Lots of insinuations about the general level of morals among her younger female tenants, and absolutely no information about Conway at all. It seems to take an explosion to pry her away from her TV set. She probably doesn't even recognize half the tenants." He opened his mouth to carry on in the same vein, then stopped abruptly. "I've missed you, you know. Painfully. It seems like a very long time since I've seen you."

"It has been," said Eleanor. "Since last summer, I believe." She looked at him steadily, then dropped her eyes back down to her glass. "I'm really not as hard to find as you are. I did consider dialling 911 to see what would happen, but I was afraid that someone else might take the call."

Her attempt at humor had the paradoxical effect of tightening the already tense atmosphere. Sanders stared into his glass. "Someone else would have." He tried to smile in turn. "It's not a very efficient way to reach me. I've left Marie, you know."

"Oh," said Eleanor. "No, I didn't know. When?"

"Last weekend, actually. And I don't see why you would know. No one does, I suppose, but Dubinsky and the switchboard, who have my new telephone number. It's funny, though. The first thing that happens is that I run into you again. You don't know how many times I've almost called you, but didn't."

"Why not?" asked Eleanor. "It never occurred to me that I was that terrifying. No one else seems to find me even slightly alarming." She leaned back in her chair, arm along the back, with her head resting on her hand and her fingers thrust through her untidy red curls. Her expression hovered halfway between amusement and hostility. "You're not being wildly convincing."

"Dammit, you know perfectly well that I'm not terrified of you. Can't you understand the position I was in? You could credit me with some conscience at least."

"Oh, really?" said Eleanor in polite disbelief. "That certainly wasn't the impression that I got last summer. Isn't tormented loyalty a new line? I wasn't all that aware of it before."

"Christ almighty, you can be exasperating. I'm not trying to say that I never looked at another woman. But the women I run into in my line of work are a pretty mixed bag" — he ran his fingers through his hair and looked perplexed — "and they're not like you. You were — I don't know — a problem."

Eleanor shrugged and waved her hand dismissively. "What the hell. We can argue about that later. What are you doing now? Where are you living?"

He signaled the waitress for another round and sighed. "I sublet a one-bedroom apartment downtown for six months. It's a strange sensation to walk in at night to an empty house. Sort of like the feeling you get after a toothache disappears — a feeling that something's missing, but you're not sure that you care. Anyway, I'm not really living anywhere, it feels like. Basically, I'm camping out behind my desk. We're pretty busy most of the time, and now with King Kong out there ——"

"King Kong?"

"Your local rapist. The one who kills them and then carries them around for a while before he dumps them somewhere. We're going crazy. That's two women in your area now."

"Listen," said Eleanor, "if someone else has already been attacked out in that ravine, why isn't it filled with cops? How many women does it take before you start sending in patrols?''

"Patrols!'' He choked into his beer glass. "We have so many guys in there the rummies are complaining about lack of space. We even have guys in old clothes, clutching wine bottles, armed to the teeth. He is obviously very cautious. He waits until there's no one around — a patrol can't be everywhere at once — and then attacks. For all we know, he goes out every day, checking four or five different areas. This guy is very mobile and, in his way, pretty smart.''

"Why don't you let people know the ravines are being patrolled? Wouldn't it make them feel better?''

"We don't want them to feel better. We want them to stay the hell out of the way until we catch him. You may not believe it, but it's turning me into a nervous wreck. When they called us to the ravine this morning I just sat in the car and let Dubinsky go in ahead. I didn't want to walk in there and see a lot of red hair spread out on the ground. I'm beginning to lose my grip, I think.''

"I wouldn't worry about that if I were you,'' said Eleanor without a flicker of sympathy. "Everyone says that he likes them short. He probably couldn't reach up high enough to hit me on the head. Besides, I told you, I'm so fast and strong now that I can handle anything. Look at that,'' she said, flexing her right bicep.

Sanders laughed for the first time that afternoon. "Okay, Wonder Woman, show me.'' He put his right elbow on the table, arm up, in classic stance. Eleanor solemnly moved the empty beer glasses out of the way and positioned herself to meet the challenge. Slowly their palms joined, and Eleanor started to push. For a second she gained ground, and then she felt her tortured muscles give slightly, and her arm being steadily dragged down from its position. Suddenly she noticed the waitress hovering over them, her tray heavy with filled glasses. Laughter robbed her of any remaining strength and she gave up just in time to avoid knocking over the next round.

"That's no fair," she said, as she caught her breath. "You've probably been sweating it out in some jock gym for cops for fifteen years, and I just started two weeks ago."

"Naw," he said, shaking his head. "Just my innate male superiority." He ducked to avoid her fist. "No, really, I am just a bit bigger and stronger than you are. You're not bad, though." He picked up her hand again, almost absent-mindedly. "I wish you wouldn't assume that this guy is a ninety-pound weakling. He can't be that feeble, you know. It looks as though he might have carried some of those women a fair distance, while they were either dead or unconscious." A new thought flickered across his mind, but he kept firm hold of her hand still. "Tell me something — why would a woman lift weights or run while she was pregnant? Wouldn't she figure it was bad for her?"

"I'm not sure," said Eleanor slowly. "I've known a couple of girls who kept up with their running while they were pregnant on the theory that it would keep them healthy. It seemed to work for them, anyway. But lifting weights — that sounds like another thing altogether. It puts quite a strain on your system, I think. But you shouldn't ask me. I was the sort that just lay around and vegetated while I was carrying Heather. The guys at the health club probably know more about it than I do. Why do you want to know? I assure you I'm not pregnant."

"Maybe not, but Jane Conway was. That's why I was so surprised to hear that you had run into her at a weight-lifting establishment. But as far as I know, maybe all these places are filled with pregnant women bench-pressing three hundred pounds. I have trouble keeping up in some areas."

"How pregnant was she? She didn't look it to me, but then I didn't examine her closely. Wasn't she divorced or something?"

"Separated, according to the principal. And that doesn't prevent women from getting pregnant, you know. Anyway, she was only two or three months along." He took a long swallow of his beer. "We'd love to know who the father is, though. You're pretty cosy with the teachers at the school. I don't suppose you heard any gossip about who he might be?"

"I didn't even know she was pregnant, remember? And I don't see why you're worrying about it. If she was killed by your King Kong, he wouldn't care who got her pregnant, surely."

"We can't just assume that each one of these victims was killed by the same man — we still have to nose around and see what we can find. You wouldn't like to keep those lovely ears open for any gossip, would you?" He looked up, and then shook his head. "God, but I'm stupid. Forget I said that. Thirty minutes ago you were barely speaking to me, and now I'm asking you to . . . I'm sorry. You must have things to do, and I'm keeping you here in ridiculous conversation."

"Well," she said, "I am pretty hungry. And if you aren't going to go somewhere to dinner with me, I'll have to go and get something to eat before I faint from starvation. It's a long walk home on an empty stomach."

Chapter Six

Friday, April 13, dawned before John Sanders' day ended. He had spent a bleak and restless night, falling into profound slumber as the first light began to pick out the Toronto lakefront, the long-awaited sleep thus depriving him of a magnificent view from his downtown apartment. The alarm dragged him painfully to consciousness, and habit got him dressed and out of the door. By 8:45, as foul-tempered and foggy as the weather, he was facing Ed Dubinsky across their desks. He reached for the sheaf of papers on the Conway woman. His coffee spilled over two Break-and-Enters and some as yet unclassified mail. "Shit!" he muttered, looking wildly and haplessly around for something to mop the coffee up with. Dubinsky heaved himself out of his chair and disappeared, returning seconds later with a roll of paper towels.

"You don't look all that bright this morning," remarked Dubinsky. "Everything okay?" This was the closest he'd got to alluding to Sanders' domestic imbroglios.

"Everything's fine. I just didn't get all that much sleep last night for some reason. Too much work, too much coffee — I don't know." He drank the half-inch left in the styrofoam cup and threw it into the waste-basket. "Anyway, let's see where we are, as of now. Any word on Parsons?"

"Collins was up there this morning."

"And?"

"Nothing. She's still unconscious. The neurologist thinks we're wasting the taxpayers' money keeping a man there."

"So what in hell are we supposed to do? If she regains consciouness and there's no one there to take a statement we'll be in a helluva mess. Besides, she can probably identify him — and he must know that. And since he seems to be invisible, he could probably get in there and finish her off."

"Okay," said Dubinsky. "I never said she should be left alone." He shook his head. "If she buys it, that's five in four months. One guy. I can't believe it."

"If it is the same one. That's what I find hard to believe."

"This last one looks close enough," said Dubinsky. "Everything was the same — except no knife marks and she still had her clothes on. He was probably interrupted again."

"Yeah," said Sanders, "But it just doesn't have the same smell to it. I went through the newspaper accounts last night. Everything that was done to that woman has already been published in the papers. It could be a copycat."

"You think we've got two rapists running around the ravines now?" He got to his feet again. "That's really great, isn't it? You want some more coffee?"

"Sure." He looked down at the papers on his desk, spread them out a bit, and thought. Dubinsky put a fresh cup of coffee on his desk, out of range of his elbow, and sat down. "Thanks. We still don't have anything positive on her background, do we? Did we get anywhere on next of kin?" He lifted his cup cautiously to his mouth. "You'd think she was some rubby or sailor on a spree. No one seems to know anything about her except her name."

"Well, I did talk to one woman at the school who seemed to know her, but I haven't been able to follow up on the details yet." Once again he flipped slowly back through the pages of his notebook. "A Miss Madeleine O'Connor, part-time teacher of Russian and German. She said that she talked to her a fair amount because they had a spare period together every day. And that she felt sorry for her, because she was having a hell of a time with the kids and with the department head, and no one was really willing to help her. Then she went on about how teachers treat newcomers and so on. Pretty bitchy, if you ask me. And she never shut up. None of them did. I never heard anything like it." He paused to shake his head. "Anyway, Conway's husband is a graduate student at the University of Toronto, in the Department of Biology, and they're separated; she and this O'Connor woman had a lot in common because they were really graduate students, not teachers like everyone else on the staff. Whatever that means. The husband's name is Doug. And that's all I got, except that they used to go out for a drink once in a while after work." He sighed. "And if there are any other women at the school to interview, I wish you'd do it. They seem to be more your type than mine."

"So all we know about her is her name, and her husband's name, and where she worked. Great. Someone must have recommended her for the job — I have it here somewhere" — Sanders searched through his notebook — "Right. Recommended by Professor George Simmons of the Department of Physics, University of Toronto, who apparently said that she probably knew enough to teach high-school kids, as long as no one asked her too hard a question. Jesus. There's a sweet guy.'' He thought for a moment. "But we know more than that," he said finally. "She used to work out at a gym near the school. They might know something about her there. Anyway, call the Department of Biology and see if you can locate Mr. Doug Conway, and then we'll go through that apartment for whatever leads we can pick up. Otherwise off to the gym. Okay, let's get moving."

Dubinsky and Sanders stood at the entrance to Jane Conway's apartment and looked around. It wasn't quite ten o'clock; they had a promise they would be able to find the elusive husband at two o'clock in the Biology Department, and it was quite possible that it would take them the full, boring four-hour interval just to go through her papers, looking for background material. The apartment had a dreary, faded look with the spring rain trickling down the window panes. The furniture was dark and heavy; the rug an old, bleached-out red Persian. Dubinsky looked resigned, Sanders depressed. At last he turned and spoke. "Why don't you start with the bedroom, and I'll get going on that desk." They moved off in separate directions and started in to work.

Sanders began with the brown leather briefcase leaning against the side of the desk. It contained two brutally large textbooks, which he flipped through. They appeared to be just that, but tarted up with more pictures than he remembered from his schooldays. Under them was a large red notebook, each page of which was dated and ruled off in eight or nine sections. The pages were filled with abbreviations and page numbers that meant nothing to Sanders, but were more likely to do with teaching than with her private life, he suspected. On the other hand, there might be something there — he put the book to one side, just in case he wanted to go over it with someone who could tell him how much of it referred to school. There was nothing else. On the desk he found a bundle of tests, partially marked, and the usual desk-top paraphernalia — telephone, note pad, Toronto phonebook, an electric typewriter, carefully covered, with nothing in it, and a little circular container filled with pencils and fineline markers, with pictures on it of lambs gamboling among spring flowers. He picked it up in astonishment. It seemed so unlike anything else in that sober room. He noticed some laconic scribbles on the top piece of notepaper and picked it up carefully, stared at it a moment, and put it to one side.

He cleared everything off the top of the desk and started to go through each drawer, removing everything from the drawers so that they could be checked for odd bits of paper caught in corners. The top drawers were tidy and characterless, containing miscellaneous stationery, typing paper, pens, pencils, a stapler, a Dymo labeler, three sets of mathematical instruments, and an expensive-looking calculator. She certainly was neat. He thought of the chaos in his desk and shook his head. When he pulled the brass handle of the next drawer, he found a deep and capacious file drawer, legal size, filled with neatly labeled file folders. He yanked it out to its fullest extent, pulled the comfortable typing chair up to the desk, and started to go through the files, one by one. The eight folders in front were completely useless to him. They contained notes for courses she was teaching and from courses she had taken. After flipping through each one briefly he gave up. Her notes were neat and legible, however, much neater than anything he had ever taken down himself back during his brief fling as a student. There were only two folders behind them, and they seemed much more promising. One was marked "Van Loon and McHenry" and the other "Correspondence: Personal". He pulled them both out and settled back to read them in comfort.

Van Loon and McHenry was a legal firm with offices on Church Street, not far from Rosedale, according to their letterhead. She had several pieces of correspondence from them, dating back to October: one pointing out that her new will was ready for signature, and the next one confirming the points discussed in a previous meeting and stating that she would have extreme difficulty in blocking her husband's action for divorce, should he institute proceedings. Sandwiched in among these were a few bills, in which she was also charged for advice given by telephone. Sanders carefully put all these documents back and placed the file on top of the red notebook. The personal correspondence file was bumpy with bundles of letters tied together still in their envelopes. Some of them he didn't bother to read — the postmarks were from years ago and the paper was yellowed. Two bundles had fairly recent letters on top, both sets postmarked Cobourg. He undid the first one. Those letters were all the same, each one page in length, neatly written, thanking her for something or other and talking about the farm, and signed, "Uncle Matt". He put them to one side with the other things. He picked out a few from the large bundle in his hand. They were long, misspelled, and had a frenzied quality to them. They spoke of love, and eternity, and passion, all in appallingly banal terms. The dates went back five or six years; they were all signed "Mike". Sanders sighed and put them to one side as well. A thought occurred to him. Maybe this guy was — when were the last letters written? He flipped quickly. There were none after January 10th. He took that one out and read it:

My darling Jane,
   I was so happy to recieve your letter, I had almost given up hopeing that you would write me again. But I was very upset to hear how unhappy you are. You must

not let people push you around that way, of course they are going to be mean to anyone as nice as you are. I was talking to my father about it and he says that I should come down to be with you. He doesn't need me until the summer season starts again so I will be down as soon as I can get my bags packed. I will find someplace to stay, don't worry, I know how you feel about people just droping in.

All my love,
Mike

So Mike had come to Toronto in January — depending, of course, on how long it took him to pack his bags. That would cut things rather fine, if Melissa was right in her dates, but if he had scurried right down after writing that letter, he could have fathered the child. And what nasty things had she been complaining about to her gallant would-be protector? He would like to speak to Mike, whoever he was. That bundle joined the pile. The rest of the letters were loose and made no particular sense, but he took out the ones that had been written in the past six months and added them to his pile.

He looked up as Dubinsky came in. "Find anything interesting?"

"Some papers," Dubinsky said. "And a bank book — savings account with the Royal Bank." He handed it over. Sanders looked at the figures and whistled.

"That's not a bad little nest egg for a girl to have tucked away, is it? How do you suppose she's managed to salt away over a thousand a month since last summer?" He reached for the slip of notepaper. "And what do you make of this, Dubinsky?"

There were two notations: "M. — 3 — Tues." and "G. — 5 — Tu." They were written at different slopes, as if they had been jotted down at different times. Dubinsky shook his head. "She was going to meet someone at three o'clock on Tuesday — maybe her mother? Then someone else at five?"

"Sure — her grandfather this time. Or how about 'M' for Mike?" He handed Dubinsky the letter. "The trouble with that, though, is that she worked. How would she meet someone at three?" He took the slip back. "It might not mean a thing, or then again, maybe it'll fit in with something else." He stood up and began collecting the various papers she had set aside. "Here, this is her lawyers' number. Give them a call and tell them we'll be over to see them. I want to know what she discussed with them that doesn't turn up in her file here. I'm going to take another look through the place."

He wandered through the empty apartment into the kitchen. He opened the refrigerator — not that he expected to find any serious evidence there, more from a mixture of curiosity and a professional desire to find out something, anything, about this woman. It was clear from the contents that she drank beer and orange juice and ate rye bread and mayonnaise. But, on the other end of the diet spectrum, she also seemed to consume tins of liquid diet food. There was something about this that depressed him and, after checking all the cupboards, he left the kitchen as quickly as he could. He sat down at an old-fashioned white-painted dressing table in the bedroom and began to open up the drawers, expecting to find make-up, jewelry, underwear, and the like. The top drawer was empty.

"Hey, Dubinsky," he called. "Did you check this little table?"

"Yeah," he said, coming into the bedroom. "That's where I got the bank book and statements and things like that. The second drawer is full of paid bills and receipts, and the bottom drawer seems to be filled with tax stuff. Very neat. It was all locked, but the key was on her ring. I took out the stuff that might be interesting and left the rest for you. Anyway, about the lawyer — he left last weekend for a couple of weeks in Mexico. He won't be back until after Easter. His secretary hasn't the faintest idea how to reach him" — Dubinsky mimicked a high-pitched voice charged with great drama — "because he doesn't like to be disturbed when he's on holiday."

"Great," muttered Sanders. "Just one more thing to make life easier. Anyway, did you find an appointment book or anything like that? Something that might explain what she was doing on Tuesday?" Dubinsky shook his head. "Did you check her purse?"

"Come on, what do you take me for? Of course I checked her purse, and every drawer of that white thing there, and the drawer in the night table. Also the cabinets in the bathroom, her dresser drawers, and her closet. She has lots of towels and underwear, but I didn't see an appointment book. Are you sure it isn't in the living room on her desk or something?"

Sanders glared at him. "Yes, I'm sure. And she doesn't seem to have an address book or anything resembling one. Did you check her pockets?" As soon as he said that, he headed for the closet by the front door, opened it, and started to go through the pockets of all the coats and jackets hanging there. Nothing. He emerged again, shrugging his shoulders. "She might have left it at work. Let's check back there before heading on to see the husband."

Ginny sat perched on the edge of the chair in Dr. Rasmussen's office, clutching her large purse tightly on her lap. She tried to cross her knees casually, and then uncrossed them again quickly as her legs began to tremble. The doctor swept in, the light bouncing off his bald head. His mouth beamed at her while his eyes flicked over her in rapid assessment.

"Well, now, Mrs. Morrison, so far so good. I don't see anything really alarming at this point." He read the sketchy details on the new chart in front of him. "I think that Dr. Smith mentioned that you were working? Could I ask what you do?"

The sympathy she read into this comment finished her. Tears spilled down her cheeks; she scrambled furiously for a Kleenex and hauled herself back together. "Yes. I'm an assistant manager at Austin's — in the toy department. It's a good job, and I really can't afford to give it up. My husband was laid off last November, just before I realized I was pregnant. His unemployment insurance doesn't go very far, and we'd be stuck if I quit." She assumed her most mulish and independent glare.

"And that means you're on your feet most of the time?" She nodded mutely, her eyes filling up again with tears. "It's very premature to talk of quitting, Mrs. Morrison. It certainly hasn't come to that, yet. But you get sick leave, don't you? Even assistant managers can get sick. You must get off your feet and into bed. Rest is still the best way to stop the cramping and spotting. Ten days in bed, then come back and see me. Can your husband look after you?" Ginny stared, appalled. "Is your mother in town?" She nodded. "Then you should go to your mother's and let her pamper you a bit. And tell her that I want you to gain some weight. You know, at 115 pounds you're a bit thin even for a lady who isn't pregnant. I'd like to see you closer to 135 or even 140 before this baby is born. Off to bed, now, and I'll see you in ten days. Call me if things don't improve by Monday." He turned to her file and his notes as she fled the office in relief.

Ginny fished through her purse in fruitless pursuit of another quarter. Dammit, she muttered, I know I have one here somewhere. Ah, there it was — caught in the fold where the lining had ripped. She forced herself to calm down, breathe deeply, put the coin in the slot slowly and carefully, and then dial with deliberation. The phone rang and rang. He must be in that bloody garage again, she thought; she refused to hang up. Finally a slow, groggy voice answered her.

"Glenn? Where were you? Never mind. I just left the doctor's. He says I'll probably be okay, but I have to stay in bed for ten days." A pause. "I don't know why he said ten days. You can call him yourself and ask, if you want. That's what he said. Anyway, he doesn't want me doing anything so he said I should go to Mother's. You can look after yourself for a couple of weeks, can't you?" She held the receiver away from her ear slightly, with a look of exasperation on her face. "If you can't figure out how to do your shirts, take them over to your mother's. Anyway, I'll go to the bank on the way home and then pack my stuff and drive myself over there." She frowned. "Of course I'll need the car. What would you need it for? You've got the —— Well, if you think so, then you can drive me over to Mother's and take the car home. Anyway, I'll be back in about half an hour. Don't go out. 'Bye."

In the living room of the neat, multi-layered townhouse, he put the phone back on the hook and turned his gaze once more to the three daily papers spread out on the floor in front of him. "Terror Stalks City as Mad Rapist Strikes Again" screamed the headlines of the morning tabloid. "Another Victim in Metro Rape-Murders?" asked the sedate morning daily in a secondary headline, tucked under the latest international news. "Action Demanded in Toronto Deaths" cried the crusading voice of the afternoon paper. The stories, however, were all the same: a woman in her twenties was attacked and killed while out jogging in the Rosedale Ravine — identification withheld pending notification of next of kin. Metro police spokesman Daniel Kennedy agrees that it could be the work of the person who raped and killed three other woman and seriously injured another in the period of January to April this year and continues to advise caution for women out alone, especially in remote areas. He picked up each paper in turn and re-read the stories slowly and carefully, shook his head and smiled slightly, then neatly folded them and carried them out to the garage before his wife had time to come in the door.

Sanders and Dubinsky now stood in front of a plain door with four names tucked into little metal slots nailed to it. Their visit to the school had produced nothing but a welcome diversion to twenty-four giggling girls who watched, fascinated, as Sanders went through all the drawers in the physics lab. When he had produced the red notebook in order to ask Mrs. Antonini if there was anything in it that did not pertain to the school day, she had snatched it up with cries of glee and was most unwilling to give it back. She finally agreed to photocopy it and return it to him, saying most discouragingly as she flipped through it that it looked like a normal daybook to her, and that Jane's replacement was going to need all the information in it. So much for that hope. Perhaps this visit would produce more.

Doug Conway was the first name in the alphabetized list of occupants. Sanders knocked, a casual voice called out, "Come in", and the two men entered. The room was just barely large enough to hold four desks jutting out from opposing walls and to leave a narrow passageway through to a large window. The spaces on the walls not filled with desks were covered with utilitarian steel shelving, crammed with books, papers, and what appeared to Sanders to be junk. The desks themselves were piled to overflowing with books, coffee cups, plants, photographs, and computer read-outs in catholic disarray. There seemed to be only four chairs, one for each desk.

"Do come in. Sorry for the mess in here — it is awfully cramped — but just grab a couple of chairs. You're not in my section, are you?" He gave them a puzzled glance.

Sanders returned the look and introduced himself. "I

understood from your secretary out there that you were expecting us. I mean, she told us to come this afternoon at two. Apparently you didn't get our message?''

"Oh, Lord," he said. "Police. I'm sorry, but that girl is absolutely hopeless. She has discovered that the easiest thing to do with messages is to throw them out. This is when I have office hours; that's why I'm here. Otherwise I'd be in the lab. I mean, we don't really do much work in this office; that's why it looks like this. We just store books and see students here. We're all TA's.''

"TA's?''

"Teaching Assistants. Anyway, what can I do for you? Brian Jones over there is the one who deals with most of the forensic problems that get referred to us but I'll do what I can.''

"Forensic problems?''

"Isn't that why you're here? I'm sorry, maybe we should start one more time from the beginning.'' He smiled and settled back in his chair, his long frame perfectly relaxed, but his high forehead slightly crinkled, and his dark eyes fixed intently on the two men. Sanders began to feel like a specimen of some sort. He pulled over a chair and sat down. Dubinsky cautiously shoved aside a few papers on someone else's desk and perched on the edge of it, notebook in hand, filling the office with his bulk.

"No, I'm afraid that what we came over here for is rather less pleasant. There has been a most unfortunate'' — Sanders searched for a word. He hated this sort of thing anyway, and when a man is separated from his wife, one has no idea whether he's going to be crushed or relieved at the news. Or perhaps, not at all surprised — "occurrence concerning —''

"Who — ?'' he said sharply, his face changing. "What's happened?''

"Your wife, Jane Conway.''

"Jane?'' He sounded relieved. "What's happened to

her?'' Sanders wondered whose name he had been expecting to hear when that expression had crossed his face.

"You may have seen in the papers — there was a woman killed while jogging in the park late Wednesday. I'm afraid it was your wife."

"Running." He spoke automatically. "She hated the term 'jogging'. Poor Jane. She never did have much luck with things." He picked up a pen and put it down again. Sanders continued to look at him, trying to gauge his reaction. "I won't pretend that I'm grief-stricken, you know. But I'm terribly sorry that something like that should have happened to her. Was she badly hurt? That's stupid — I mean, before she died. She was a real coward about sickness and pain, poor thing."

"No. She seems to have died instantly." Sanders paused a moment. "We would like to ask you a few questions." Conway smiled agreeably and nodded. "I take it you were separated?" He nodded again. "For how long and why?"

"Since last summer, actually. Around the beginning of August, I think. I came home from the lab one evening and she wasn't there. Why she left is a harder question to answer. I think there were a lot of reasons." He paused for a second. "I've thought about this quite a lot. We got married the year she was at O.C.E. — teachers' college — at Christmas. That was in 1980. There weren't many jobs around, but she managed to get one up in the Bruce Peninsula. We only saw each other on weekends, but I was working very hard on my doctorate, and as a research assistant, trying to impress the hell out of the big boys — which I did — so only having her around on weekends was great as far was I concerned. But she really hated teaching. The kids just ate her for breakfast, I guess, and she didn't seem to be able to figure out what to do about it. Anyway, she got fired at the end of the year and I talked her into going to graduate school. Well, I had sort of forgotten what a slog she had found university when we were both at

Queen's together. Anyway, she started in, and after a while had to drop a couple of courses because she couldn't manage a full load, and by spring it was clear that when she did finally get a degree, it would be a terminal MA — sounds like a terrible disease, doesn't it? That's how she felt about it.''

"What is it?"

"A degree with marks too low to get you into the PhD program. It's just another way of failing, 'really, if what you wanted was a doctorate. Meanwhile, of course, I was going great guns. Professor Griffiths took me on as a graduate student — he's the really big man in the field around here — and people were inviting me to give papers and stuff like that. I think she started to hate me for it. Anyway, she began to screw around a bit. But by this time we hardly saw each other, except that we sometimes went running together. I hadn't slept with her for months; she couldn't stand me talking to her, much less touching her, and I had struck up a friendship with a terrific girl. That was all it was at the time, anyway. I think Jane was involved with some guy, though. At first, she just came on strong with almost anyone at parties; it was kind of gruesome in a way, but then that stopped, and she started disappearing for the night from time to time.''

"Didn't you object?" Sanders looked at him with interest. He seemed to take his wife's infidelity with extraordinary detachment.

"It's hard to explain, but I was finishing up my course work for my doctorate and getting preliminary materials for my dissertation. I had just landed Griffiths as a supervisor, and between the lab and the library I was working at least twelve hours a day. Jane was so bitchy whenever I saw her I began to avoid her as much as possible. Christ, I didn't have the energy left over to cope with her soul-searching. I don't know what it was about Jane — she just whined on and on about life being unfair, and she never got off her ass and did anything about it. The only thing she was good at was attracting men. I think that was the only thing she really enjoyed. Not that she liked them much after she got them, though. You'd see some poor bastard she had hooked on Friday come bouncing up to her at a party on Saturday and get brushed off like so much dandruff." He chuckled.

"Did you make any attempt to get her back after she left?"

"Are you kidding? That was such a load off my mind. I felt so guilty about her, as if all her bitching and whining and misery was my responsibility, that when I read her letter I dashed back down to the lab and collected everyone I could find and dragged them off for a drink. Including Karen, whom I dragged off for the weekend on Friday. That's the girl I was talking about." He leaned back again. "And that's about it."

"Have you see her much since the separation?"

Conway shook his head. "Hardly at all. I called her a couple of times about her stuff, and I gave her a hand packing it up and taking it over to her new apartment, that's all. I was going to get in touch with her this month about divorce proceedings, but I hadn't got around to it yet."

"Did you think she'd give you a hard time?" Sanders cocked his head to one side.

"Nope. With no kids, no assets, and her walking out on me, there's absolutely no way she could hold things up."

"Her apartment is in a fairly expensive area of the city, I notice. Were you contributing to her maintenance?"

"Me?" Conway stared at him in amazement. "I'm living on a grant in low-cost housing. She was healthy and able to work and walked out on me. Even Jane didn't have the nerve to ask me for money."

"Was she getting money from her family, then? To help her along?" Sanders asked.

"I doubt that. She didn't have much family. Her parents are both dead, and her nearest relation is her Uncle Matt; he owns a small farm. I don't imagine he could spare much cash for anyone. No. Jane was always poor as a kid, I gathered." Conway's eyes were bright with curiosity.

"Did your wife ever think of staying at home and having a family? Since she didn't seem to like working?"

Conway laughed. "Jane was absolutely horrified at the idea of children. She wanted to have her tubes tied, except that it involved an operation, and she was even more terrified of doctors and knives than of ruining her lovely body with a baby." For the first time, a tinge of bitterness flavored his speech.

Sanders gave him another measured glance. Dubinsky, pen in hand, interposed. "Could you give us the name and address of this Uncle Matt? If he's Mrs. Conway's next of kin?"

"Well, his name is Jameson, Matt Jameson, and I don't know his address — just 'Cobourg' might reach him. Anyway, his address should be in Jane's book."

"Her book?" asked Dubinsky,

"That little green three-ring binder in her purse. She carried it with her always. The front half is a diary/appointment book, and the back half is addresses and phone numbers. You must have found it." Sanders nodded noncommittally. "He'll be in it, and all her friends, and, I suspect, all the guys she was going out with."

"Do you know who she was seeing recently?"

"The last ones I knew about were Grant Keswick — he's an actor of some kind — and a Mike somebody from Cobourg who she knew in high school." He shrugged his shoulders to plead ignorance. "If you want more information about her, you could always try Marny. When Jane took a year off after university and went to Europe, she worked with Marny after she got back, and they were great pals. I couldn't stand her — not my type."

"Does Marny have another name?"

"No doubt, but if I ever knew, I forgot it as fast as I could." He tossed this off cheerfully. "She might still work for Pronto Secretarial Services, though. She was office manager last I heard of her. They should know where she is."

As Sanders and Dubinsky rose to leave, Conway looked at them curiously. "If you don't mind my asking, why did you want all that information about Jane? I mean, except for her uncle's name — I can see you needing that. The papers seemed pretty clear that she had been killed by some rapist — the guy who did in those other girls."

"Oh well," said Sanders vaguely, "we still have to look round a bit, just in case someone took it into his head to try to get rid of her and push the blame off on someone else." He stood up to leave. "By the way, what's your blood type?"

"O positive," said Conway. "And the estranged husband is the first person you look at, isn't he? Well, I can't exactly mourn her, but I never would have killed her, or even wished this end on her. And you can believe that or not, as you like. Do you want my alibi?"

"It may come to that some day, Mr. Conway. Let's not worry about it for now."

Sanders and Dubinsky emerged into sunshine and Sanders looked around him at the slowly greening campus. "Pretty cool type, isn't he?" he asked. "A true scientist — you know, the detached observer, and all that crap."

"He stinks," said Dubinsky. "Where are we going?"

"To Pronto Secretarial Services. We'll see if the mysterious Marny likes him as much as he likes her."

Sanders stopped and scanned the list of occupants in the smallish red-brick building on St. Clair Avenue East. There it was: Pronto Secretarial Services, Room 201. He looked quickly at his watch and headed in the door. It had taken Dubinsky at least five minutes to find even an illegal parking space this close to five o'clock on a Friday afternoon. That woman had better not have left yet. Streams of people were already pouring out of the doors and elevators; there was no time to wait around. He dashed up the stairs, two at a time, followed by a heavily perspiring Dubinsky. Room 201 contained a pleasant reception room and a severely elegant blonde who was engaged at the moment in putting on her coat. She gave them a distinctly chilly smile and an almost inaudible, "May I help you?"

"I'm looking for your office manager — uh, Marny ——" he paused, hoping for some help.

It was obviously the sort of remark the receptionist would have expected from someone crude enough to arrive at 4:59 on a Friday. "I'll ask Miss Huber if she can see you. Your name?" He handed her his card. It did not impress her. She handed it back and muttered swiftly into the phone. "If you would care to sit down, Miss" — the stress on the "Miss" was exquisitely calculated — "Huber will be out in a moment." She finished putting on her coat, reached under her desk for a small, tasteful red purse, and flashed by them, in small, tasteful red shoes that were carefully contrived to set off the otherwise purely black and white perfection of her clothing.

Miss Huber emerged almost as soon as the blonde vision had cleared the door. If Sanders had been subconsciously expecting a further manifestation of blonde ice, he was pleasantly surprised. She was on the tall side of average and robust-looking, with olive skin and a thick cap of black hair that swung down around her ears. She had a slightly Slavic cast to her features, and at that moment her mouth was set in a rather ferocious expression. Cop-hater, thought Sanders. Nothing you can do about it.

"Yes?" she asked, in a flat, neutral voice.

"You were a friend of Mrs. Jane Conway, I believe," said Sanders.

"Were?" She looked puzzled.

"Is there somewhere less public we can talk?" A group of three women were emerging from a door behind the receptionist's desk, all yelling " 'Bye, Marny" as they hurried out.

"Come into my office, then. It's through here." She pointed to a door at right angles to the first. It opened onto a corridor with several doors leading to glass-partitioned offices on the left, and, on the right, a low wooden partition which separated off a large room filled with desks and activity. He looked at his watch again. She remarked stiffly that on Fridays they worked late, so that the girls could come back and pick up their pay, and then ushered them into a spartan office. "Now what is this about Jane?" She glowered at him.

"Mrs. Conway was killed while out jogging on Wednesday," he said bluntly. "Her name hasn't been released to the press because we haven't been able to contact her next of kin." He kept his eyes carefully on her as he let the flow of inconsequential information cushion his words.

She stared at him, her face gray and her body still and stiff with shock. "Are you sure? Are you sure that it's Jane?" She continued to stare. "I can't believe it. Jane wouldn't let herself be caught by someone like that." She stood up suddenly. "Would you excuse me a minute?" Without a pause she picked up her purse and raced out of the office.

"Well," said Dubinsky, "it's nice that someone is upset because she got it. I was beginning to think that the whole world couldn't have cared less if she lived or died." He stretched his feet out in front of him and wriggled his toes in relief. They had done a fair amount of running around so far.

A minute or two later, she came back in the room, looking calm and self-possessed. "And in what way can I help you?"

"Mrs. Conway's husband suggested —"

"That bastard!" she interjected in a matter-of-fact tone.

"— that you might have seen her more recently than he had, and that you could tell us something about her present friends and associates."

"What do you mean by that?" The hostility in her voice was palpable by now.

"Only what I said, Miss Huber. Nothing else." She leaned back in her chair. "For example, when did you see her last?"

"When did I see her last?" She seemed to consider for a moment the wisdom of answering this question. "I suppose it was Tuesday night."

"This past Tuesday? The day before she was killed?"

"Yeah." Her tone dared him to make something of it. "I had a little sort of party at my place and she came."

"Who did she come with? Anyone in particular?"

Marny shook her head. "Not that I know of. I think she came by herself."

"Were there many people there? Wouldn't you have noticed who she came with?"

"Not necessarily. There were about fifty or sixty people there, I guess. But I do know that she left early. She had to work the next day, she said, and couldn't stay late."

The door to her office opened with a crash and a small head with yards of brown hair hanging from it poked in. "Oh, sorry! I thought you were alone." She smiled winningly at the two men. "I just wanted to ask if you were coming to my opening tonight, Marny. Because if you were, there's a party at Bill's afterwards, and we'd be expecting you. Do come — to both, that is." She grinned in a disembodied way and disappeared again, shutting the door behind her.

"A lot of our girls are actresses who work for us when things are a bit tight. She's playing the second lead — the ingenue — in something opening tonight." Marny's voice reverberated with the pleasure she got from the reflected glamor of it all. "Now, what did you want to know?"

"We'd like to know about the men in her life — in her recent life, that is. Did she go home from the party with anyone, for example?"

"I don't think so. You mean, did some guy take her home that night?" Then she shook her head definitively. "No."

"Do you know of anyone she had been involved with in the past two or three months, then?" Sanders was getting exasperated at this waste of a Friday evening.

"Nope." She leaned back and crossed her arms — the attitude said that she would be unforthcoming. Then she relented and moved forward a bit. "She used to go out with Grant Keswick, but that was washed up long before Christmas. And there was that funny guy from Cobourg, Mike Somebody-or-other. He was always hanging around her. He was creepy. I could never figure out why she let him stick around. But she said it was nice having someone around who'd do anything you wanted. There were always lots of guys crazy about her all the time, but she was really choosy. She didn't go out with a lot of people." She stood up. "I'm sorry, but I have to get out there and make sure that everything is winding up all right. I really can't tell you anything else about her anyway." She ushered them out of the office, pointed their way to the exit, and hustled into the large room.

Sanders picked his raincoat up off the chair and began to struggle into it. One of the crowd of girls from the back office emerged through the door and smiled at them. "Is anything wrong?" she asked hesitantly. "I mean, the girls said you were from the police. We were wondering if there had been an accident or something." Her eyes sparkled with fascination and malice. "Miss Huber looked so upset when she came out of the office."

"We're investigating the murder of a friend of hers. She

seemed to take it hard," said Sanders, with deliberate and callous indiscretion. "Maybe someone here should keep an eye on her and make sure she's all right," he added casually as he did up his coat. "The friend who was looking after her before — when she left the office the first time, a few minutes ago?"

"Oh no. That wasn't what she left for," said their little informant. "She dashed over to telephone someone. Probably someone else who knew her friend." She looked expectantly for another tidbit. Sanders smiled and left her standing there.

"Well," he said, as they sauntered casually down the stairs. "I wonder who she called? I'm not sure that it was simple grief that made her react so poignantly to her friend's death." He caught sight of a telephone booth in the lobby. "You take the car on downtown. I'll grab the subway later. We should get onto Cobourg tonight, and Mr. Keswick."

There was no answer at Eleanor's apartment. He deliberated briefly and then looked up her cousin Susan's number. Susan owned the house the scattered crew of them lived in and was generally to be found lounging comfortably in her study on the second floor. He identified himself rather hesitantly and was surprised to be greeted with sleepy enthusiasm. "Sorry," said Susan, yawning. "I'm studying for exams, and I fell asleep over some particularly obscure and turgid philosophy. Thanks for waking me up — otherwise I probably would have slept all night. Aunt Jane believes that if you're sleeping, you must need the sleep. Which is kind, but awkward at exam time. What can I do for you? Looking for Eleanor?"

He admitted that he was. "She doesn't seem to be upstairs. I thought perhaps she might be down with the rest of the family."

"So you called me to avoid getting stuck in a long conversation with Aunt Jane. And got stuck in a long conversation with me instead. Well, she's not home; she is over at Kate Abbott's. Do you want me to yell for her out the window?" Susan's study overlooked the side garden of the large house, and when the trees weren't in leaf, she could see right into the Abbotts' windows.

"You don't have to do that — but maybe you could give me Kate Abbott's number. Unless you think she'd be upset if I called there."

"Kate wouldn't be upset," said Susan. "And you probably know better than I do right now if El would be." Susan gave him the number and finished up with a cheerful "See you."

Eleanor had just set down her empty cup and yawned when the phone interrupted the desultory conversation in Kate's living room. "It's for you, Eleanor," Kate said and dangled the phone in her direction. "A customer?"

Eleanor reached lazily for the receiver, totally unprepared to hear John's voice. "Look," he said urgently. "I'm tied up here tonight with stuff that has to be followed up on — but could I see you tomorrow night? I really will be off for the weekend by then. Perhaps we could ——"

"Oh no!" said Eleanor, before he could explain what it was that they could have done. "I'm going out tomorrow night." At this, Kate tactfully picked up the tea things and hustled herself and her niece out of the room. "One of Susan's friends — one of those theatrical types she inherited — wants me to go to a party and I said I would. At the time," she said pointedly, "I hadn't anything better to do."

"I see," said John. "An old friend, is he?"

"Not an old friend of mine certainly — probably an old friend of hers. Anyway, from Grant's description of the party, it sounded deadly, so if you had something particularly interesting in mind, I might be able to wriggle out of it."

"Grant?" That name was on his current checklist.

"Yes. Grant Keswick. An actor. You've probably seen him in TV commercials. I think he's the one with the beer bottle in one hand and a blonde in the other as he shoots the rapids above Niagara Falls, or something like that. All done in the studio, of course. Anyway, he's an egotistical bore — in fact, a lecherous, egotistical bore, so I'd just as soon get out of it, come to think of it."

"No, don't do that. I'm terribly interested in Mr. Keswick. It seems he's an old friend of your weight-lifting associate. I'd certainly like to know more about him. Why don't you go to that party and listen and be sweet, and remember everything he says, especially about Jane Conway? Or anything anyone else says about her."

"You mean I'm supposed to be an informant?" she asked. "You going to pay me fabulous amounts of money to betray my friends and acquaintances?"

"That's just on television. We're much too cheap to pay people when we don't have to. I'll call you on Sunday and see what you found out."

"Wait," she said. "Did you know where Jane Conway spent Tuesday night? Because I just heard."

"So did I," he said. "At a party."

"That's not what I heard. According to Kate's niece, she spent Tuesday evening (or part of it, anyway) at the After Hours, which is, I gather, a rather steamy sort of joint downtown."

"Are you sure about that?"

"According to Amanda, one of the girls in her class saw her there. The kid was downtown with a parent or something — not actually in the bar. And she asked Conway about it in class. Anyway, Jane Conway got very upset and annoyed, which the kids took to mean that she actually was there. And that's all I know. See you later."

"Thanks," he said thoughtfully. "That's a very interesting place for her to spend her evenings in. I'll call you."

Chapter Seven

Grant Keswick and Eleanor stepped out of the elevator into the hotel corridor. They had no trouble figuring out which of the function rooms they were heading for — waves of sound punctuated by shrieks of laughter led them directly to it. Grant plunged into the room and headed directly for the bar, dragging Eleanor after him. She stumbled over feet and caught her high, narrow heels in the broadloom, until finally they reached the drinks table relatively unscathed. In her ridiculous shoes, she towered over Grant, but he had insisted that she wear them. "When I take out a tall girl, I want the whole world to see that she's tall — the effect is marvellous. If I want to look tall myself, I'll kick you and you can sit down somewhere while I find myself a shrimp to stand beside." It had been at this point that she had begun to doubt the wisdom of accepting his invitation. If John Sanders hadn't been so excited about her going to this party she wouldn't be here.

But here she was, with a vodka and tonic in her hand — this was a government affair, and the wine looked suspiciously domestic — her feet hurting, trying to be sparkling to a lot of people who were all talking about things she knew nothing about. And only because her cousin knew everyone in Toronto theatrical circles and had introduced her to Grant Keswick and he had decided that he wanted a tall redhead for tonight. For reasons that would become clear later, no doubt. And she was supposed to look excited about a mini-series that she had not watched and be overwhelmed by the knowledge that a bigwig from a U.S. network was here and seriously considering buying the series to show in the fall. From the general euphoria exuding from everyone, it was obvious that most of those present saw themselves already on the magic carpet, being rapidly transported into the big money and the even bigger prestige associated with acting, designing, directing, or even fetching coffee for a big American network.

Eleanor found herself trapped between a large chair and a medium-sized girl, who was mouthing something at her. "I beg your pardon," she said. "It's so noisy in here I can't hear what anyone is saying."

The girl whispered a bit louder. "I see you came in with Grant Keswick. Did he bring you?" Eleanor decided that this was a trick question. She nodded brightly and kept her mouth shut. "I've been going out with him ever since we started the series, you know," she said as she stared through Eleanor. "I think he's a bit old to be playing the juvenile lead, don't you? But he's trying to look as young as possible. That must be why he invited an older woman tonight. For the contrast. He always thinks of things like that."

It seemed to be an unanswerable comment. Eleanor remembered her mission and attempted to edge away from this sweet creature, looking wildly about for her scheming escort. She saw him finally in a quiet corner talking to a man dressed soberly in gray. Not an actor or director, then. Probably from the Canada Council, or a politician or civil servant. There were enough of those around. She squeezed in between the chair and the girl as expeditiously as possible without knocking either one down and without pausing to observe the effect of her sudden departure on Grant's erstwhile love.

She was heading for an enormous chair in the vicinity of the two men, close enough to appear to be with them, yet not so close that she would intrude on their conversation. She should be able to hear Grant's clear actor's voice from there. Three more closely knit groups of people and she should make it. Suddenly a bony hand grasped her around the upper arm, and a too-familiar voice squawked in her ear: "Eleanor! How wonderful to see you! Is Susan here with you?" This was why Susan had ducked the party. She knew that her old boyfriend would be here — as weedy and unpleasant as ever, and still as impossible to get rid of — and had no desire to run into him again.

"Stephen, how nice to see you." She kept her voice low and unenthused. "How's Art History? Susan couldn't come to this. She's studying for exams." As he droned on at her, she tried to peer past his long, skinny frame to see what had happened to her quarry. Fortunately, Stephen rarely listened to anyone, and an occasional grunt was always sufficient to satisfy his demands for conversational response. Two people shifted position, and she could see Grant again, still deep in conversation. She turned politely to Stephen for a moment. When she looked back, Grant and the man in gray were gone. Damn! Getting rid of this persistent idiot took real skill. He appeared to be going on about theater being the only true plastic art, citing a series of contradictory reasons that she hadn't time to make sense of.

Suddenly a deep voice cut through his monologue. "Eleanor, my love," said Grant. "Have I been neglecting you so long that you're picking up new men?" He grabbed her by the wrist and pulled her closer to him. "Come on, doll, let me parade you around and impress people. Sorry, Stephen, old chap, but she's mine tonight. Have you met Paul Wilcox? He's probably your provincial MP — except that I can never remember exactly which group of people is supposed to vote him in." Before either she or Stephen had a chance to react to this, Grant swept Eleanor into the center of the fray with one powerful arm around her waist. She wondered how much chance she would stand if it came to her strength against someone like Grant Keswick and shivered slightly as she tried, unsuccessfully, to disengage herself from his grip.

"Interesting man, Wilcox," said Grant casually. "Did you hear what he had to say about the provincial Art Council's new policy on the classification of commercial theater?"

"No, sorry, I didn't," said Eleanor. "I was caught by an intense little creature who feels she has some claim on you and was trying to put me in my place, and then, of course, by the inimitable Stephen. I always seem to miss the interesting conversations. That's why I'm never able to convince anyone that I'm an insider. I think I'll write a novel called *Life on the Fringes.*" Good God, she thought, I'm beginning to chatter brightly.

"It will sell a million copies, my dear, because everyone will think it's an exposé of the fashion industry." He maintained his hold on her wrist and gripped her even more tightly around the waist. "Let's head for another drink, and then I want you to look decorative for that man over there. See him? The one who looks like an accountant? He's the guy from the network, and he loves tall, intelligent women. And if you're good, I'll take you away after this and buy you a smashing dinner with decent wine for being such a sweetheart." Eleanor laughed, and allowed herself to be swept along through the crowd.

John Sanders was already at his desk, making rapid notes from a pile of papers in front of him, when Ed Dubinsky walked into their crowded and chaotic corner of the building on Monday morning. "You're late," Sanders said.

"The hell I am," said Dubinsky. "I'm never late. If I got here late, it would mean Sally was late getting to work, and she's never been late for anything in her life. You're early. You sick or something?"

Sanders glared at him. "Merely trying to get a grip on things around here." He pushed a couple of quarters across the desk. "Go get us some coffee and we'll get a move on." The list in front of him was growing rapidly. By the time Dubinsky returned with the coffee, it had filled a page.

"I put a pile of reports on your desk. Check through and see if anything has come in from Cobourg yet, will you? Either on the uncle or the boyfriend — whoever he is." Sanders returned to the heap of paper in front of him.

The silence in their corner was unbroken except for the occasional grunt or snort of reaction, all lost in the ringing of phones and general bustle of the morning. Finally, Dubinsky looked up. "Here are a couple of reports in from Cobourg. You want them?"

"Just give me what's in them for now."

"Okay." Dubinsky glanced rapidly over the two documents. "First of all, Matthew Jameson, her uncle, was finally contacted yesterday morning. Cobourg reports that he showed very little reaction to her death. He apparently said that he had not seen her since shortly after she left her husband, when she had come down to the farm, and he had 'tried to explain to her what a wife's duty was'. That must have been an interesting conversation. Anyway, she simply stayed away after that, although she continued to write to him as regularly as before." He looked up. "And I gather that as a result of this, identification was released to the newspapers last night. He also identified 'Mike' as Michael Hutchinson, whose father owns the Hutchinson Hardware Store in Cobourg. When contacted, Mr. Hutchinson said that he hadn't seen his son since the middle of March but had been in frequent touch with him by telephone. He said that Mike would be very upset to hear of Mrs. Conway's death, since he was deeply attached to her. And there's the name of a motel out in Scarborough where he has been staying. His father hasn't heard from him since last week — last Sunday, he thinks. And that's about it."

"I suppose we'd better get the hell out there and pick him up, then," said Sanders. "Let's move."

As the bell shrilled through the halls at 12:15 that same Monday, Kingsmede Hall School for Girls was instantly transformed from ordered industry into shrieking chaos. Amanda snaffled her brown bag from her locker and headed upstairs to eat in a corner of the far-off Latin room, patronized by a cohesive group of like-minded souls. Jenny and Leslie were already opening their lunch bags and trying to swap bits of the contents for something better. Amanda looked incredulously at her peanut butter — why had she packed that? — and took a tragic mouthful. But it was only seconds before the talk moved from food to the police. And murder. The drama of Mrs. Conway's falling victim to Johnson's mad rapist vindicated her in their eyes. It even helped wipe out the memory of those hideous physics classes. Jenny, of course, was miles ahead of everyone else, as usual. She knew exactly what had happened, and where, and what the police were thinking on the subject right at this very moment.

"There were two plainclothes cops here on Thursday and Friday for hours, and they questioned all the teachers and Miss Johnson. Her name wasn't Conway, you know, and she wasn't really a physics teacher."

"Who says that?" asked Leslie, with suspicion; she knew from experience the solid worth of Jenny's information.

"My dad, that's who. And he knows all about it. He

said that she seemed to him to be a pretty strange character when he saw her at Parents' Night, and he's going to ask for one-eighth of my fees back, because we haven't been properly taught." Jenny nodded her head emphatically.

"That's not true, Jenny," said Amanda. "I mean, I couldn't stand her, but she wasn't that bad a teacher. We learned a lot of physics."

"Maybe you did, brain," said Jenny resentfully. "But I couldn't understand a word she said, and I haven't learned a thing in the last month." Amanda opened her mouth and Jenny hastily added, "And don't say that isn't new."

The door opened again, and a plumpish, dark-haired girl came in with lunch bag in one hand and well-thumbed French textbook in the other. A murmur of "Hi, Sarah" went around, and the group returned to the subject at hand.

"Well, I don't care about that," said Leslie. "What I want to know is who was the guy in the gray car outside her apartment all the time."

"What gray car?" asked Sarah.

"There was this gray car," explained Leslie. "And you know she lived right across the street from me and down a bit. Anyway, Amanda and I saw this guy in a gray Honda — you saw the guy, didn't you, Amanda? What did he look like?"

"I'll bet he was her boyfriend," said Sarah. "And he got jealous and killed her."

"Uh huh," said Jenny. "He was probably her husband. She was separated, you know. He was probably tailing her, to see what she was up to."

"How do you know?" asked Leslie once more. "Wait, don't tell me. Your dad told you." Jenny nodded, her mouth full of salami and roll, and kept on chewing vigorously. "I'll bet it was her husband, you know. What did he look like, Amanda? Did he look like someone who would kill Conway if he got mad?"

"How should I know?" replied Amanda. "He just looked like a guy, that's all. I mean I didn't go over and ask him if he liked killing people or anything like that. Besides, she was killed by the rapist."

"How do you know? My dad says that whenever there are a string of crimes like this one, you get people knocking off their families and pretending it was done by the first guy." This from the omniscient Jenny.

"Well, she was. Because our next-door neighbor is a good friend of the cop who is investigating the murders, and she told my Aunt Kate that it was probably the same guy. And that we should be very careful." Amanda took another bite from her limp sandwich. "And so it doesn't matter who that poor wimp was — I mean, even if he was her husband, he didn't do it." There was something in Amanda's air of finality that intimidated her classmates. The conversation turned rapidly to some very cute hunks who were coming over from a local boys' school, and to whether the slim chance one would have of being tripped over by one of them would make staying late worthwhile.

But at the dinner table that night at the Martin Delisles, and the Geoffrey Smiths, and the Paul Wilcoxes, the fascinating tale of Amanda Griffiths and the man in the gray Honda was trotted out as a lure that would interest even Daddies. Martin Delisle felt that in some obscure way it proved what he had been saying all along, and he warned Jenny to be on her guard. Geoffrey Smith laughed, and to Leslie's intense irritation, dismissed it as a particularly elaborate piece of schoolgirl embroidery. Paul Wilcox even managed to look faintly interested and to ask a kind question about her observant friends. Poor Sarah glowed with delight at the implied, but unaccustomed, praise, as she prattled on.

It was well past lunch time, and Sanders and Dubinsky had been driving back and forth for some time in a thin, nasty drizzle along Kingston Road — the city's eastern strip — looking for the Blue Cross Motel. The Cobourg Police Department had apparently believed that a name and the street on which it was located would be sufficient identification. "And it would have been," said Sanders, "if they'd gotten the bloody name right. There isn't a Blue Cross Motel, Dubinsky. Turn around and we'll try the Blue Dolphin and the Bluegrass." Dubinsky started patiently back the other way. "There it is." Sanders pointed at a gaudy sign depicting a porcine and melancholy dolphin with a wary look, as if it were expecting to turn up at dinner as special of the day. The gentleman behind the counter looked even more melancholy and world-weary than the dolphin.

He twitched back the corner of his little mustache in a smile. "Yes?" he asked in sepulchral tones.

"Do you have someone here," Sanders flashed his identification in the clerk's direction, "named Michael Hutchinson?" He glanced around him impatiently. The sight of the I.D. card plunged the desk clerk into even greater fits of despair. He shrugged his shoulders helplessly and reached for the register. "Staying since the beginning of February?"

"Oh, no," he replied morosely. "Our customers don't often manage to stay until dinner time. I'd certainly remember if someone had been here that long. No. No one. Not of that name or any other. Sorry." He pushed the register back into its niche with a sigh.

"A comedian," said Sanders, as they walked back to the car. "Let's get on with it."

The Bluegrass Motel was small, shabby, and absurdly named. It was tucked in behind a large gas station and beside a tiny suburban plaza in its death throes. The nearest grass was probably three blocks away; the nearest horse, several miles. Inside the hovel marked "Management", a thin, white-haired elfish man sat hunched over a copy of a magazine which he slid rapidly under the counter as soon as he saw that he was not alone. "We don't rent rooms for half a day," he said sourly.

"Jesus, what is this?" said Dubinsky. "What the hell do we look like?" His voice became coldly unpleasant. "You got someone here named Michael Hutchinson?"

"He's out. His car ain't there, so he's out. What you want him for?"

"To talk to," said Sanders, tightly. "When did he go?"

"Dunno." He pulled out his magazine and flipped the page.

"The key," said Dubinsky, clapping his huge hand over the open page on the counter. "We'll check it out for ourselves."

"Can't do that. Not unless you have a warrant." He tried to yank the magazine out from under Dubinsky's paw, with no success.

Sanders leaned over the counter, his voice friendly and confidential. "Perhaps you'd prefer to have us come back in the evening," he said. "Every evening, say, in a nice bright yellow car, with lights flashing on the roof, just when you're trying to fill up for the night." The clerk glared at him across the counter, slowly got up, reached in a drawer for a small bunch of keys and tossed them down in front of them.

"Room nine," he said. "The numbers are on them." He turned his back on them in complete indifference and went back to his cultural pursuits.

Except for an unmade bed, room nine showed few signs of occupancy — no suitcases, no clothing hanging up on the open rack near the door. Sanders looked in the bathroom. Empty. Not so much as a rusty razor blade in the tiny medicine cabinet. Wet towels lay about the tiny room; the paper bath mat was soggy and gray. On the floor in front of the television set a morning paper lay spread open to pages two and three. As Sanders leaned over it to see what was there, the second part of a story on the death of Jane Conway stared back at him. He turned to Dubinsky. "He's gone. The bastard's gone. As soon as he saw the story in the paper he took off. All this time we've been farting around looking for disappearing rapists and husbands, and he was right under our noses. Get the license number and make of the car from that idiot out there and call it in. We should be able to pick him up if he didn't leave too long ago." As Dubinsky went out the door, he glanced back and saw Sanders standing very still, muttering at the carpet.

Eleanor pulled up in the driveway of 24 Forest Crescent and sat for a moment in the car. The spring house-buying season was in full swing, and the day had been hectic — meetings in the morning and three showings in the afternoon. Fortunately, a five o'clock appointment had canceled out, or she could have been in the office until nine. She wondered if John had called. After all, it had been his idea that she go to that crashingly boring party with Grant, and two days later, she still hadn't heard from him. Of course, she'd been presiding over an open house all Sunday afternoon, but he knew how to leave a message at the office. Damn! Sitting here stewing did no good at all.

She opened the front door cautiously and looked around to see who was about. Mrs. Flaherty was crashing around with her pots in the kitchen, a reassuring sound, and the blare of the television from the morning room told her where her daughter probably was. She strode through and discovered her mother and Heather deep in a *WKRP in Cincinnati* rerun.

"Oh, hi, Mummy," said Heather. "I thought you weren't going to be in tonight." She reached up her forehead for a kiss.

"Sorry to disappoint you, sweetheart, but my evening appointment canceled out — three houses I don't have to go through tonight. I think they've finally realized that they have no intention of moving." This remark was addressed to her mother, who also presented herself for a kiss. "So here I am. Anyone call?"

"Not that I know of, dear. But you'd better check the front hall."

"Yes, of course I will. How was school?"

"Fine," said Heather as she always did. Eleanor often wondered what it would take of triumph or disaster to make her come up with a more elaborate description. "And I need five dollars and a permission slip signed today because we're going to the zoo tomorrow and I'm the only person who hasn't got her money in yet. Mrs. Brett is really mad."

"Oh, good Lord, Heather, why didn't you tell me earlier?" Her daughter shrugged and smiled maddeningly at her.

"Are you going to be in for dinner?" Eleanor's mother asked. "I should tell Mrs. Flaherty if you are."

"I don't know. I think I might be going out again." Now why did I say that? she wondered. "Anyway, I'm going up to change. I'll see you in a minute. Heather, get out of your uniform. And have you done your homework yet?" Without waiting for replies or excuses, she fled from the scene, feeling slightly more as if her maternal conscience had been eased.

The phone started ringing as she opened the door to the third-floor apartment. She dashed up the stairs and grabbed it in a slide that would have done a first baseman proud. Her hello was so breathless as to be incoherent, but it elicited the right sort of response.

"Hello. Sorry I didn't call before, but things have been going crazy around here." Sanders' tone became tentative. "I know it's early, but how about dinner? Everything I was working on has suddenly collapsed. I might as well knock off."

Eleanor hesitated, searching for the right reaction. "Why not?" she answered casually. "We all have to eat.

Shall I meet you somewhere? Or are you going to swoop up here in a police car and convince my neighbors I've been arrested?''

"I think I'd better come and get you. You don't drive very well as the evening progresses, I seem to remember. And I have a responsibility about these things,'' he answered coolly. "Is 6:30 too early?''

"No — I'm starving already. Should I get dressed up?''

"I thought we'd go to the Pallas — if you like — and that's hardly dinner-jacket country.''

That was a low blow. The Pallas had tender associations from her first encounters with him; his comment jolted her out of her cool breeziness. "That sounds — lovely,'' she said. "I'll meet you downstairs at 6:30.''

She showered and dressed in a casual pair of pants and a large shirt. It wasn't quite the track suit she usually wandered around in when she wasn't in working dress, but at least it was comfortable enough to enable her to deal with John Sanders. She certainly didn't want to be struggling along all evening in a tight skirt and hobbling high heels. She bade farewell once again to her daughter, thinking she could have tried to look a little crushed that her mummy was going out, and went out to wait for John in the late April sun. She shivered in the chill wind. Life seemed a little too perfect this evening; something was bound to go wrong. She waved over the shaggy hedge of bridal wreath at Kate Abbott, who was just coming home, and slowly walked down the long drive to the street.

The restaurant was as warm, the food as comforting as she remembered. Eleanor took a sip of her retsina and smiled. Then she complained, "You haven't asked me about all my earth-shattering discoveries of Saturday night. What's the use of having an informant if she doesn't inform?''

"Sorry about that,'' he said, in his most off-hand way. "Did you find out anything earth-shattering? I spent quite a bit of time with Mr. Keswick myself over the weekend,

and he didn't strike me at the time as a very useful source
of information. And we seem to be chasing another rabbit
right now.''

"Who's that?"

"Her old boyfriend from home. As soon as the story
broke in the newspapers, he ran. And we haven't found a
trace of him — he's not at home, at her uncle's farm, at
any of his friends', or on the highways in between. The
O.P.P. have been looking for his car all day. If he'd been
driving around, they'd probably have spotted him. I
wasn't around on Sunday when the report came in, and
none of those bleeding idiots thought he was that important, so they left him for me this morning.'' He glared at
Eleanor as if she had been personally responsible for letting him get away and then laughed and poured some more
retsina in her glass. "So what did you find out about Mr.
Keswick? Am I grinding my molars over the wrong man?"

"Not very much, actually. He was deep in conversation
with some politician for a long time, but before I could
creep over and hear what they were talking about,
Stephen — remember Susan's creepy boyfriend, Stephen? —
jumped me and it took me forever to get rid of him.''

"Did you catch the politician's name?"

"Paul Wilcox. I didn't recognize him, although the
name sounds familiar. Grant said that they were discussing
Arts Council grants.''

"Could be. He's an up-and-coming type in government
these days. Every time you look around he's on some commission or other.'' He reached for her hand. "Thank you.
You did your best and they probably weren't discussing
anything important. Do you remember the last time we did
this?" Eleanor nodded, making an indeterminate noise in
her throat. "I went back to your place and got hit on the
head.''

"I remember that,'' said Eleanor, grinning in spite of
herself.

"Perhaps we should go back to my place then,'' he said

lightly. "And just to prove how honorable my intentions were, you'll discover that I made no attempt to clean up this morning. At that point I had no plans to try to lure you back there."

"And just when did your plans become dishonorable?"

"I think when I saw you walk through the garden in the sunshine. I always seem to connect you with gardens. They suit you." He looked at her for a moment longer. "Why don't we forget dessert and coffee. I'll make you coffee at my place. It's one of my secret domestic skills."

Eleanor stood by the window in the darkened apartment and looked over the magnificence of the city by night, and the thick blackness of the lake in the distance. "This is spectacular, John. How did you find it?"

"Luck, really. I got the tag-end of someone's lease. The place does have certain disadvantages. Because of its location, I have to share it with the upper-income-bracket pimp-and-hooker population. That sort of makes me feel at home — like my days on Vice. All those familiar faces." He moved over behind her and put his hands very lightly on her shoulders. "Eleanor, do come here," he said softly. She turned quickly and found herself clinging tightly to him, astonished at the ease with which her emotions could betray her. She had intended — if she had had any intentions — to keep this evening light and chatty, giving herself time to sort out her annoyance at having been dumped unceremoniously last year and then picked up again like an old half-read novel. Now, between the trembling of her knees and the uncertainty in her voice she couldn't have formed a coherent sentence to save her life. And she was clutching him with the intensity and determination not to let go you might find in a large, hungry dog with a very juicy bone. They sank in a tangle on the somewhat crowded couch.

"You know," John remarked some time later, looking down at her tousled head and remnants of clothing, "there is a bed. Over there in the bedroom. It has a view of the lake, too. Come on." He heaved himself off the couch, removed his arm from the one sleeve of his shirt that he still had on, and dragged her to her feet and into the apartment's other tiny room.

"I would like you," said Eleanor, stretching luxuriously on the unmade bed a few minutes later, "to admire my belly muscles. They have cost me a great deal of sweat and agony — and I feel I deserve some sort of reward for the effort."

"Impressive," he murmured, as he lit a candle. "Now, can I get you some coffee — or beer, maybe, or there may be wine, and since Dubinsky was here, there's something left in a bottle of rye. And take off that shirt. You look much better without it; besides, partially dressed women are beginning to make me nervous."

"Sure." Eleanor shrugged herself out of her shirt. "And I'll have a beer, I think. We'll leave Dubinsky the rest of his rye." Sanders retreated to the tiny kitchen and returned with bottles, glasses, and opener. "Speaking of Dubinsky, which we really weren't, I suppose, what makes you so un-Dubinsky-like?"

"In what way? It is not given to all of us to have a build like a sumo wrestler, you know. But it's a very comforting trait to have in a partner. He doesn't even have to do anything. They just look at him and melt into the scenery."

"I don't mean your size, you idiot. I mean, Dubinsky would never talk about people having builds like sumo wrestlers, would he?"

"Aah. You are referring to the thin veneer of civilization that a couple of years of English and Philosophy at University College gave me, are you? That flippant manner and brilliant use of language, you mean?"

"How did you get from there to here, then? It seems a long way from English to murder."

"But not from philosophy to crime. Well, to make a

short story too long, I was a perfectly ordinary boy from the east end with a flair, I suppose, for school. I won a scholarship to the U. of T. and went into a nice arty program, where I did all right for a while" — he turned casually away to pick up his beer again — "until I got deflected."

"Deflected?"

"After first year I got a job as a security guard back on my home turf and ran into Marie, who was pretty enticing in those days — she's still not bad, you know — and between her distracting me all through second year, and then during study week finding cause why we should get married, I didn't even bother writing my exams. And that was the end of my experiment with culture and civilization. The police force was recruiting at that particular time, which was more than you could say for a lot of other places, and it seemed like a fairly secure and interesting way to make a living, so I joined. I'm not really that different from Dubinsky, you know. The polish slips off pretty easily." He rolled over and ran his hand along her belly, and then took her beer glass from her and carefully set it on the floor.

"What time is it?" asked Eleanor. "I have to get home before it's time to get Heather off to school. I am not one of your carefree singles."

Sanders reached over for his watch. "Would you believe that it's only 9:30? That's what happens when you leave for dinner before the sun sets."

"Mmmm," said Eleanor, giving herself up to the moment, "set the alarm for two o'clock."

"Why not five?" he murmured. "I'll cook you breakfast."

Chapter Eight

It was the final five minutes of Amanda's second last class of the day, English. The sun pouring into the classroom seemed to have infected teacher and students with a spirit of lazy contentment. It had been a long, cold winter. The discussion of Alexander Pope's *Rape of the Lock* was dwindling into nothing; even the title was no longer capable of producing giggles. In that soporific atmosphere, the secretary's head poking around the corner hardly caused a ripple. Miss Whitney lazily took the proffered piece of paper, read it, and called to Amanda.

"It's a phone message. It's almost time for the bell, so why don't you go now and call? Take your books." Startled at the unusual summons, Amanda hastily gathered her knapsack and poetry text and stumbled out of the classroom down to the pay phone in the Common Room.

She looked carefully at the words on the slip for the first time. "Please call your Aunt Kate as soon as possible." Where was Aunt Kate? The number on the message was not familiar. Amanda fished out her quarter and dialed the number. A pleasant masculine voice answered with the words, "Harris and Robinson. May I help you?"

"May I speak to Dr. Abbott, please?" asked Amanda.

"And who may I say is calling, please?"

"It's her niece, Amanda," she replied, confused.

"Oh, yes. Is that Miss Griffiths? Dr. Abbott is in a brief meeting right now. Would you like to hold? She shouldn't be more than ten minutes." Ten minutes sounded like an eternity to Amanda, who could at that moment hear the bell ringing for Latin. "Wait a moment, I think she may have left a message for you." There was a pause. "Here it is. Could you please meet her at 3:30 at the corner of Mount Pleasant and Elm, the southeast corner? She is picking up your parents at the airport."

Still clutching her magic piece of paper, Amanda pelted into Latin class, no later than several of her slower-moving classmates. Breathlessly she waved the slip in front of Mrs. Cowper's face and explained her predicament. Her parents were coming in; her aunt wanted her to drive out with her to the airport to meet them; and could she leave class five minutes early?

Mrs. Cowper reacted predictably. "Of course, Amanda! How nice that your parents are coming in. Keep your eye on the clock and slip out when you need to. Leave yourself enough time to get to your locker. Have a lovely time tonight!"

It was a couple of minutes before the final bell when she stationed herself on the prescribed corner, looking intently down the hill for Aunt Kate's car to appear. She scarcely noticed the yellow police car pull up in front of her and stop, lights flashing. The handsome young constable who was driving got out and walked over to her. She looked up in surprise. "Excuse me, Miss, but are you Amanda Griffiths?" She nodded, beginning to feel a sickening sense that something was very wrong. "I was asked to pick you up and take you out to the airport — something about an accident ——'' As his voice trailed off, he smiled and put a comforting hand on her shoulder.

"Is it my parents?" she asked. "Has someone been" — she couldn't say the word that was on her mind — "hurt?"

"I'm afraid I don't know," he answered gently. "But if you'll come with us we'll soon have it straightened out." He propelled her toward the car and opened the back door. There was a man in plain clothes sitting on the passenger side, looking straight ahead. She climbed in, and only realized after the door slammed shut that there were no handles on the inside. That and the mesh between the front and back seat gave her an uncomfortable caged feeling.

Instead of heading north in the direction of the airport, however, the car turned right off Mount Pleasant into north Rosedale; it cruised along Summerhill, into a park, past the sign that said "Official Vehicles Only", and down a steep hill. Amanda opened her mouth but could not phrase a question that seemed adequate to the occasion. Besides, terror had taken away her voice, and she was grappling to maintain an outward appearance of calm. The car stopped, and the driver got out. He opened the door and bent over to peer in. She shrank back automatically. He turned away from her; when he turned back to her he had a handkerchief in his hand, with a sickly, sweet, chemical smell to it. As she opened her mouth to scream he clapped it over her face, soaking wet and cold. She struggled for an instant.

Eleanor sat with her mother, lazily drinking tea and letting her thoughts float idly where they would. Her mother was chewing over a problem having to do with the planting of some perennials at the bottom of the garden and the apparently related question of whether the tenant who was renting the coachhouse over the garage for a handsome sum should be allowed to buy a puppy. A standard poodle was what he had in mind, and the various strengths and weaknesses of the breed — as understood by Jane Scott — were being canvassed minutely. "You see, dear, poodles dig. I know they do, because they're just like terriers, and it's impossible to keep a garden if you have a terrier. So what do you think I should do?"

Eleanor paused and looked at her mother. She hadn't been listening carefully enough to know which problem had actually been tossed in her lap, and besides, it seemed obvious to her that her mother would plant what she liked and that Susan, who owned the house, coachhouse and all, would not object to anything her new tenant wanted to do of such an innocent nature. "Well," she temporized, and was saved by the sight of Kate Abbott waving through the living-room window and striding around to the side door. "Kate," she hailed, "come and have some tea."

"Well, I don't really think I should," she said. "I just came over to see if Amanda was here. She wasn't home when I got in, and it occurred to me that she might have wandered over."

"She's not here," said Eleanor. "But we can ask Heather. She might know where she was going after school." She called upstairs and was finally greeted by an answering shout and the appearance of her daughter. "When did you last see Amanda, dear?" asked Kate. "And did she say anything about where she was going?"

Guilt compounded with alarm spread itself over Heather's face. "I haven't seen her," she said. "I waited with Leslie for the longest time, and then one of the other girls said that Amanda had gone already, and so Jennifer and Leslie walked me home. They said it was all right." Heather's eyes swam with tears as she felt the weight of the awful responsibility they felt for one another on these trips back and forth. "Maybe she's still at school waiting for someone to walk home with; Miss Johnson said she'd suspend anyone who walked home alone or didn't make arrangements.''

Kate gave her a reassuring hug and said that it was perfectly all right, that Amanda had probably arranged to do something else, and that she, Kate, had forgotten all about it. That had happened before. But after Heather, relieved, had run off again, she turned a very alarmed face to Eleanor. "Do you suppose she is still at school?" asked Kate. "Perhaps I'd better go over and see."

"No," said Eleanor. "We'll call the school, and if I can't get anyone there, I'll drive over. You want to stay at home so you'll be there to scream at her when she walks in. Who's that girl that lives around the corner — the one who walked Heather home?''

"Leslie — Leslie Smith. She lives on MacNiece. They'll be in the phone book. We just have to find a Smith on MacNiece."

"Don't be silly," said Eleanor. "There's an easier way. Heather! Get me your yearbook! Her number will be in there. It's a lot easier than plowing through four pages of Smiths." Heather appeared, book in hand. But Leslie Smith, although easily located, had no more help to offer.

"I'm sorry, Dr. Abbott," she said. "But all I know is that someone — I think it was Kim — said that Amanda had left early and so we shouldn't wait. I figured she had a doctor's appointment or something like that."

"Why don't we go over to your place," suggested Eleanor, "and take the yearbook with us, and see if we can track her down?''

Jane Scott, who had been listening quietly to all of this, nodded in agreement. "You go back, and Mrs. Flaherty and I will come over with a bite for you to eat.''

But half an hour later, at 5:45, they were no further ahead. No one had answered at the school office, so Eleanor had driven over. But Amanda was not among those dressing after late soccer practice, or on the stage polishing up their routines for the music show, and none of these girls had seen her. Jennifer knew no more than Leslie, and Kim vigorously denied having said anything about her whereabouts. Baffled and frightened, they looked at each other over a plate of sandwiches, untouched, and a bottle of sherry, sitting on the coffee table between them.

Eleanor checked her watch and decided it was time to take more decisive action. "Are you really worried?"

"I'm terrified. Not only am I fond of Amanda, but I keep imagining my brother's face if something has happened to her. But it's only been a couple of hours since she got out of school. If I call the police they'll laugh at me." She pushed her long hair back into its fastenings and composed her face. "You see, she's never done anything like this before, and she and her friends are very careful about letting you know where they are these days, even if it does irritate them to have to do it."

"Right," said Eleanor firmly. "I'm calling John. He'll know whether we should worry or not, and he certainly won't laugh."

"John?" said Kate. "What can he do?"

Eleanor shrugged impatiently. "My only problem is that I've never called him before — at work, that is." She turned pink with embarrassment. "I always have visions of getting eight police cars and an ambulance if I call the department, so I've never tried."

That elicited a slight smile. "Well," said Kate, "let's try now. Just look up 'police' in the phone and avoid any number that says 'emergency'."

"I'll try his apartment first." Eleanor took out her little book. But the phone rang uselessly in his empty bedroom. "Well, then, here goes." She took a deep breath and dialed. It only took five minutes to get someone on the line who grudgingly admitted that he might know where John was and reluctantly agreed to fetch him. "Thank God," she breathed into the receiver at the sound of his voice.

"It's me, Eleanor. I'm at Kate's, and we need your help."
Her explanation tumbled out in an almost incoherent jumble of words.

"When did you say she was last seen?" he said at last.
"Three-thirty? Wait there. I'll be right over."

It took him less than twenty minutes to pull up in Kate's
driveway. Eleanor dragged him in the door, spluttering
apologies as she went. He raised his hand dismissively.
"Don't worry about it. Just tell me exactly what you know
so far." He sat very still and watched them carefully as he
listened. "Now," he said calmly after the story had trickled to a halt, "first let's find out what happened at school.
Why did her friends think she had left early?"

"I don't know," said Eleanor, "except that some girl —
unidentified — said so, and everyone accepted it, of
course. But I suppose that we could call Roz Johnson and
see if she knows anything."

Amanda was dreaming in garish color that she was flying
through a brightly painted department store filled with
overstuffed furniture upholstered in various shades of
bilious green and yellow. Suddenly, something went wrong
with her flying mechanism, and she crashed, unable to save
herself, into a particularly hideous couch that trapped her
in its feathery depths. Her first thought at this point was
that she was going to be sick. She gagged and retched and
tried unsuccessfully to move. Her apparent paralysis
panicked her completely, and she thrashed unavailingly
until she was conscious enough to realize that her hands
and feet were tied, and her mouth closed with a tight bandage. Voices floated in and out of her awareness.

"Undo that gag — come on, she's going to be sick.
Move it!"

"What for? Who cares? It's not your goddamn car."

"What for? You fucking idiot, she could choke to
death, and then where'd we be?"

"Who the fuck are you calling an idiot? You said she'd

be out for hours. Give her some more of that stuff.''
Hands grabbed her, yanked the gag off her mouth, and
pulled her upright. She opened her eyes, saw grass and the
edge of a car seat wavering in front of her, and was very
sick. Hands held her up as she retched and retched until
her agonized stomach muscles could produce nothing
more, and she sagged down with her head sitting against
the greasy edge of the car door.

Then the hands grabbed her hair and yanked her head
back. Out of the corner of her eye she saw a flash of white,
then a double blur of white: then, blinking and concentrating, she saw the handkerchief. She took a desperate last
gasp of untainted air before it hit her face, and in the only
defense measure her blurred brain could think of, she
slumped inertly at once. The voices faded and echoed, far,
far away, and once again she floated, lurching helplessly
through a void that was at once black and harshly brilliant.

Eleanor sat aimlessly at the typist's desk in the general office at Kingsmede, watching Roz Johnson and John trying
to track down Amanda. They had abandoned a distracted
Kate with Jane Scott, leaving instructions to call if
anything happened.

"If she left early," said Roz, "she should have signed
out. They're not allowed just to leave, even if they have a
good reason. Although of course some of them do.'' She
was running her finger up the list of names in the sign-out
book as she spoke. "But Amanda has never been one of
those — so far, anyway. No, she's not here.'' She paused
for a moment. "Well, we have to find out when she left. If
she was in class last period then we'll have some idea of the
time.'' She looked wildly about her. "Where in hell do
they keep the student timetables these days? Sorry to appear so dim, but I'm used to screaming at someone else for
information like this.'' She sorted quickly through sets of
files and notebooks. "Ah, there they are.'' And she picked

up a huge blue three-ring binder filled with computerized timetables. "Let's see, today is Wednesday," she muttered, "so she had Latin last period. Good. We call Isabel Cowper and see if she was in Latin. That's simple — we'll get there soon." Roz disappeared into her own office and returned flourishing a typed list of names and addresses. "This shouldn't take long," she said. John moved over and sat on the desk next to Eleanor.

"Who's staying with Heather?" he murmured.

"Susan. She got home just before I went over to get mother. Large families are terribly useful in a crisis." She stopped to listen as Roz made contact on the phone.

"She isn't? Do you know where she is?" A pause. "Do you know where they went for dinner? It's important." Another pause. "Well, did they say when they'd be back? This is Rosalind Johnson, from Kingsmede, where she teaches." An excited burst of noise from the receiver. "Yes, hello, Cynthia, it's nice talking to you, too, but I must reach Mrs. Cowper." Exasperation showed in Roz's face. "I don't suppose they said which movie they were going to, did they?" Despair settled on her features. "Well, if she does call, tell her I must speak to her at once. And, in any case, she's to call me as soon as she gets in, either at the school number or my own private number. She has it." Roz listened again to a spate of high-pitched noise. "Fine, Cynthia, and thank you. Now don't forget, it's important." She put the receiver down. "God help us, I think that woman's salary should be cut for going out and leaving her kids with the vaguest idiot in the Grade Ten class. Anyway, she's out to dinner somewhere, and then going to a movie somewhere, but she might call in to check on the kids." She reached over for the blue book again. "So, what did she have before Latin? That might help — you never know." She stared at the timetable. "English. Now who teaches her English — oh God, it's Anne Whitney. Young and single. She's probably out too." She picked up her phone list. "You know, they always tell me that they have so much work to do that they never have a chance to leave their desks until midnight. Ha!" She dialed carefully, and they all waited. And waited. No response. "Damn," said Roz finally. "Okay, I'd better call Sylvia. She runs the office here and generally knows what's going on. Then I'll just keep trying the others. They can't stay out all night, you know. They have to come to work in the morning."

"John, we can't just wait here and watch Roz trying to telephone, can we?" asked Eleanor. "I mean anything could be happening to Amanda. Shouldn't people be searching or something? Shouldn't you get in touch with the department?"

"I did, darling. And they're watching for her. But if she was picked up by him, and unless we accidentally stumble across him, it's probably already much too late. I'm sorry — not that we won't keep trying." He reached out and took Eleanor's hand. She turned and stared, white-faced at him.

"That poor kid! And poor Kate. I can't bear it." John handed her his handkerchief as tears poured down her cheeks.

Amanda swam back and forth between consciousness and black lurching oblivion. Voices rose and fell; each time they penetrated her conscious mind they were clearer and made more sense.

"We've got to get her the hell out of this car," said one voice urgently. "The only time I can get it back in the garage without anyone noticing is between 8:00 and 8:30. Where did you leave yours?"

"I told you, Rick. It's in a lot at the Chester Street subway station. And we'd better get a move on." Amanda's stomach gave an ominous heave as the car veered and speeded up. She breathed as deeply as she could through her nose and gradually the nausea eased.

"Where can we switch her over? It's going to look god-damn peculiar if someone sees us dragging a girl out of a patrol car and dumping her somewhere else." The voice called "Rick" sounded worried.

"I've got it all worked out, Rickie baby. Not everyone is as stupid as you are." The other voice was venomous in its contempt. "You just let me out at the parking lot, go round the block, and follow me again. When I drive into the garage, come in after me. Then we'll switch her."

"Jesus, Jimmy, what if someone sees us?"

"No one will see us, okay?"

There was a ruminative pause as the car bucketed and bounced over potholes and obstructions. Amanda's head began to ache fiercely. "Did you hear her? I think she's awake again." Rick's voice was edgy, nervous.

Another pause. Amanda lay as quietly and still as she could, breathing, she hoped, with the languor of one heavily doped. "Naw. She's out for the count. Listen, she's coked up to here on that stuff."

"I wish you'd give her some more. It gives me the creeps thinking she might wake up on me when I'm alone in the car."

"For Chrissake, Rick. If I give her any more, it'll kill her. Haven't you heard of autopsies? You are the stupidest goddamn cop in the entire bloody force. They can tell what someone dies of, you know. And she isn't supposed to die from too much chloroform." The meaning of his words was slow to reach her, but when it did a wave of cold, hideous panic swept through Amanda.

"Well then, I don't see why we have to wait. Why not bash her head in now? She makes me nervous."

"Look, Rick, you do what you're told. I've got this all worked out, and you're sure as hell not going to fuck it up now. Shut up and drive."

Roz came back into the office with a pot of coffee and three cups. "I hope black is okay," she said wearily.

"There doesn't seem to be any milk left." She poured coffee and passed the cups over the desk, then sat down. She looked progressively more haggard as the evening wore on. "Let me give Anne another try," she muttered. "It must be fifteen minutes since I called her last." She let the phone ring as she dangled the receiver from her fingertips and continued to chat. "I wonder if this is the most efficient way to go about things — Oh, hello! Anne? Roz Johnson here. Look, we have a problem. Was Amanda Griffiths in class today? Sure, go and check." She looked up. "Well, she's home. She sounds a bit cheerful, but she's gone for her attendance book." Roz spoke into the phone again. "She was. You're sure." Another pause. "What sort of message? Are you absolutely certain? Of course." She raised her eyebrows. "Well, we can't find her at the moment." A pause. "We tried that. If you think of anything else, call me here at the office, or at home, if no one answers here. Thanks."

Roz hung up the receiver and looked rather unhappily over at John and Eleanor. "According to Anne, Amanda got an urgent message to telephone her aunt as soon as possible. She let her leave class early. And that's all she knows. But I guess she didn't use the phone in the office or Sylvia would have mentioned it. I think. I'd better call her again and make sure." With a sigh she reached for the list once more. "And you can use that phone if you want to check with the aunt. Not that I think for a minute it was a genuine call. It wouldn't be the first time people have used faked messages to try to get the girls out for one reason or another."

The car lurched sideways; there was a screech of brakes and loud horns. Maybe they would get into an accident. Amanda prayed for a car to smash into them, preferably on the side her feet were wedged against, not her throbbing head. Then the car pulled up and stopped. She rocked back and forth on the floor between the front and back seats.

"Is this it? Look, will you check and make sure she's still out?"

"Goddammit, Rick, she's still out. If she comes to, she'll make a lot of noise and stuff — like the last time. Stop worrying."

"Well, hurry up, then. I don't want her moaning and throwing up back there." She felt the car shudder as the door slammed, then the monotonous bumping along the pitted road surface started up again. The horrible black swirl of unconsciousness started to take hold of her again, in spite of the pounding of her head and the ache of her pinioned arms. I mustn't, she thought, I mustn't fall asleep. Must stay awake. Awake. She was dimly aware of further stops and starts. Time telescoped; the surface beneath her heaved up and down. Then the vibration under her stopped. The change shocked her awake again just as the door beside her head was opened.

"Here, grab her," said the voice she recognized as "Jimmy". Again she tried to breathe like one profoundly doped. Hands grabbed her shoulders and dug cruelly into them, then yanked. In spite of herself, she stiffened as her head cracked against something hard. "Shit, Rick, you don't want to bash her brains out all over the car. Be careful."

"Well, give me a hand then. She weighs a fucking ton."

Amanda bristled a little at that. "It's just because she's dead weight. Here, I'll get her around the waist." She forced herself to lie totally helpless in their grasp as they pulled, pushed, and jostled her out of the back of the yellow patrol car. Suddenly she was in the air, then dropped, her back on something soft, her feet trailing on the hard ground. The short pleated skirt of her uniform flipped up, and she could feel cold, damp air on her unprotected thighs. Then she felt a pair of cold, damp hands on them, moving upwards.

"Just a minute, Rick. How much time you got? I mean, she's just lying there, and no one can get in this garage. She's supposed to look like she's been raped, anyway." Jimmy's voice sounded hoarse and far away as the hands started tugging at her underwear.

There was the noise of feet. The hands abruptly left her thighs. "Shit, Jimmy, now who's being stupid! Don't you know those bastards can tell who raped somebody? It wouldn't be the right guy. Christ! Go buy yourself some tail if you can't wait. I can give you some great names." Amanda felt herself being hauled up into another car. "And don't mess around with her while I'm gone. I gotta go now and return the car. I'll meet you at 8:45 outside the park."

The door slammed against her feet. She heard the slam of another car door and the starting of another car engine. Her protector — as she now identified him — had gone. Leaving her alone with a disgusting voice and slimy pair of hands called "Jimmy". She tried to wriggle herself into a more comfortable position without moving noticeably. The car door by her feet opened again. She felt the agonizing crunch of a bony knee covered in coarse material on her calf, then an elbow pressed on the seat beside her. Heat radiated from the body poised above her, and a hoarse voice whispered in her ear, "Don't worry, sweetheart. We'll wait till little Rickie isn't so nervous, and we have a little more time." A huge hand clutched her; then she was abruptly dumped over the edge of the seat onto the floor, wedged face down on one shoulder.

The living room of the suburban townhouse was no longer brightly neat. Opened newspapers were scattered over the floor; grease and egg yolk congealed on plates scattered about the room. Various items of clothing lay where they had been taken off, and the television set flickered on, unheeded. He was sitting on a large chair with the walnut-veneer coffee table in front of him. Beside him on the floor were his colored markers in their plastic case. He pushed the table out of the way, went out of the room; down the three steps, he made a right turn into the kitchen. The table was covered with more dirty dishes. A carton of milk sat, warm and sour-smelling, on the counter beside a dirty frying pan and some used coffee cups. He reached into the cupboard and took out the last clean glass, put it down, and reached into the refrigerator for a large bottle of Coke. When he turned back to the counter, there was no space to put the bottle down; with a gesture of impatient rage, he swept the counter clear in a welter of flying glass and sour milk. He put the bottle down, and there was no longer a clean glass waiting. He hit the counter with the bottle, and then stood, trembling, clutching the bottle in both hands. Finally, he walked carefully over to the far cabinets, his feet crunching on broken glass, and carefully lifted down a dusty tumbler from what was obviously a "good" set, poured his Coke into it, and returned to the living room.

His last failure still rankled. Not since the very beginning had he been humiliated this way, and he was sure that it must have been a matter of insufficient preparation on his part. He would pick a site tonight and, tomorrow, would inspect it carefully. Friday was plenty of time to act. He could certainly wait until Friday. He picked up his red marker and started to wave magic circles above the map. He chose, he rejected, he chose again. Finally he took out his yellow marker and made a little dot beside a green space. Then he took out his operations notebook and jotted down a strategic route. When he finished he leaned back in his chair and stared at a spot on the wall above the draperies, his mind empty of conscious thought, but filled with flickering, garish images.

Amanda strained her ears to pick up what was going on but heard nothing except the distant hum of traffic. After what seemed an interminable time, the garage door was thrown up once more, the door to the car opened and slammed, and the key turned in the ignition. She had been lying with her face pressed into the space under the front seat, choking on the fine dust of the floor, terrified of moving lest she attract Jimmy's attention once again. The garage must have been built on a dirt laneway of ancient and epic disrepair; with every enormous bump her head jerked and she scraped her nose against the seat back. Finally they reached pavement again and the car maneuvered along the uneven streets, screeching to halts and spiraling in an endless series of turns. They finally pulled up with a nauseating bump. The door opened once again.

"It's about time you got here. Christ! Where have you been? And what in hell were you doing? Listen, if you were messing around ——"

"Don't worry," said Jimmy soothingly. "I wouldn't mess around without giving you your chance, too, Rickie baby. Anyway, I had to make a couple of phone calls that took me a little longer than I thought. We don't want to do this too soon. It'd be better to wait until everyone's gone home to bed anyway."

"Wait! Shit, Jimmy, I have to go on duty at eleven. It's going to look pretty funny if I don't turn up on time. And I want to take a shower before I go on."

"A shower! You're kind of weird, aren't you? I mean, thinking of showers right now." Jimmy's voice was light and mocking now. "Well, here we are."

"Just a minute. I'll move the barricade."

"Isn't that going to look funny?"

"Naw. The guys who patrol around here always move it. And half the time they don't bother putting it back. It just has to be moved for the next car. No one will notice." The car door opened, cold wind blew in; then it shut again, and the car bounced downward.

The car crept slowly onto what must have been dirt or

grass. It bumped its way cautiously along and then gently stopped. "Okay." Jimmy's voice was clear, authoritative now. "We get her out of the car onto the grass. Untie her and take off the gag. There's a big rock under the seat on your side. Got it?" There was a murmur in reply. "Okay. As soon as she's untied, we toss her in the bushes and bash her head in. And don't screw up. Just a minute. You see anyone?" There was a pause. "Okay, let's go, and don't waste any time."

The back door opened. Amanda was frozen silent with fear. "Jesus," whispered Rick. "She's awful quiet. Think she's dead?" A hand felt for her throat, pressed down on her jugular.

"She's alive." Hands grabbed her everywhere and dragged her, scraping and banging her against the sides of the car until she was clear of it and then flung her onto the grass. She felt an intolerable tugging of the constraints on her ankles as they were sawn away by something. Her legs fell slightly apart. "Here. Take the knife and get her wrists and the gag." Jimmy's hand fell on her thighs again and flipped her pleated skirt up as Rick hacked away at her wrists and yanked the gag from her face. Blood surged painfully through her arms as Rick carefully moved them into a more natural position.

"Would you quit that, you bastard. Someone's going to come by here and that'll be the end." She felt herself being lifted by the shoulders. "Grab her feet, you creep, and let's go."

"Have you got that rock?"

"How in hell am I supposed to carry her and the rock? I'll go back for it when I put her down." Amanda took her first deep breath in hours. If she had a chance, it would be now. She sagged artistically in their grasp until she felt Rick start to loosen his grip on her shoulders. "Here, this'll be good enough. Drop her."

As they dropped her, she flung herself sideways and rolled, landing on her shaky feet and hands; she was just able to push herself up. She staggered two steps, got caught by some bushes, thrust them aside fiercely and plunged forward, helplessly, down the side of an abyss.

Chapter Nine

Amanda was sitting on a large bus that was traveling over an enormously high, arched bridge. The bus skidded suddenly and swerved, and then turned into a huge recalcitrant pony that bucked and threw her off its back and down toward the deep blue-black water beneath. She plunged miles and miles through the blackness. Her mouth felt dry and muffled, stuffed with thick black cotton wool; her head buzzed and echoed and her stomach heaved. Then she was awake and aware only of a stabbing agony in her arm and shoulder. Memory trickled back slowly. She knew she must be very quick, and very quiet, but she couldn't remember why. From up above her she became aware of furious whisperings and muted scuffles. That was it. She had fallen and left them up there. She remembered it all now. She must have passed out when she landed. How long had she been unconscious? It felt like a very long time, but if they were still up there discussing her, it couldn't have been for more than a few moments.

It was time to explore her position. She was lying on her left side, with her face very close to some slimy-feeling substance and with something very hard pressing into her spine. Gingerly, she wriggled her toes, and then tried to move first one leg, then the other. They both seemed to function. She tried to dig her toes in to push herself upright, but her shoes caught on something that gave and left her with nothing under her feet but empty air. The movement caused a rustling from the branches and twigs she had dislodged.

"I heard her move," hissed a voice from above. "She must be all right."

"Go back to the car and get the flashlight out of the trunk — the big one. The keys are in the ignition. Quick!"

Panic seized Amanda once again. She had to get away from here before they came to get her. She tried to move her whole body, but it was clear that she was too tightly wedged; by the feel of things she was between a very unyielding tree trunk and the damp bottom of a gully. Automatically she put her hands down and tried to lever herself up. The throbbing pain that she had been living with for the last few minutes rapidly changed into ex-cruciating agony. She gasped and felt tears pouring down her cheeks. She stopped and rested, panting with shock. Think, Amanda, she screamed silently to herself, think! You have to get yourself out of here. Push with your other hand. She scrabbled around in the dirt to get her right hand under her and pushed. Nothing happened. She never had been able to do push-ups in gym class, and one-handed push-ups were simply impossible. Suddenly there was another noise from above, and a huge beam of light began to move back and forth around her. She had to get away from here. Move Amanda, you idiot, you twit, you . . . She couldn't come up with the words needed to spur herself on.

"There she is — down there. See?" The hiss chilled her.

"That's not her. Damn those goddamn green clothes they wear. They're impossible to see. Keep looking. She must have fallen somewhere close to here."

"There's a path over there that goes down to the bottom of the ravine, Jimmy. We're better off down there. Let's go."

"Wait. You go. Take the flashlight. I'll stay here until you get under me. Otherwise we'll never know where she went down. And stay there until I get down."

Rick's heavy footsteps moved away at a rapid pace. For a few moments, anyway, they wouldn't have that light near her. She couldn't push herself with her feet; her knees were too wedged-in to be of any use; she couldn't lever herself with the one arm that worked. She reached out ahead of her. There was ground, steeply sloped, but solid; her hand caught a branch. She gave it an experimental tug and it held, at least for the moment. She pulled frantically and her body moved out of its vise an inch or two; she retched with the pain. She pulled again, moved another few inches, and her body turned at the same time, ever so slightly. For a moment she could think of nothing but the pain. Then she heard Rick's ponderous footfalls, this time below her. I must get my knees under me. I must. Come on, Amanda, pull — to hell with the arm, pull! She yanked again, moved another six inches, heeled dangerously over on her left side now that the tree trunk no longer provided support, and lay there sobbing in pain.

"Hey, Jimmy. Where the hell are you? She's somewhere up above me, but I can't see exactly where."

"Just a minute. I'll be right down. Shine the goddamn light back on the path." More sounds of feet, lighter, this time, and faster. "Shine the light on the path, you idiot." A crash and scuffle. "Not in my goddamn eyes you bastard, on the path."

Desperate, Amanda clutched her branch and slowly drew one knee forward. It found a niche to rest in, and she brought up the other knee, positioning it carefully against her old enemy, the tree trunk. With a heave she was in a more tenable position. Not exactly on all fours — her useless arm was dangling painfully. Nancy Drew would have improvised a sling at this point, and then probably some sort of defensive weapon. Amanda could almost smile at the idea.

From her more upright position she was able to look around her and try to figure out where she was. Far below her she saw the powerful flashlight beam illuminating the path. Dizziness washed in and then receded as she realized just how high up she was. Then the light stabbed the darkness around her once again. They must both be below now. The beam traveled over the steep slope beneath, slowly and regularly, sweeping back and forth, starting way ahead of her and moving back over every inch of ground. With each horizontal sweep it moved higher and higher. She crouched to present as small a target as possible. Suddenly it was level with her, up ahead, throwing the rough terrain into dramatic relief. She saw that she was on a narrow ledge that ran level for about fifteen or twenty feet and ended in a tangle of thick undergrowth, probably another fissure in the surface of the slope. Then the light caught her. It moved on, then stopped. It moved back.

"There she is. Way up there. See that white? It's her. She must be hurt — she isn't moving. Let's go." With ferocious scrambling and muttered curses they launched themselves at the slope.

The din made by two full-grown men hurtling up a steep wooded slope in the dark hampered by a large flashlight that bumps and crashes is impressive, and certainly adequate to cover the noise made by a terrified and rather small fifteen-year-old girl crawling rapidly along a fairly level ledge. Amanda tried very hard not to think of the height and sheerness of the drop beside her; she wished fervently that her functioning arm had been on the other side to save her in case she started to fall, but terror pushed her on regardless. She moved at a sort of crouching run, steadying herself with her good hand every step or two and falling down on her knees for support every five or six steps. It was a surprisingly speedy method of getting from place to place. Suddenly her hand reached for the ground and encountered nothing but a handful of small branches. She moved her knees up to the edge and felt over. It was another bottomless pit as far as she could tell, but it was the only place to go. Soon those two would have made it up to the ledge and would start searching for her again — they had the advantage: four arms, four legs, and a light. She waved her arm back and forth over the void until it encountered something solid — a branch, or perhaps a sapling, growing in the cut. She turned around and flattened on her belly, edged herself over, feet first, reached out and grabbed the branch. She slid, slowly at first, then faster; the branch snapped in her hand and she landed with a sickening thud on her feet, then sat down, suddenly.

Amanda hurt in so many places that the pain in her arm no longer preoccupied her. She sat for some time, panting from exertion and terror, listening to the now muted crashing of her pursuers. She couldn't stay here. When they got to the edge they would simply shine their light down and there she'd be, caught. She was tired of falling downward, and so she started to crawl painfully up the crevice she had landed in. It was wet, cold, and muddy. A small stream coursed along the bottom. The pebbles, roots, and rubble under her were clawing at her knees, and her one good hand was raw from the pull of branches and twigs. The bushes were getting thicker as she moved up; suddenly she got to the point where the effort of pushing her way through the tangle of stems and branches was more than she could manage. She began to cry, long racking sobs that tore at her bruised ribs and aching throat, and she stopped moving. For a long time she remained immobile, crouched on her knees, her chest heaving and tears flooding her cheeks. Then she lay down on her good side and drew her knees up to her belly under her kilt as tightly as possible. The cry of "See that white?" still echoed in her brain, and she was determined to hide under kilt and blazer, so providentially made of ample quantities of hunting green wool. With her good hand she twitched down her skirt as much as possible, then attempted to arrange her injured arm in a comfortable position. Pain throbbed throughout every nerve, and she slipped once again into black, whirling oblivion.

Night had fallen quietly in the townhouse in the suburbs. Oppressed by the silence and the tension, he suddenly leapt up from his chair. He could wait no longer. He leaned over and switched off the ten o'clock news. There could be nothing on it tonight that would be of any interest to him. He needed action. Perhaps the last time he had not chosen his site carefully enough. This time he would reconnoiter in good military fashion, probe the weaknesses of the enemy, and choose the best place to strike.

He picked up the map, the pens, and the notebook, grabbed his jacket, and headed for the garage. He opened the overhead door very gently, bending over and peering out to see if anyone was watching him. All clear. He hoisted it completely, rapidly backed the van out onto the driveway, and swiftly closed the door again. He reversed onto the street with the slow deliberation that he had cultivated as a driver, turned, and set out. It was good that he was alone in the house, with no one to ask him where he was going, no one to get suspicious, no one to betray his position to the enemy. But if she was the enemy, could she betray him to it? No. She was already — that was too confusing. She was a spy. That was it. It had been a good idea to get rid of her.

He swung on and off Highway 401 with the same steady caution that he always used; then he drove along a busy street, turned, and headed slowly toward a long space without housing. He stopped. This was it. But as he began to open his door he saw in the park entrance a familiar yellow car. The interior light went on as the front door opened, and two uniformed officers were captured in blinding clarity. That was close! He drew his door shut again and very gently pulled away, proceeding at a measured pace to the next intersection. He turned right, stopped, looked around, and pulled out his flashlight. He examined his map with care, and finally marked another yellow dot against another patch of green. He carefully traced with his finger the network of roads that led from one green space to the other and put his map away again. He sat motionless in the dark for a very long time, alert for the sound of pursuit, like a hare who hopes to baffle the hounds with rocklike immobility.

At long last he turned the key in the ignition and pulled away. It was a cautious fifteen minutes from the first area to the next, and he arrived exactly within the time estimated. This time he made a preliminary reconnaissance excursion the length of the road that skirted the green space, and when he came to the small track used by the parks department for maintenance vehicles he was horrified to see two patrol cars sitting on the grass, overhead lights on, officers chatting to one another through their open windows. This was it. They had worked out his tactics, and the squeeze was beginning. He had always known that it would only be a matter of time before the enemy deduced his plan of action and tried to forestall him. His head pounded with excitement. But they couldn't have worked out the full extent of his strategy. They wouldn't know that he was also capable of attacking close to home. He turned carefully and headed back in the direction he had come from.

The long bridge over the Humber River in the farthest northwest stretches of the city was absolutely deserted. He stopped the van on the bridge and waited for fifteen minutes for signs of pursuit. None. He opened the door on the passenger side and climbed out. Still nothing. He peered over the edge of the bridge down into the black ravine to the even blacker narrow band of water at the bottom, noted with satisfaction the one heavily treed slope, and mentally fixed in his brain the location of the footpath that shimmered slightly in the light of the almost full moon. He was right. They hadn't been able to work things out this far. He would still be able to act, although it would be dangerous. He felt dizzy with elation. He would have to return on Friday, however, to find a suitable opponent, as he had planned. He climbed back into the front seat of the van and headed sedately home.

Amanda awoke groggily, and then shrank back in terror as a bright beam of light shone directly in her eyes. She shut them tight, waiting for the blow. Nothing happened. When she opened them again, the light still shone, but all was quiet and tranquil. Its source rode peacefully above her in the heavens — the moon. She was soaking wet and bitterly cold. Every part of her ached except for her arm. It screamed in pain. She was thirsty, and her stomach twisted and rumbled, whether from nausea or hunger she could not tell. She slipped back into unconsciousness.

The next time she woke up the bitter cold was the first thing she felt, then the thirst and the pain in her arm and chest. She shivered uncontrollably and slipped back into the void. After what felt like a minute she opened her eyes and realized that she could see. The sky was silver and birds were chattering in the dawn. What time was it? This seemed to be the most important question of her life. If it were almost sunrise, then when does the sun rise? Tears trickled down her face as she tried desperately to think.

She shifted position and moved her arm; it reacted swiftly, burning into her consciousness with pain. With a cry, she grabbed it and felt the watch on her wrist. But she could neither bring her arm to her face, nor force herself to sit up and look at it. She tried to raise her head far enough to see it; the moon swam dizzily and blackness closed in again.

Something warm and bright touched Amanda's cheek, and her dream of fires and comforting things rapidly changed to one of hot, burning, destroying things and she awoke again. The sun was shining brightly through the budding branches, and stray warm beams touched her here and there. It took a long time for her to understand why she was lying in a pool of water, trembling with cold, with a burning pain in her arm and chest. But it was daylight. Surely nothing dreadful could happen to her now. Someone must come and rescue her. She thought of the long painful crawl up to this point, of how far down it was to the path below, and of how impossibly far up it was to the park above her. Despair caught her. Then through the singing of birds and chattering of squirrels she heard a confused murmur of voices. She listened sharply. They were male voices, but she didn't recognize them — yet. There seemed to be more than two, but it was impossible to say whether Rick and Jimmy had gone to bring back friends. Then individual words rose out of the general babble and drifted up to her. The voices were apparently down on the path. "Take this side and divide it up — you three. We'll try up there" floated up to her. It was people looking for her.

She raised herself up as far as she could and tried to scream. Nothing came out. "Up here," she said, but it was just a croak, and the searchers were making so much noise by this time that it would have been a miracle if anyone had heard her. The excited barking of a dog, who seemed to be rushing back and forth, added to the noise and confusion. Tears of frustration fell down her cheeks as she realized that the searchers were moving farther away from her. Then, from relatively close by, she heard a voice, a voice she knew very well, saying, "I'll just try up here — you go on ahead, sir." Amanda pushed herself up to a sitting position with her good hand, pain dulled by terror. Through the branches she could see a young, handsome man, a little tired and in need of a shave, but very familiar, making his way up the mud and gravel of the spring stream bed. "No!" she screamed. "Not him! He's the one ——" and once again she hurled herself down the precipice, rolling wildly past the startled figure of Constable Rick Gruber, who stood silent, then dropped the rock in his hand. Amanda landed on the path at the feet of an astonished John Sanders.

By nine o'clock Thursday morning Eleanor was sitting in a small waiting room at the Toronto General Hospital, hoping for news of Amanda. She yawned fiercely, absolutely exhausted by a night in which she had caught only moments of sleep in a large chair in Kate's living room. It had been eleven o'clock before they had been able to establish with certainty what had lured Amanda out of school, when the errant Mrs. Cowper had told them what the false telephone message had been. Roz Johnson had turned white with anger. "That is an obscene thing to do. Nothing else would have made a girl like Amanda wander off alone." Then the matter had been left entirely to the police. They had left Roz to catch what sleep she could and returned to Kate's. And Kate, pale with guilt and anxiety, had called her brother and sister-in-law in California to let them know that their only daughter, clever and pretty and well-beloved, had been abducted on the way home from school.

John Sanders had been in and out all night, once staying long enough to catch an hour's sleep on Kate's couch. The news that there had been a plot to abduct Amanda had infused him with energy and guarded optimism.

"You realize, don't you," he had said briskly to Eleanor, "that this is the first hope we've had."

She shook her head in bewilderment. "I don't understand you at all. It doesn't seem particularly hopeful to me."

"Well, the rapist seems to grab his victims entirely at random — and when he attacks, he kills." Sanders paused. "I don't know why someone wanted to snatch this particular girl, but there is a chance that it was for some other reason than killing her. And so she might be alive."

Eleanor had shuddered. "Do you think Kate realizes that?" she had asked.

"I suspect so. She's a very clever woman."

Eleanor yawned one more time. If someone didn't turn up soon, she was going to fall asleep here in the waiting room. As she started to nod off, the door opened, and Kate appeared.

"How is she?" asked Eleanor groggily.

Kate smiled broadly in relief. "She's all right. Relatively. She has a badly fractured collar bone and a sprained wrist, and she's a mass of scrapes and bruises. She's suffering from shock and exposure, but they're very cheerful about it in there. They say she'll be fine in no time. Except for the collar bone. She's out like a light still, and they won't let us disturb her." The door swung open once again, and John Sanders walked in, looking rumpled and dark-jowled. Kate looked at her watch suddenly in alarm. "My God. Eleanor — David and Suzanne are coming in on the 10:15 flight, and I have to meet them. They don't even realize that Amanda has been found. They'll be sick with worry. Could you stay here in case she wakes up? It would be awful if no one was with her."

"Sure," said Eleanor heroically. "Just tell them I'm a temporarily authorized visitor, that's all."

"Thanks," said Kate, and disappeared.

"Don't worry," said John. "She won't be alone. We still want to know what's going on, and we haven't had a chance to talk to her. She was screaming something about 'No, no, he's something-or-other' when she passed out at my feet, and I'd like to know what she was talking about. It's clear she was running away from 'him'. It would help if we knew what happened last night." He sat down on a large couch and pulled her down beside him. "Why don't you go home and get some sleep?" He gave her a long look. "Or better yet, go to my place and get some sleep. It's very quiet, and maybe I can get back there this afternoon."

She snuggled her head sleepily on his shoulder. "No. Kate will expect me to be here when she gets back, and people will start talking if I don't go home sometime." She kissed him on the neck and settled herself more comfortably against him.

Sanders looked up and caught the eye of an embarrassed young constable standing in the door of the waiting room. "I think they already are," he said.

Chapter Ten

The embarrassed constable, torn between tact and necessity, was making a valiant try to catch John Sanders' attention without appearing to notice him. He looked infinitely relieved when Sanders finally made his way over.

"Excuse me, sir, but it's about the girl. She's awake, sort of, and the doctor says we can talk to her for a little while if we have to, but she's — she won't cooperate."

"What do you mean, won't cooperate?"

"Well, every time Collins tried to say something, she just kind of shrieked and the nurse got very upset. I think she's scared of something, sir." He looked back over his shoulder. "Then Sergeant Dubinsky tried to talk to her, but she just kept staring over at Collins and blinking sort of funny. The nurse said that maybe she wasn't really awake yet. Sergeant Dubinsky would appreciate it if you could come and — uh — assess the situation."

"Thanks," Sanders said abstractly. "I'll be along in a moment." He turned from the door and went back to

148

Eleanor. "Apparently she's awake, but she's too nervous or frightened to talk. Is she a terribly shy girl?"

"Not that I've noticed," said Eleanor. "She's rather quiet, but she doesn't run out of the room in terror at the sight of a stranger."

"Why don't you — she knows you, and you might reassure her a bit."

"Of course," she said, with a yawn. "Anything to oblige. Let's go."

Amanda was in a private room, with her left arm and shoulder encased thickly in plaster, and an intravenous feed clipped into her right hand. She looked pale and groggy, but Eleanor's face, swimming into focus above her, elicited a smile.

"Eleanor," she said thickly. "That's nice. Where's Aunt Kate?"

"She's gone to the airport. To pick up your parents."

Amanda's eyes widened in horror. "Oh, no! That's ——"

"It's all right, sweetheart," interrupted Eleanor soothingly. "We know all about that. But this time she really is there, and your parents really are on that plane. How are you feeling?"

"Awful. But not as awful as I did before." Her voice began to sound stronger and not as thick.

"Terrific. Now, I've brought John Sanders in to talk to you. He's a friend of mine, but he's also a police detective, and he's trying to find out what happened to you. We know about the fake phone call, but that's all." She waved John over to the bed. "Here he is."

Amanda's good right hand, intravenous and all, reached out and clutched at Eleanor. "Are you going to stay?"

"Of course I am, if you want me to." She tried to smile reassuringly. "But John is very nice, even for a cop. Really he is. And you'll be perfectly safe with him here."

Amanda looked from one to the other doubtfully. Finally

she spoke, but with hesitation in her tone. "It was a cop who kidnaped me. A cop in uniform."

Startled, Sanders turned to her. "A cop? Are you sure?" he said abruptly. "A real police officer? Not just someone dressed up in a rented uniform?"

Amanda cast him a withering glance. "He was in a bright yellow car marked 'Metropolitan Toronto Police', and all that, with big red lights on the roof. Flashing. He picked me up on the corner of Mount Pleasant and Elm. He said that my parents — no, actually, he didn't say — he just said that there had been an accident, and I was to go out to the airport with him."

"Did you get a good look at him?" Sanders' voice was hostile, challenging. "Would you recognize him again?" Eleanor glared at him.

Amanda paid no attention to the tone of his voice. "Yes. I'll never forget that face, let me tell you. Anyway, I saw him again. He was the one that came along on the search party looking for me. That's when I tried to run again, only I fell — again."

"Are you sure he was the same one?" Sanders' eyes never left her face.

"Positive," said Amanda steadily.

"Really? Because you screamed when you saw Constable Collins out there, and he wasn't the one who kidnaped you, was he?" Sanders' voice bullied.

"I couldn't see his face. My eyes were all blurry, and I just saw this uniform coming for me, and I screamed. I'm sorry. But I really did recognize the one who kidnaped me. His name is Rick. Or that's what the other one called him."

"Just a minute. I'll be right back." Sanders strode out of the room to where Dubinsky was lounging against the wall talking to Collins. "Ed, I want the names of all the people who were on the search party looking for the Griffiths girl this morning — all of them. Look for someone named Rick or something close to that. Fast.'' Dubinsky headed off to the nearest phone.

Sanders stuck his head back in the door. "We're on our way. Would you mind if Collins comes in and takes notes? I'll put him where you don't have to look at him.''

Amanda laughed, her voice clearer and more cheerful now. "No. That's all right. I feel safe with Eleanor here.''

Sanders grabbed a chair and pulled it over to the bed. "You said 'the other one'. There were two men who kidnaped you?'' Amanda nodded. "Did you recognize the other one? Would you know him again?''

She shook her head. "I didn't really get a look at him, and I think he had a hat on most of the time — one of those tweed, checked sort of Irish hats. Most of the time I was asleep, or trying to pretend that I was, and I didn't dare open my eyes and really look at him.''

"Maybe we'd better start right from the beginning and get it all down in order. How are you feeling?''

"Pretty good. I'm thirsty, but my head is clear.'' Amanda took a sip of the proffered water and started in on her long recital.

Most of the time the three people in the room listened in silence; the only interruptions were the scratch of Collins' pen and his occasional request for repetition of a word. When she came to describe what they planned to do to her finally, however, Sanders made her go back several times. "And you're sure they meant to kill you?'' She nodded vehemently.

"Yes. They were quite clear that I mustn't get too heavy a dose of whatever it was because that would kill me and the autopsy would show the wrong cause of death, but they certainly planned to kill me. They were going to bash my head in, was the way Jimmy put it.''

"Did either one of them try to attack you in a ——'' John's voice trailed off at the poisonous look from Eleanor.

Amanda laughed. "Really, Eleanor. I'm not a baby.

Yes. Jimmy tried." She shuddered. "He was awful. But the other one — Rick — wouldn't let him."

"Well, at least the cop wasn't a complete bastard, then," murmured Sanders.

"Actually, it wasn't that. He said that they'd be identified if they did."

"Jesus," he muttered. "Vicious and stupid."

Amanda went slowly and carefully over the details until she got to her desperate escape. Aside from commenting that her mother would be furious because she'd certainly have to buy another school uniform, she hastily glossed over that awful night before the search party arrived.

"How did you know where to look for me?" she asked. "I mean, they could have taken me anywhere."

"It was all that crashing around you did that put us on to it. A Mr. Cottrell who lives across the ravine heard a great deal of strange noise; he thought you were a pair of raccoons fighting. But when he heard on the six o'clock news that a girl had disappeared and that we were searching everywhere, especially the parks and ravines, he called us. Just in case. It was the first real lead we had, and so we tried it."

"By the way — where was I?"

"I think you were about fifty yards from St. Clair Avenue. If you'd had a rock, you probably could have tossed it onto the bridge and hit a car."

"No, I couldn't," said Amanda. "Not even to save my life."

Dubinsky thrust his head in the door and beckoned. "I've got what you want, I think," he said, looking down at his notebook. "There were nine people on the preliminary search party, as you know, and I've got all the names. But there was only one named Rick — a Richard Gruber, known as 'Rick,' usually. He's with the uniform branch on nights, patrolling, these days. He turned up when the party was being organized, said that he had heard about it, had been looking out for the girl all night while on patrol, and wanted to volunteer for the extra shift to help. Nobody was very surprised, since a lot of guys feel pretty strongly about this sort of thing, and he went along in your group. That's it. I asked them to get his file together." He snapped his notebook shut.

Sanders moved without hesitation into higher gear. "What I want now is a picture of him and about five other guys in uniform — all around the same age. And throw in a picture of Collins too. Bring them back here, see if we can get a positive identification. I'm going back to the school to clear up a few details. Call me if you get anything before I get back."

"What do I do if she starts screaming when one of us walks in?"

"She won't. Not now."

Three people turned the corner and raced rapidly down the corridor. Kate Abbott was in the lead, with a tall, lanky man and a small determined-looking woman in full cry behind her. They swept into the room without a word; John stuck his head in after them and beckoned to Eleanor. She picked up her purse and raincoat and left Amanda to her family.

With unnecessary gallantry, John Sanders swept open the front door of the blue unmarked police car and helped Eleanor in. She lay back on the seat, head tilted, her chaotic red curls pouring over the headrest, eyes closed. "I'm taking you home," he said. "Don't worry, it's on my way."

"I'm not worrying," she said. "I'm past worrying about anything right now except how long it's going to take me to get into bed." She yawned. "Where are you going?"

"Back to the school — to tidy up some details; then I'll check up on this Rick and maybe I'll get some sleep. Dubinsky can take over the rest." Eleanor fought a brief battle to stay awake, lost, and sagged against the door frame. The gentle bumping of the car as it hit a rough spot in her driveway woke her up.

"Omigod, we're here. I'm sorry. I couldn't manage to stay awake. I don't know how you do it." She sat up, shook her hair free of her coat collar, and tried to smile without yawning. Sanders leaned over and kissed her, lightly at first, then with sudden strength. Her body sleepily molded itself into the bends and folds of his, and she clung.

He finally pulled himself back, holding her away from him. "I feel like coming upstairs too. But I won't." He kissed her nose, still holding her away from him. "But I'll call you later — or will you be asleep?"

"It doesn't matter. Just let the phone ring until I answer it." She tried a vague smile. "It was a horrible night, but I'm glad you were around." She opened the door and left him quickly, walking briskly into the house without a backward glance.

It was near noon when Sanders stuck his head in the principal's office and asked Annabel if he could talk to the people who would have taken the phone message for Amanda. She pointed him laconically in the direction of the General Office with hardly a pause in the rhythm of her typing.

Neither of the hard-pressed occupants of that spot admitted to having taken the phone call, however. "I delivered the message when I got back in the office," said Ruth, "but I didn't take the phone call. I was off on a tour — showing a pair of prospective parents around the school," she added, by way of explanation, "and it was sitting there along with a couple of others." She looked over at Sylvia. "You were on late lunch, weren't you? Who was on the phone? Annabel?"

"Don't think so. She might know, though," and Sylvia rapidly dialed through on the intercom. "Who was on the phones yesterday afternoon when everyone was off — was it you?" A pause. "Oh, of course. Thanks." She put the receiver down. "That explains it. It was Joyce. We never take a call for a student telling her to get in touch with someone at once without some explanation. It interrupts classes if it isn't really important, and if it is something truly serious — a death or something — we want some control over the situation. And, of course, boyfriends — and others — do try to reach the girls sometimes."

"What do you mean 'others'?"

"We have some girls here from fairly wealthy families, and we have to be careful about messages sending them off to a rendezvous — especially if we don't recognize the caller's voice. And it seems to me — yes, a couple of days ago, someone called, all full of politeness, you know, and wanted Amanda's address. He said it was because she had lost a parcel at his restaurant and he wanted to mail it to her."

"What did you tell him?"

"To mail it to the school — that we would be delighted to give it to her. And I thanked him ever so for being so thoughtful. It might have been genuine; you never know. But we don't give out addresses." She turned back to the pile of envelopes she was stuffing. "But Joyce is new — she's the assistant in the infirmary; it was nice of her to help on the phones, but we wouldn't have taken such a vague message and passed it on. And you can see why. Amanda's the first girl we've actually had snatched from the school area that I can remember, and we've had quite a few vulnerable ones over the years." She smiled competently at him. "If you want to talk to Joyce, I'll get her on the phone." She dialed again, assuming that he would, of course, want to talk to Joyce, if only to make her feel that she should think, the next time, and be more cautious.

Joyce had nothing to add but apologies; the message had been just what she had written down. The caller was male, and no, it had not occurred to her that it was odd that a man should be calling on behalf of Amanda's aunt. Sanders hoped fervently but silently that she was a better nurse than she was a receptionist and hung up, no further ahead than he had been, except for the added knowledge that someone might have made more than one attempt to get at the girl.

Sanders glared with distaste at the corned beef sandwich and coffee sitting on his desk in front of him. They seemed to be looking back at him in much the same frame of mind. He pushed them aside and decided that there was no use in attempting to carry on; it was well past one o'clock and his mind had long since ceased to function. The door opened silently; Dubinsky glided in and tossed his coat down on a chair.

"I went out there myself. Absolutely nothing. I had picked up a warrant and we managed to get into his apartment without too much trouble. You should see it. Must cost him at least a thousand a month. And there's several thousand just sitting there in equipment: the stereo, TV, VCR, with piles of porn tapes. Anyway, the super said that his parking space is empty, but that's all he knows. He says he doesn't bother tenants if they don't bother him, and so on. We got hold of his sister; she says he drives a new Corvette, and no, she hasn't the faintest idea how he paid for it. She assumed he bought it on time, like anyone else. Sure — on a beginning constable's salary, it would only take him twenty years or so to pay for it."

"Could you tell if clothes were missing? Has he packed up and left?"

"Who knows? There's enough stuff in the closets to keep me in clothes for ten years. But there was probably room for some more. And there wasn't any shaving stuff in the bathroom, so I guess he packed something before he went."

"Get a description of the car from Motor Vehicles, and

put it out along with his picture. Better cover the border posts, airport — not that he'll still be around there. But it would be enlightening to discover that his car is in the lot at the airport. And contact the O.P.P. up north — he might have headed for cottage country. I want to talk to his partner; he should have had enough sleep by now. Tell him to drag his ass down here. He must have known about the goddamn Corvette — someone like that doesn't keep all that stuff a secret. I want to know where that money came from — and why. And why we haven't heard anything about it. And if anyone else around that division seems to have too much money as well. Christ! This is going to have to go upstairs before we get too far into it." He slumped back in his chair and picked up his cold coffee. "And help yourself to the sandwich if you feel like it. I'm not sure I'll ever be able to face food again."

Gruber's partner was as slight as recruiting regulations permit. Carruthers had an eager, anxious face, like a nervous kitten's. He was somewhat older than the man he worked with, but the impression his light blue eyes and hesitant smile gave was of youth and naivety. He was sandy-haired, freckled, and homely in a pleasant sort of way, and obviously much taken with Gruber's style.

"Yeah, I mean, we knew he had a pretty fancy car. He sort of said he got a real deal on it. I never asked him about it. He was a really nice guy, always got along with people — you know, great at handling complaints and making old ladies feel good, that sort of thing."

"Did he have a girlfriend?" asked Sanders, his voice sharpening with dislike.

"I don't think so. I mean, not a regular girlfriend. He went out with lots of girls all the time — I went along with him a couple of times — real knockouts." Carruthers' voice became wistful with nostalgia. "But I don't think he had a steady girl."

"It never occurred to you that he lived in a pretty extraordinary manner for someone with his salary? You must have known about how much he made.''

Carruthers squirmed slightly under Sanders' gaze. ''Well, I never really thought'' — his glance slid past Sanders to the desk — ''I mean, you can never tell if people have actually paid for things, you know. I mean, all that stuff could have been on credit cards and ——''

''Only it wasn't, was it? And you damn well knew about it, but you didn't want to get him in any trouble, did you? Because you thought he was a really great guy, and he tossed you his left-over girlfriends and garbage like that.'' Sanders stood up abruptly. ''That's all. This will all get passed upstairs. You might be sorry you thought he was such a great guy. But it's not my baby — I'm just looking for Gruber, your dear friend, who kidnaps helpless fifteen-year-old girls and tries to kill them. I'm glad he wasn't my friend, Carruthers.''

Sanders watched the shaken Carruthers walk out of the small interview room and threw his pen down on the untouched pad of paper in front of him. Let someone else sort through all this crap, he thought, and get the unlovely details down. He had lost interest as soon as Carruthers had admitted that he hadn't the slightest idea where Gruber might be. Maybe California, he had said, Rick had always admired the California style. He dropped his head into his hands. As anger drained off, fatigue came washing in like a Fundy tide. He could have fallen asleep at that moment, sitting bolt upright at the utilitarian little desk, but the enormous shadow of his partner spread across the paper in front of him. ''You get anything more?'' he asked, yawning himself awake again.

''Not on Gruber,'' he said. ''But Cobourg just called.''

''Well?''

''They found Hutchinson. Or at least, they found what was left of him. Up north. He blew most of his head off with a hunting rifle.''

''Goddamit,'' said Sanders. ''Goddamit to hell. I

wanted that man. If he was up north where they could find him why didn't they do it before he blew his head off? How did they find him anyway?''

"His father finally got worried about not hearing from him and told them he had a little cabin up on Lake Kashagawigamog. That was where he was. The O.P.P. found him. He left a note. They need it for the inquest but they're willing to send it down afterwards if we think we want it.''

"I don't suppose you went so far as to find out what was in the note, did you, Dubinsky?''

His partner ignored the heavy sarcasm in his tone. "Yeah. I've got it here. You want to hear it?'' Sanders repressed the reply that rose to his lips and merely nodded. "Okay. Here it is.'' Dubinsky stared down at his notebook. "Dated Tuesday, April 17. 'Dear Dad. I'm sorry about this but after Jane I can't face any more. I should have had more understanding about the fix she was in. It was my fault she died, I know it. Try to explain to Mum, and you should let Bill have my share in the store, he hates his job. Say good-bye to Elaine. Your loving son, Mike.' That's it.''

"What does he mean it's his fault she died? Are you sure that's what's in the note?''

"That's exactly what they said. And I guess maybe he's saying he killed her. Which wraps that one up.''

"It's a pretty funny way of putting it, if that's what he meant. Who in hell are Bill and Elaine?''

"Elaine's his sister. Bill's her husband.'' Dubinsky shrugged.

"She must have told him she was pregnant. What other 'fix' could he mean? And does that make him the father — or an old friend you tell your troubles to? What a mess,'' said Sanders, his voice hollow with fatigue and depression. "Get in touch with Cobourg again and ask them to let us have everything they can, will you? Coroner's report, ballistics, blood type, and anything they can get out of the family about him. Are they sure it's all genuine? The note, the set-up?''

"So far. But they're poking around a bit still.''

Sanders yawned again and blinked in an effort to clear his head. "I'm going off to grab a couple of hours' sleep. Call me if anything else exciting happens. Then maybe we can start chasing down some of Gruber's pals. Get me a list of everyone he's worked with since he started, then go home. I'll take over later.''

Sanders woke up with his mouth dry and his heart pounding, his body tensed to defend itself; he lifted himself halfway to a sitting position and then collapsed again as he recovered a sense of his surroundings. With a muffled groan he looked at his watch. 6:30. A.M. or P.M.? The way he felt it could have been either. The soft light filtering into his bedroom didn't give much of a clue; he flipped on the radio and listened for a minute. P.M. He flipped it off and reached for the phone.

The ringing came to Eleanor from far, far away. She shrugged irritably and tried to brush it off, but its pestering insistence continued. She reached over and picked up the receiver. "Oh, hi. It's you.'' She yawned for the hundredth time that day. "I know I told you to call me — I never said I'd be awake when you did, though. God, I feel awful.''

"Then how about feeling awful together for a while,'' he suggested. The warm tangle of his bedclothes increased his desire to transport her bodily at once to his side. "Why don't you come over?''

"Mmmm,'' said Eleanor. "I'm thinking about it. Let me take a shower and see how things are around here. What time is it?'' She picked up her watch and peered at it. "Say in an hour and a half? Is there any place safe to park around that place you live in?''

"Take a cab. I'll drive you back." He placed the receiver gently on its cradle and headed for the shower.

Eleanor looked at Sanders over a large bowl of Armenian black bean soup with a doubtful cast to her eye. "Are you sure this is really what I need?"

"Believe me. When you're a cop you spend too many days and nights without any sleep, and you learn to cope. This stuff is worth bottles of pep pills and tranquilizers. I live here when things get really tense."

The light was dim, the music very soft, and vaguely Middle Eastern, the waitress a quiet, slow-moving motherly type. Eleanor took a cautious spoonful of the dark, strange-looking liquid. It was hot, savory, and fiery. Her mouth and throat burned, but the butterflies in her stomach quivered once or twice more and settled down to sleep. She smothered the fire in her mouth and throat with a large swallow of beer, and suddenly felt as if she could now proceed with her life. "You're right," she conceded. "It works." She nibbled on a piece of warm pita. "Is everything all right now? Have you heard anything new on Amanda? I couldn't reach Kate before I left."

"As far as I know, she's okay. They're all probably still over at the hospital," he said, gesturing in that direction with his soup spoon. "This whole thing worries me, though. We're really not much further along, and I don't like the look of it so far. I can't see a clown like Gruber organizing to that extent just to kidnap a girl like Amanda. Her family isn't rich — not rich enough to tempt someone like him — and they aren't famous — no one should even have heard of her. Usually when a girl like that gets abducted it's a straight rape case or some kind of demented boyfriend — the marry-me-or-I'll-kill-us-both kind — but according to her, they seemed to have planned on getting rid of her from the start."

"Isn't it more likely that it's connected with Jane Conway?" Eleanor leaned forward to make her point. "I mean, that's the only connection that Amanda has had with anything criminal that I can see."

"Yes, but how? Is someone going around mopping up all her students? That doesn't seem likely. And there is very big money in this somewhere. Someone has been paying Gruber a lot — his apartment looks like a pimp's delight, he's driving a Corvette, he's had money to burn. But the Griffiths kid seems too young — and clean — to be mixed up in anything." He went back to his soup.

"Mixed up in something? What sort of something?"

"You know — drugs, prostitution, anything that's organized by the big boys. She doesn't have any connections that I can see. I mean, her father isn't involved in manufacturing stuff, is he? He does work in a lab."

"I doubt it. From Kate's description, it wouldn't seem to be the right kind of lab."

"Anyway, killing his daughter is a pretty drastic way of warning him off. It doesn't smell right." He pushed aside his plate. "And that leaves only the Conway case. But the connection escapes me. Conway's boyfriend from the country killed himself, you know. And left a note saying that it was all his fault."

"You mean that he killed her?"

"No, that her death was his fault. Does that sound to you as if he killed her? Dubinsky is inclined to think it does, but he's a lazy bastard most of time."

Eleanor shook her head. "It sounds as though he forgot to do something — you know, didn't get the car brakes fixed and she drove into a truck — something he blames himself for. Funny way to put it. I wonder what he meant? But let's get back to something more important. Is Amanda safe now?"

"Until we find Gruber, and this guy Jimmy who was

with him, and figure out why they snatched her, no, she isn't. But there are people on at the hospital keeping an eye out for her. She should be okay."

"But what if someone you put on to guard her is another one of them? I mean, how can you tell?"

"Don't worry. I've hand-picked them all. They all have wives and kids, frayed collars, and big mortgages. They're safe." He wished he felt as confident as he sounded.

Chapter Eleven

He checked his equipment one last time. It was ten o'clock.
Almost time to leave. One last trip to the bathroom.
Careful visual check of his appearance. Neat, and clean,
but not too slick. Hair washed and shiny but curls a little
tousled. Clean shaven, no cuts, no funny shine to his skin
from too much attention or shaving lotion. He practiced
his pleasant and open smile one last time in the mirror, and
then turned abruptly and headed for the garage. As he
backed out slowly and carefully, he saw the young woman
who lived next door, out for a walk with her infant in a
stroller. He smiled and waved. "How's Ginny?" she called.

"Getting much better," he said, with warmth and
sincerity. He liked that ring of truth in his tone. But he'd
better not let this bitch hold him up. He hadn't allowed for
too many delays. He reversed onto the street and pulled
away, a little faster than usual. The streets were strangely
quiet for a Friday morning.

He pulled into the spot he had chosen the day before.

10:25. He slowly arranged his equipment where it would be needed then began his careful hunt. There were fewer people than he would have expected. The weather was good for operating; there should have been young housewives out for walks between the development and the mall. No problem, though. He had allotted himself an hour before the lunch-hour rush from the local school made maneuvering impossible. The window on the passenger side was open, and his sharp ears strained for the right sort of sound. Far-off voices were merely an irritation to be classified and discounted. Then, coming up the footpath he heard the unmistakable sound of steps — one set, perhaps light enough to be the right sort.

She was panting from the effort of her rapid climb up from the river and grabbed a branch to pull herself up the last couple of feet to the sidewalk. She stopped for a minute to scrape the mud off her shoes and wipe the sweat from her forehead, looked back down the path a second, and started along the sidewalk. Her way was almost blocked by a pleasant but puzzled-looking young man, leaning on the open door of his shiny new van, squinting at a road map in his hand. "Excuse me, Miss, but do you have any idea where Hawthorne Crescent is? It's supposed to be in one of these subdivisions, but I don't seem to be able to find it." He waved the map slightly toward her, and she automatically stepped back a pace, but good-naturedly glanced down.

"I don't really know the neighborhood," she started, "but my ——" Then her quick eye caught the flash of black in his fist, and she ducked as he swung and tossed the map into the van at the same time. The blow glanced off the thick braid on the back of her head, and she reeled as he grabbed her with his left hand. He threw the pipe after the map and reached for her inert body. What he faced, however, was screaming fury. Before he could grab her free arm, a clawful of fingernails raked his cheek. He lunged for her and got only her upraised foot in his grasp just before it landed. All the while she was yelling incoherently but lustily. Her scream ended in a loud gasp as she lost her balance and fell backwards, loosening his grip on her arm, but still caught by one foot. When he looked up from the ruin of his enterprise, he suddenly realized that three people had materialized from the footpath. He let go of her foot and threw himself into the front seat of the van. In seconds he was in gear and lurching toward home. On the bridge, two people helped her gently to her feet, while the third stared after the retreating van.

In less than an hour, Sanders was standing in an interview room looking down at four robust, lively young adults in jeans and heavy sweaters. The smallest of the four, a girl with long brown hair half pinned up in a braid, looked a bit dusty and muddy, but otherwise in excellent condition. "You are" — here he glanced down at the names hastily scribbled in front of him — "Miss Karen Dodds? You are the one that ——"

She nodded vigorously. "That's right."

"Did he hurt you?" he asked quickly. "Has she been looked at by anyone?" he said, turning to the young constable in the corner of the room.

"I'm fine," she said. "They tried to drag me off to the hospital, but really, there's nothing wrong with me. I fell on my backside, that's all. I've done that plenty of times before."

"I thought you said he hit her on the head," said Sanders, turning back accusingly to the man in the corner, who reddened slightly as he opened his mouth to protest.

"He missed," she said. "Hit my hair, that's all. It's probably a mess." She automatically reached up and patted the straying braid back into place. "I saw it coming and ducked. I almost got him, too." She flashed a triumphant smile at the large young man hovering over her. "Did you see that, Dave? If I'd had boots on instead of these things," she said, pointing down at her running shoes, "he wouldn't have felt much like driving off. The bastard."

"You were very lucky, Miss Dodds. If you had been alone" — he paused to fight off the image of that lively face turned to pulp by savage pounding.

"Luck has nothing to do with it," she said. "He'd have had some doing to pin me down in broad daylight even if the others hadn't been there."

Dave looked down at her in smug satisfaction. "Karen's a great gymnast," he said. "And a dancer. She's fast and strong. He sure picked the wrong one this time."

"How good a look did they get at him?" asked Sanders, turning back to the young constable in the corner.

"Pretty good sir," he said. "We've put it out." He flipped back a page or two in his notebook. "He's taller than average — about six feet — in his twenties, light brown curly hair, medium length."

"And he should have some pretty good scratch marks on his cheek, too," said Karen, who looked pleased at the thought. "I think I drew blood."

"Did you include that in the description?" asked Sanders impatiently.

"No, sir, but I will, right away." He hurried on with his report. "And he's driving a new van, probably North American make, light brown or tan, with a license plate number that has a nine in it."

The other young man looked up apologetically. "By the time we realized what was happening and made sure that Karen was okay, the van was a long way down the road. But we're pretty sure of the nine."

"Right," said Sanders. "We'll get in touch when we find him. We'll need you to identify him."

"Do you think you'll find him just on this?" asked Dave. "There must be thousands of vans out there."

"Even if there are," said Sanders, "we'll find him."

He sat in the garage, still trembling, clinging to the wheel of the van with sweat-slimy hands. The door had clanged shut and was firmly locked, but the safety it offered was illusory. What had happened? He hadn't even heard the others coming up the path. He had failed again. Miserably, disgustingly. "Failed again, failed again" echoed in his skull in that thin, nasty, mocking voice that was going to drive him wild. He slowly picked up the crumpled map and smoothed it out. He studied the folds carefully and then restored it meticulously to its original shape. Clutching it in his hand, he eased himself out from behind the wheel and stepped heavily down onto the garage floor. Slowly, slowly, he locked the van door, opened the door to the house, and moved up the stairs to the kitchen. The powerful stench of rotting food seemed to make no impression on him as he walked through the room, his feet crunching on the broken glass on the floor. He picked up a box of salted crackers from the counter and walked up the stairs to the living room. In a corner the television set flickered on soundlessly and endlessly. From a table beside him, the telephone rang, and rang, and rang. His hand crept up to his right cheek. His fingers slowly measured the long red gouges running down his face until the ringing stopped. He stared, unseeing, into the far corner of the room.

Nine o'clock Saturday night at the Toronto General Hospital had come and gone, and Amanda was sitting up in bed flipping channels on her television set in a desultory manner. The hospital, as is the way with such places, was already concentrating its efforts on bedding everyone down for the night, and an atmosphere of weary boredom had taken over. She sighed and flopped back down again. Nothing on. She was already getting sick and tired of being there and was eager to get back to Aunt Kate's. She even itched to get back to school, cast and all, just for a change of scenery. The door was flung open suddenly, heralding the arrival of a nurse; Amanda had observed that each class of person at the hospital entered a room in a distinc-

168

tive way — the cleaning staff gingerly, the nurses abruptly, the doctors coyly, and so on. This was a new nurse. They changed with dizzying frequency, and when Amanda had commented on it, she was told that it was a consequence of landing in hospital close to a holiday weekend. She smiled vaguely at the nurse, who was proceeding toward her briskly.

"Now, love, just roll over, and we'll soon have you feeling better. Come on." She grabbed the corner of the bedclothes to flip them back.

"Hey! What's that?" said Amanda, sitting up and pointing at the wicked-looking hypodermic needle in her hand.

"It's your injection, dear. Now roll over."

"I'm not supposed to get an injection. Stop that!" she said loudly as the harassed nurse tried to roll her on her side. "Stop! Al! Help!" She was screaming by now. Into the room raced two hundred and ten pounds of well-muscled, uniformed policeman. He grabbed the nurse by the arm.

"I'll have to ask you not to do that," he said apologetically, not loosening his grip. "Not until I get authorization from someone. She's not supposed to get anything that I don't know about. Sorry," he said, looking nervously at the nurse's face, which was rapidly shading from scarlet to purple.

"Well," she said. "I'll get the doctor who ordered the injection, and perhaps you won't attack him!" She stormed out of the room, muttering something that sounded unprofessional.

"Thanks," said Amanda. "I'm getting tired of people doing things to me these days." He winked at her.

Five minutes later the door opened, a trifle more gently this time, and a white-coated resident, young and brisk-looking, poked his head around and said, "So this is the young lady with the pain, is it?" He smiled. Amanda was sitting bolt upright, bright-eyed and determined. "You don't really look as if you're in pain, though. Is it better?''

"Better? I'm not in pain. I haven't been in pain all day. I'm fine," she said fiercely.

"Then you really shouldn't have asked for an injection, you know. It's not good for you to have these strong drugs if you don't need them. If you're having trouble sleeping we'll give you something for that — no need to ask for a needle. Isn't that true, nurse," he said to the woman who had followed him in. His gently condescending voice was immensely irritating.

"I didn't ask for an injection, I tell you. I'm fine. I've been fine all day, haven't I, Al?'' She turned to her protector and star witness. "So you can keep your drugs and injections to yourself.'' She tried to wave her huge cast in their direction, muttered a silent ouch, and settled back on her pillows.

"Well, I was just doing what I was asked to do," said the nurse, huffily. "Dr. Weatherill ordered an injection and I came to give it.''

"I ordered the injection because I got a call from the nursing station that the patient in 526 was screaming in pain. Why else would I do it?'' Now he glowered at Amanda, then at the nurse. "I have enough to do around here without medicating patients who don't need it. If you knew the kind of load I had on a holiday weekend you'd realize I don't go around treating other people's patients just to amuse myself.'' His voice was low and bitter now.

"Who called you, may I ask?'' said Al hastily, before Weatherill could get any further in his catalogue of complaints.

"I don't know. It must have been Miss Beatty here," he said.

"Wasn't me," she said, rapidly tossing the responsibility as far away as she could. "I just got back from my break and there it was — the order for the injection. So I got it ready. I know nothing about it. I haven't been on duty for days. I just got back this evening.'' She glared at Dr.

Weatherill. "It must have been one of the others." At that she flounced out of the room.

"I'm going to have to call someone in to look into this, Dr. Weatherill," said Al. "You understand that this young lady is under police guard because an attempt has already been made on her life."

"Well, investigate away," he replied, offended. "But all I know is what I told you." As he left, he brushed against an orderly hurrying past, and saw but did not see an innocuous-looking man leaving the room across the hall, saying good-bye tenderly and affectionately to an empty bed and two unoccupied chairs.

Sanders was standing, keys in hand, vehemently pointing out to Eleanor that a woman of her age should be able to spend a night out without worrying what her mother might think. "Dammit, Eleanor, has she ever said anything?" he whispered. They were standing in the corridor of his apartment building and making half-hearted attempts to keep their voices down. She paused to consider for a moment.

"Stop trying to steam-roller me," she complained. "You're entirely too used to pushing people around. It's not good for you." Before he could think of a reply, the phone on the other side of his door began to ring.

"Dammit." He fumbled with the lock, cursing under his breath, flung open the door and dashed to answer it. For a long time he simply listened. "Did you call Dubinsky? Okay. Tell him I'll see him there right away." He turned to Eleanor and shook his head. "Okay, sweetheart. You win this time. Someone made another try to get at Amanda. She's fine — they bungled it — but I have to go down and see what's up." He kissed her on the forehead. "I'll drop you off on my way."

"That's not exactly the way I had hoped to win this particular fight," she said. "Losing would have been more fun."

Chapter Twelve

The mills of justice, in their own way, like the mills of the gods, grind on, even on holiday weekends and in unlikely places. Easter Sunday morning dawned bright and clear in southern Florida — the birds and the tourists sang and fluttered in the early morning sun. In fact, many of the birds, like many of the tourists, were on their way back to Canada and were making the most of the friendly climate while they were still there. But in the minor resort town of Pidgeon's Bay, a clutch of motels and beach houses outside of Fort Lauderdale, things were dull and dreary in the sheriff's office. The drunken students were gone, the hordes of tourists were slowly dwindling, and the sleepiness of summer was beginning to pervade the atmosphere. Des Hepworth sat in lonely splendor, staring at a cup of coffee and the various papers that had hit the desk since Friday, when he had last been on. Among the long lists of stolen cars and wanted fugitives one stray item caught his attention. The words "1984 Corvette — white" leapt out at him. That was what he wanted with all his heart and soul. A white Corvette. So did Lindy. When he had made his unsuccessful bid to transfer her from beach blanket to motel last night, she had distracted him with shrieks of delight at the white Corvette parked outside the Flying Fish Motel. "Look, Des," she had squealed, "isn't that the most gorgeous car! I wonder who it belongs to?" And he had dragged her away again, almost forgetting what they were supposed to be there for. Or had she done it on purpose? Damn that girl. You could never tell what she was up to.

He read the rest of the item — Ontario license number SYW 567; driven by Richard Gruber, 6'2", light brown hair, age 23, weight 195 lbs. Wanted for kidnaping and assault. Bastard, he thought. Kidnaping. He rested his hungover head on the chair back. That license number seemed somehow familiar. Shit! He reached for his phone, moments later for his car keys, and was out of the door.

And so it was that one *aficionado* of sexy white cars and lively women met up with another — only these two, who should have been soul mates, ended up in a spirited battle in room sixteen of the Flying Fish Motel. Des had the back-up, however, and by Monday morning Rick was at the Miami airport, sullenly awaiting a free trip home.

When Sanders came in on that Monday morning, he found Dubinsky already hard at work. He looked up from the pile of things on his desk and nodded. "I heard about Saturday night. Sorry. I was at my niece's wedding. I wouldn't have been much use to you by the time they called, anyway." He shrugged apologetically. "Did you figure out what happened?"

"Sort of. If you put everything together. It looks as if someone came out into the corridor outside room 526, all excited, saying that his daughter was screaming in pain and no one was answering the bell. He grabbed a nurse who happened to be passing by from another ward. She passed the message on to Miss Beatty's relief, Mrs. O'Connor. She assumed that the first girl had gone in and looked at 526, and so she put in a call for the resident who ordered a standard dose of painkiller. Very simple. He obviously counted on the floor being slightly short-staffed because of the holiday. It's harder to tell exactly what he had in mind from there, but someone had been camping out in the empty room across the hall. There were sandwich wrappers and some empty coffee containers in the garbage. And a couple of orderly's outfits — one of them worn. I suppose they were going to try to take out the man on duty and get at her when she was unconscious. It's a damned good thing the Griffiths girl is getting very suspicious of people in uniforms," grunted Sanders as he headed for the door. "Anyway, let's get out to the airport and meet our dear friend Mr. Gruber. We wouldn't want him to be kept waiting.

Sanders and Dubinsky faced a new Rick Gruber, stripped of whatever status he might have enjoyed, sitting on the wrong side of the table in the interview room. He was pale and bedraggled, but stubbornly defiant still.

"I had some time coming to me, that's all. I was tired, so I took off for Florida." He attempted a casual shrug of his shoulders and winced. Des had inflicted a few nasty bruises before he got finished. "So is that a crime? I mean, I should have gotten permission for leave, but that's no reason to haul me back like a bloody fugitive."

"You left in a hell of a hurry for someone who just thought he had a few days coming to him, Gruber," said Dubinsky. "Not very convincing."

Gruber looked at him with one raised eyebrow and said nothing.

Sanders brought his fist down on the table in front of him with a crash. "Get the hell off the pot, Gruber. Let's stop playing games. The girl has identified you. That was a pretty stupid thing to do if you didn't want to spend the next twenty years in maximum security. You know what they do to cops in there, Gruber? It's not very nice. You don't want to spend twenty years watching out for a knife in your back every time you turn around.''

"What girl?" said Gruber. "I don't know what you're talking about."

"The girl you went off so nobly to help us find on Thursday morning, Gruber. The one who screamed as soon as she saw you again and ran like hell. Why do you suppose she screamed, Gruber?"

"I don't know, sir," said Rick. "I suppose the poor kid was confused."

"No — she was the one you were planning to murder, only she got away from you. You bungled it, Gruber, and you got caught." Gruber looked at the ceiling, apparently fascinated by some non-existent pattern traced on its plain white surface. Sanders' voice got lower and lower until it was almost a whisper. "She was awake, Gruber. All that time you were farting around figuring out how to finish her off, she was awake. And listening. Your little friend, Jimmy, gave you bad advice about putting people out. You didn't give her enough, and she woke up. And so we know what you were going to do, only we don't know why. And that's what you're going to tell us, Gruber. You're going to tell us why, and you're going to tell us the names of everyone else involved in this." He stopped to let it sink in. Gruber continued to stare at the ceiling, apparently oblivious to his surroundings, happy to sit quietly and observe.

"I think maybe we should just leave him for a while to think about things, don't you, John?" said Dubinsky, in a pleasant, reasonable tone of voice. "I mean, like he has to think up a story about where he got that car from, and all that fancy equipment in his expensive apartment. That might take him a while, don't you think?" Sanders nodded, and Dubinsky went to the door and signaled to the constable waiting outside.

"We'll be back," said Sanders. "Soon. Think about what you're going to tell us, Gruber. It had better be good." He turned to the man coming in. "Give him some dinner. We wouldn't want him to complain about the way we treat prisoners in here. We'll be back in an hour."

"You eating?" asked Dubinsky, as they headed for the collection of little fast-food stands and restaurants in the complex near by.

"Not yet," said Sanders, sliding into a quiet table. "Get me a coffee while you're up there, will you?" He flipped him two quarters.

"I think," said Dubinsky, when he had finished with his chow mein, "that he's ready to do a deal, don't you?"

"I'd say so. He knows we've got him and he's worried. I hope he knows it, anyway. By the way, has anything come in on the Parsons woman today?"

"Kranik said that they were going to try to operate on her head again, maybe tomorrow morning. They're surprised she's still alive — think maybe if they get the crud out of her skull" — Sanders looked greenly at him — "bone chips and stuff like that, you know. Anyway, Kranik's word, not mine."

"Do you think she'll regain consciousness?"

"Maybe. There's a chance it'll work, I guess."

Half an hour later they were back in the little room. Gruber didn't look as if dinner had improved him much.

"Let me put it this way, Gruber," said Sanders, quiet and confidential. "We might be willing to believe that kidnaping the Griffiths girl wasn't your idea in the first place. I mean, you're probably not bright enough to have worked out a plan like that. And we have lots of evidence that you're on the take, Gruber. You're going to have trouble explaining all that money in your bank account, all those expensive toys in your apartment. Have you considered what we have on you? Kidnaping, attempted murder, accepting bribes, just to start with. But you're a very small minnow, and we want the big fish, Gruber. Who is he?

What was the idea behind kidnaping the girl? Who's Jimmy? We would like to talk to Jimmy, Gruber. We really would." His voice trailed off. He smiled at Gruber.

There was a long pause. Gruber looked from Sanders to Dubinsky. "I want a new identity," he said, suddenly. "And immunity from prosecution."

"You won't need a new identity if we catch the big fish. He won't be around. And I doubt, somehow, that I could get immunity past the Crown. Not for a police officer. The public doesn't like its police on the take. But I might get charges reduced. Maybe even enough to make you eligible for a provincial institution. You don't want to go to a federal institution, do you?"

"Christ," he muttered. "You guys don't realize what could happen to me if I open my mouth."

"We'll do our best, Gruber," said Sanders. "But you should bloody well have thought of that before you got involved in this."

"I don't know that much," he whined. His thin mustache was soaked with sweat. "I don't know who the big fish is. I only dealt with Jimmy."

"Jimmy who?"

"Jimmy Fielding. I don't know where he lives. He has an office on Dundas Street West, above a crummy Chinese restaurant, The Golden Apple. Only a couple of blocks from here."

"What does Mr. Fielding do in that office?" asked Sanders.

"He's an agent — for all sorts of things. He does some importing, and runs a translation service and that sort of thing, and acts on behalf of immigrants who have problems."

"You mean he smuggles in illegals? And then slides them into the States for a bit extra."

Rick squirmed a bit. "Well, maybe. I don't know."

"And where did you fit into his little business?"

"Well — I didn't have to do much. Sometimes I just

turned up when he was talking to someone and stood there. He just liked to have someone in uniform there; it made him feel safer, he said. Jesus, it's just like the super-market people hiring an off-duty to stand in the goddamn parking lot. It wasn't anything to worry about.''

"Sure," said Sanders. "Only in the office was some poor bugger who didn't understand English and was ter-rified of people in uniform, and Fielding used you to extort what he wanted from him, didn't he?'' Gruber shrugged. "And what else did you do, besides intimidating illegals?''

"Well — sometimes I just carried packages around. I don't know what was in them, but they were packages he didn't want anyone to steal. So he figured no one would knock off a cop, you know.''

"Shit!" said Sanders. "Packages. Come on, Gruber, you're not that stupid. Just what in hell was he importing? Heroin? Where did you pick it up from? The airport?'' Gruber nodded. "Carried in by innocent-looking tourist types, I suppose.'' Gruber nodded again. "And you were in uniform? And driving a patrol car?'' Gruber nodded for the third time. "Christ. That's all we need.''

"I don't think it was heroin, though," said Gruber.

"Oh, good," said Sanders. "What was it?''

"Coke.''

"That's nice. It's much classier, isn't it? Goes with the apartment and the silk shirts.'' He stuck his head out the door. "Hey you. Get someone to come in and take Mr. Gruber's statement. We're off to find a friend of his.'' Then he turned back. "By the way, Gruber, why did you snatch the Griffiths girl?''

"I dunno," he said. "Jimmy said the boss wanted her out of the way, and it had to be done in just that way. You'll have to ask Jimmy.''

"I will," said Sanders. "I will.''

Mr. Jimmy Fielding was sitting tranquilly in his large, grubby office, that, with bathroom and kitchen attached,

formed the entire second floor of the building that housed
The Golden Apple. Smells of old grease and newly burned
food wandered up through various cracks and crannies in
the floor and reminded him that he had not as yet had his
dinner. But he was waiting for a client. Because of the
nature of his business dealings, which were many — those
that Gruber had known about were only a small sampling
of the rich variety of his services — he often worked evening hours. To accommodate honest working folk. Tonight
he was pleased with life. Gruber had screwed up, but
Gruber had had the sense to disappear. If he had done
what he was told, he should be in the Cayman Islands by
now, happily living on what had been banked there for
him. And when that ran out, he could be useful at the
Caribbean end of things. But he was going to have to find
another cop — someone as greedy as Gruber, but a touch
cleverer.

At the sound of a step on the stair, he looked at his
watch. Right on time. Good. That meant he was anxious
and would be easier to deal with. "Come in," he called
jovially as soon as he saw a hand raised to the milky glass
of the door. His feet abruptly left his desk and the welcom-
ing grin his face when he saw his two visitors.

"Well, now gentlemen, may I help you? I have a client
arriving very soon, so ——"

"Well, well," said Dubinsky, "if it isn't little Jimmy
Feldman. I haven't seen you for a while."

"Good evening, Sergeant. It is Sergeant now, isn't it?
But what brings you here? Surely it's not a crime for someone to change his name and embark upon a life of hard
work and legitimate endeavor, is it?" He smiled.

"Certainly not," said Sanders. "but we're here to talk
about a kidnaping. As well as various other little enter-
prises."

"Kidnaping?" said Jimmy, in tones of astonishment.

"Yes, Mr. Fielding. The kidnaping of Miss Amanda
Griffiths. We've got you, you know. She identified

Gruber, and Gruber fingered you. You can't trust anybody these days."

"Gruber?"

"Yeah." Dubinsky leaned casually against the door. "Constable, or should I say, ex-Constable Rick Gruber, your partner in this alleged kidnaping."

"Oh. That Gruber. Yes, indeed." Fielding paused for a while, the pleasant smile sitting poised on his face. "An over-anxious and not very clever young man, I'm afraid. I fear he jumps to conclusions and misunderstands the simplest requests."

"He does? In what way did he misunderstand you, Mr. Fielding?"

"Ah well. It was a simple custody case — you know, one of these instances in which children become the pawns of warring parents."

"You're about to make me sick," said Sanders. "Get to the point."

"Well, a very unhappy man came to see me a little while ago, with a very sad story. His beloved daughter had been snatched by his wife — a dreadful woman, apparently, with no morals to speak of — and had been placed in an expensive girls' school where she was miserable. The place is a veritable prison. He hadn't been allowed to see her or even to speak to her. He asked me if I could help him — out of pure charity, of course — regain custody of this poor girl." He spread his hands in a gesture of resignation. "How could I refuse? And it seemed a simple thing to do, merely picking up a girl after school and delivering her to her father."

"In a police car? Taken from a police garage without authorization?"

"No!" said Jimmy, quivering with amazement. "He didn't do that, did he? I told you, he was a man of more good will than brains. You see, my car wasn't functioning well that day, and Constable Gruber offered to help me out by driving her to her father. I don't know what happened. The girl must have misunderstood what was going on. We thought her father had had a chance to explain the plan to her. Or, you don't suppose that Constable Gruber forgot himself and tried to take advantage of her, do you? He is a very young man, you know. Anyway, he called me in the evening to say that when he tried to take her to her father's car, she panicked and ran away, and he was dreadfully afraid that she had fallen and hurt herself. I think he must have spent the rest of the night torn with remorse and trying to find her, poor chap."

"You mean, you weren't there?" said Sanders. "Not at all?"

"Oh, I was there when we picked the girl up, but I had other things to do, and Constable Gruber dropped me off on his way to the rendezvous. I'm afraid I don't know what happened after that. Except what I've told you." He smiled gently at the two of them.

"And who was this poor deprived father, may I ask? Do you think we could discuss the matter with him? After all, if he had a custody order, we might be able to help him have it enforced."

"Well, the document he showed me was from the State of Maine. He said it was a custody order. But I don't believe he gave his last name — it must, of course, be Griffiths, mustn't it, if that's the girl's name. His name is Pete, and I think he's staying at the Park Plaza Hotel — close to his daughter's school, to catch a glimpse of her if he can. Is the girl back at school, might I ask?"

"No, you might not," snapped Sanders. "The girl's whereabouts is classified information. In case someone else tries to get custody of her." Sanders leaned beside the door of the office, and Dubinsky wandered casually over to the space between the desk and the entrance to the filthy little kitchen behind. "It was a lovely story, Jimmy. I enjoyed every minute of it. Only it was a crock of shit from beginning to end. Unfortunately for you, the girl was not unconscious. Someone should have told you how much of that stuff you have to give a person her size to keep her under that long. She heard it all. And Gruber has confirmed her story. We've got you."

Fielding slowly started to open the drawer of his desk, without looking to either side. His right hand moved gently into it. "Look out!" yelled Dubinsky, throwing himself at him, as Sanders ducked sideways and tried frantically to extract his gun from the tangle of his suit jacket.

"Gentlemen, please," said Fielding. "I was only trying to get my gloves out of the drawer." He held up a pair of gray leather gloves and slammed the drawer shut. He reached for his Irish tweed hat and his raincoat from the stand by the desk and smiled.

Dubinsky pulled at the handle. The drawer was locked. He gave it a ferocious yank and it sprang open. "Do you have a license for this?" he asked, picking the revolver up gingerly and checking to see if the safety was on. Fielding shrugged and moved toward the office door.

Marny slowly scanned the dimly lit, smoky restaurant from her position by the door. There he was, sitting with a man almost as casually elegant as himself. She tossed an incoherent mutter at the hostess and bore down on the table. "Hi, Grant," she growled, as brightly as she could. "I thought I might run into you here." She half-smiled with blank eyes at his companion. "That answering machine of yours gives me the twitches, and so I decided that I really needed a drink anyway. I wish you wouldn't put such cute remarks on it. I can never think of anything to say back."

Grant's expression remained carefully neutral. "What a pleasant surprise," he said, in a very unsurprised voice. "Have you met Geoff Porter? He was in the series with me."

Marny's head whipped around. "That must be why you

look so familiar," she said. Now warmth dripped from every syllable. "How are negotiations going with the U.S. networks and all that?" she asked cosily.

"Nothing much happening at the moment," said Grant. Geoff raised an eyebrow in his direction and then lifted his glass to drain his drink.

"These things certainly do get stalemated," he said agreeably. "But I had better get going. I fear I am already a little late for this evening's jollification. Thanks for the drink. And the interesting discussion. Good-bye-uh, nice to meet you."

"Sorry," said Marny, as he picked his way between the tables, "I guess I chased him away."

"Not really," said Grant with a slight yawn. "I think he actually did have somewhere he had to get to. Some sort of reception or other that's due to finish in about half an hour. But why did you come searching me out? I take it that's what you were doing. After all, Giuseppe's isn't your usual stomping ground, is it?"

"Look, Grant, I have to have a talk to you. Is this place safe?"

"As safe as any, sweetheart. Talk away." He looked both amused and faintly bored.

"Well — it's just that ever since Jane died — I mean, I'm having a party on Friday night, like usual, you know. And there are going to be a lot of people there. I used to have two contacts, but one fizzled out on me, and lately I was relying on Jane. I mean, I only used her for emergencies and extra stuff like that before, because she was more expensive than this other guy. But he's gone to Florida, and I mean, I don't think he'll be coming back. Look, Grant, those people are going to be expecting to buy from me, and my only two sources have dried up." Her voice was low and nervous; she stabbed the air between them in her eagerness to be understood. "You have a source, don't you? Do you think you could put me on to him? Your source wasn't just Jane, was it? I never got the impression it was." She glanced quickly around the room, stopping to look closely at the people at the tables closest to them. The sudden voice of the waitress in her ear sent her several inches into the air until she processed the familiar words. "Yeah, thanks. I'll have a rum and Coke."

"Well, it used to be," said Grant. "Although I did get a line on her supplier. He's a useful guy. I don't know just where he fits in in the larger scheme of things, but he does do his own importing. I imagine there's someone higher up bankrolling him, of course. One doesn't like to ask about these things." His voice drawled, unconcerned. "In fact, I was about to do a deal with Jane concerning a certain expansion of interests — increased marketing, you might say, tapping a demand that certainly is there. But that is something that you and I might consider at a later date, supposing we decided that we could work together in peace and harmony."

"Jesus, Grant, if you could work with Jane, you could work with anybody. The two of you fought like drunken Finns."

"No ethnic slurs, if you don't mind. I'm an ethnic myself. And Jane and I had a certain common set of interests beside business that kept things going, you might say." He smiled.

"Yeah. Bed. Anyway, can you give me the name of your contact?"

"No, ma'am. He wouldn't like that very much. But I'll give him your name and home telephone number. He'll call you if he's interested. If you don't hear from him, there's not much I can do." Grant shrugged.

"Great." Marny dropped a couple of bills down on the table between them and left, just as a rum and Coke was set down in front of her empty chair.

Eleanor sat in the spring twilight at her desk. She stared out the window of the elegantly redone red-brick Victorian house that was home to Webb and MacLeod, Real Estate, trying to avoid the clutter that had accumulated in the past few days. It had not been a terrific time to be *non compos mentis*, apparently. Several people, obviously desperate for housing, had been trying to get in touch with her over the weekend. She felt a pang or two — one of guilt and one of regret for probable commissions lost — and sorted out her messages. In the midst of this dreary contemplation of opportunities missed, her phone buzzed. At the same time, Frances, on her way out the door, stuck her head in the office and said, "Phone. It's a man. A friend, I think." Frances spent her days trying to marry off all the unattached agents in the firm.

"Hello. Eleanor Scott speaking," she said cautiously, more afraid it might be one of those people she was supposed to have called back several days ago.

"Hello to you, too. Are you busy?" Without waiting for a reply, he went on. "If you're not, I'm going up to see Amanda once more and then out to eat. Want to come?"

"Yes, I am," she said firmly. "I have to make a living." She paused a second. "On the other hand, I would like to see how she's doing." She crumbled completely. "Well, okay. I'll meet you up there." Her face brightened as she swept everything off her desk and slammed the drawer shut.

Amanda was sitting up in bed, much encumbered still with plaster, but looking very lively and tackling an enormous bunch of grapes with one hand. She waved the grapes at them in a gesture of welcome. "Hi. Mom has gone to take my father to the airport; he has to get back. But she's staying until I'm out of here. So I'm all alone. Except for my friend out there. Do you know that he won't let me eat anything except stuff my parents and Aunt Kate bring me? It's awful." She gestured at them to sit down. "And I suppose it's all your fault, too," she said, looking accusingly at Sanders. "Leslie brought me a box of chocolates, and I couldn't have them."

"Better safe than sorry," he said, unrepentant. "But if

you're not too annoyed, I have a favor to ask." She grinned. "Would you look at these pictures and see if you recognize Jimmy in any of them? I know you say you didn't get a good look at him, but we think we know who he is; it would help if you could confirm it for us."

"Sure," she said, eating another grape and putting down the bunch. "But I really didn't see him, you know." She wiped her good hand on the sheet and spread the pictures out on the bed in front of her. She looked intently. "Hey!" she exclaimed. "Is that ever funny. I don't recognize Jimmy, but look at this one! It's the man in the gray Honda!" And she picked up the picture of James Feldman, also known as Jimmy Fielding.

"Did everyone know about the man in the gray Honda but me?" asked Sanders over a plate of goulash in the closest Hungarian eatery. "That might have made things hang together a bit, you know." He glared at her.

"Don't harangue," she said. "This is the first I've heard of it. Heather probably knows more than I do."

"Terrific," he said, irritated. "And I wonder what the significance of 'all the kids' is in the statement 'all the kids knew about it'. The whole school?"

"I wouldn't think so. Just her friends and anyone they told it to. Shouldn't take more than a month to figure it out," she said with a laugh. His glare checked her mirth. "Sorry, but you couldn't imagine the speed at which news travels in a girls' school. I doubt if you'd ever figure out who knew one piece of information at one particular time. But I'm sure that Roz will do anything she can to help you. Of course, you'll have to wait until tomorrow. Unless you want to go around and try to see all Amanda's best friends and see what they say."

"No," he said. "That's probably a waste of time. I think I'll concentrate on Mr. Fielding himself, and see what he can come up with in the way of an explanation."

Chapter Thirteen

Sanders walked into the familiar room and headed toward his desk with the profound conviction that he had never left it. The sight of Dubinsky, yawning and bleary-eyed, only served to heighten the illusion. It had been after three when they had finally decided that they were going to get nothing from Jimmy Fielding. For six hours he had sat and smiled and referred all questions to his lawyer. A sleepy nurse on night duty had thought that maybe Fielding's mug shot represented the face she had seen in the hall outside room 526; but, then again, she hadn't noticed him that clearly. Sanders' jaw still felt stiff from suppressing his anger. He yearned to get the man alone for a few hours, to see if he could shake that complacent grin off his face, to evoke just a flash of fear in those bland eyes. Dammit. If they hadn't been in such a hurry to hustle him downtown so they could get a positive I.D. on him from the Griffiths girl, he could have — but no. Whoever it was that Jimmy worked for would be a hell of a lot more terrifying to him than John Sanders, Detective Inspector, could ever be since Sanders was unlikely to carve him up and feed his guts to the gulls, no matter how tempting the idea might be. "Hi, Ed," he yawned. "How's it going? Any word on Parsons?"

"Not yet," said Dubinsky. "McInnis is on. He'll call if she comes to."

"I think I'll drop over to the hospital and keep an eye on things. We'd better take a copy of that sketch — if it's ready — in case she can identify the bastard. And maybe we can get something new out of the Griffiths girl while we're waiting." He flipped half-heartedly through the mail on his desk, opened some, dropped the rest into a drawer, and then turned the leaf of his desk calendar. He peered at the cryptic scribblings on it. "What do you know," he said. "This is the day Conway's lawyer gets back from Mexico. Call him, eh, Dubinsky, and tell him we'll be over this morning. Don't give him a choice. I have something to pick up first. I'll meet you downstairs."

Dubinsky fell into stride beside Sanders along Dundas Street. The weather, which had spoiled Easter with wind and cold, was tormenting office workers by being warm and sunny now that the long weekend was over. "I couldn't get him," he said finally, as they headed the few blocks over to the hospital. "He's not getting back to the office until tomorrow, she says. And she hasn't the slightest idea where he is." Dubinsky grunted in disgust. "Which she seems to think is pretty funny. If I was that guy I'd get another secretary."

Sanders noted the empty chair outside room 526 and scowled. He flung open the door, half expecting to find Amanda's mangled corpse inside. But she was sitting tranquilly up in bed, watching a game show, with a young police constable in the chair beside her. "Working hard?" said Sanders, and jerked his head in the direction of the door. The young man fled. Sanders pulled a brown paper bag out of his pocket and dumped it on Amanda's bed. She picked it up doubtfully and glanced inside, then pulled out three large Swiss chocolate bars — a hazelnut, a nougat, and a praline. "I hope you like those kinds," he said. "I'm sorry about the food."

"Mmmm," she said. "I love them. But you really didn't have to. Did you come all the way over here just to bring me chocolate? I'd feel awful if you did." She was trying to open each one as she talked and to sample all three flavours, not an easy task for one hand.

"Well, no. I had other reasons." He forced his fatigue-numbed facial muscles into a smile. "We'd like you to try to remember everything you can about Jimmy." Amanda nodded. "First off, how often was he there?"

Her slightly freckled nose wrinkled in concentration as she considered the question. "I suppose once or twice a week, after school, usually. He'd just be sitting there in his car. We used to stand around on Leslie's front porch talking, sometimes for a long time, and he'd be there all the time."

"Can you remember when he first started showing up?"

"We first noticed him about five or six weeks ago, but he could have been around before that. You don't really pay any attention to cars just parked there, you know. In fact, we probably never would have noticed him except that one day Mrs. Conway walked by the car and he called out something to her. She stopped and looked at him for a second, and then went right on. That was when we decided that he was following her, and we started making up these crazy stories about who he was and what he was doing. As a joke, you know." She laughed. "Our best one was the oil sheik — he was a filthy rich oil sheik, dying of passion for her, and was waiting there to abduct her and carry her off to the Persian Gulf where she had to teach his other wives physics." By this time she was giggling wildly, and Sanders and Dubinsky were staring blankly at her. She took a deep breath. "That was because one day a police car came by while he was there, and he took off right away — so, obviously he had something to hide, you see."

Dubinsky looked up sharply from his notebook. "Looks like a drop, doesn't it?"

Sanders nodded. "More convincing than the thought that little Jimmy was dying of love for her." He shook his head. "Who's he connected with, Dubinsky? You know him from way back, don't you?"

He shook his head. "That's hard. He always seemed to be a loner. But he's been mixed up in a lot of mob-connected stuff."

"Then we'll have to work at it from the other end," said Sanders, turning abruptly back to the girl. "Who knew that you knew who was in the gray Honda?"

Amanda stopped to consider for a moment. "Well," she said, "Heather did. And she could have told her mother, I suppose." He glared at her. "And Leslie. She saw it too, lots of times, although she didn't walk by it, the way Heather and I did, so she couldn't see in and recognize the guy. But aside from them, we talked about it at lunch one day."

"When?"

She shook her head. "I'm not sure. One of the days after Conway was killed. I suppose Monday or Tuesday. It wasn't right after, I know that. Probably Monday or Tuesday."

"Who was there?"

"That's harder. Leslie must have been there ——"

"Leslie who, Miss Griffiths?"

"Sorry. Leslie Smith. And Jennifer — she always eats lunch with us. Jennifer Delisle. And I think Sarah Wilcox was there, too." She shook her head again. "Jessica Martin might have been in the room, too. She usually eats lunch with us."

"Do you know if any of those girls told anyone else?"

Amanda tried to shrug her shoulder and failed. "Probably. I never asked them not to tell anyone. But you'd have to talk to them."

Sanders snapped his notebook shut and stood up.

"Thanks. Would you like that miserable specimen out there to come in and keep you company?" She nodded. "Okay. I'll send him in. Don't feed him all your chocolate."

It only took them four minutes to travel between the lively Amanda and the surgical waiting room. McInnes was sitting there patiently, among the anxious parents and spouses, flipping through a magazine. "Any word?" asked Sanders.

"No, sir, not yet," he said, getting to his feet. "I brought a tape recorder — they said we could try it in the recovery room, in case she comes to." There seemed no response to this, and a gloomy silence fell over the room again.

It was at least twenty minutes before they were beckoned to the door by a tired and irritable-looking man. "Sorry," he said. "We did what we could, but there never was much of a chance, you know. It was a miracle she hung on as long as she did."

"You mean she's dead?" said Dubinsky, startled.

"That's right," replied the surgeon. "And I trust you'll find who did it to her before I have to treat any more like this." His voice was cold and angry.

Thirty minutes later four very apprehensive girls were ushered into a small seminar room at Kingsmede Hall. They relaxed visibly at the sight of a pair of plainclothes policemen. A group summons out of class like this usually got you Miss Johnson and a whole lot of trouble; this looked like twenty minutes' relief from sweating through some dreary novel. They giggled themselves into four chairs and prepared to waste time. All four reluctantly denied knowing anything useful, however. Jessica Martin had to deny knowledge of any Honda or anyone in it. She had been sick last week and couldn't possibly have been at lunch that day.

"I remember that conversation, though," interposed Leslie. "We were trying to figure out if the guy was her husband or her boyfriend — only seriously, this time. But I don't think I ever told anyone about it. Honest." She looked at him with innocent brown eyes. He sighed and wished he were better at distinguishing truth from falsehood in adolescent females.

"Wasn't it Amanda who said that a friend of her aunt knew someone in the police who said that the murder was done by the rapist?" asked Jennifer. "So the man in the gray Honda wasn't important and it didn't matter who he was. I told my dad, but he didn't believe me."

"What didn't he believe? That Amanda's aunt ——"

Jennifer broke out in fits of giggles. "No," she said, gasping for breath. "That Amanda had seen someone outside the house — Conway's house." She giggled again. "He said that girls our age have very fertile imaginations and we probably couldn't tell the difference between a gray Honda and a beige Pinto."

"I told my dad, and he thought it was clever of Amanda to notice something like that," said Sarah, blushing furiously. "But I never told anyone else. I mean, except my mom and little brother, too."

Sanders looked intently at the four faces in front of him. "Thank you," he said morosely, "you've been a big help," and watched them swarm from the room.

"So," said Sanders, "there we have it. Not one of them, if you can believe them, told anyone except members of their own families. I wish I knew if they were telling the truth, or if they think they'll get into trouble by saying they told other friends. They all sounded as if they were lying through their teeth. If I got a performance like that out of a suspect, I'd be on the phone to the Crown, working up charges."

"I think," said Dubinsky, "that they giggle and blush even when they're telling the truth."

"They also do it when they're lying," growled Sanders. "But let's assume we heard the truth. Then we'd better find out something about their parents, wouldn't you say?" He strode off in search of the principal.

Roz was standing in the hall watching uniformed bodies hurtle by her on their way to class. Sanders raced to grab her before she disappeared again. "Do you have information on those girls' parents? Like what they do and where they work? We're trying to establish a link between Amanda and the men who attacked her." Roz looked at him doubtfully for a moment, and walked back into Annabel's office.

"Pull the admission files for those four girls, please, and bring them into the seminar room. Thanks." She turned to him. "I hope that's what you need," she said, then she smiled dismissively and left.

In a matter of minutes, Annabel dropped four file folders on the table in front of them. "That's confidential information, you know," she said tartly. "Ordinarily we don't let anyone look at it. If there's anything you don't understand, ask me." With a mildly poisonous look, she swept out.

"Okay," muttered Sanders. "Eliminate the Martin girl, since she wasn't at school — although I suppose we should check that." He placed her folder to one side. "Right. Smith. Mr. Geoffrey Smith." He scribbled down both addresses, home and business. "He's an architect; they live on MacNiece Street, a few houses away from the victim's apartment building." He picked up the next folder. "Delisle. Dr. Martin Delisle. A plastic surgeon. I wonder if he makes millions doing face lifts." He continued scribbling. "And last, Wilcox. Mr. Paul Wilcox. Well, look at that — Wilcox the MPP. They have everything at this place, don't they?" He looked up. "Which one of these guys had any connection with Jimmy, do you suppose?"

Dubinsky shrugged. "Could have been any of them. I'd put my money on the politician, though. A man with Jimmy's connections could be very useful to someone like that.''

"How about the architect? I'd be willing to bet Jimmy's network extends to construction and building contracts, wouldn't you?'' He piled all the files neatly once again. "Or, of course, it could have been any one of them telling somebody else, or it could have been someone connected with one of the other girls who passed it on after she heard it through the grapevine." He yawned again. "Let's go back to Mrs. Conway's old friends and try out the trafficking scenario. I like it — it seems to fit some of them very nicely.''

It was one o'clock in the afternoon when he stumbled out of his sweat-soaked bed and into the bathroom. The face that peered back at him from the mirror belonged to someone else. It was flabby and covered with stubble; the right cheek was hideously disfigured with claw marks. He shuddered in disgust. He had fallen alseep in his underwear; now he reached over and pulled on a pair of wrinkled cords and a sweatshirt, picked up his dirty socks and dragged them on. He grabbed a pile of quarters from the change on the dresser and stumbled down the winding stairs, yanking on boots as he passed the door. His destination was the row of newspaper boxes at the corner. He blinked as his eyes hit daylight. For four days now he had been sitting inside the house with curtains drawn, sleeping erratically and infrequently, sending out for pizza on the few occasions that he noticed hunger. He was living besieged, surrounded by enemies, enemies so powerful and clever that they could manipulate the news. They were lulling him into a false sense of security in order to set traps for him.

He had already fed the first coin in the slot before he noticed the front page of the afternoon paper. His gut twisted in a spasm of pain. He took a deep breath, carefully opened the box, and took out a paper, then fed more coins into the morning paper boxes and took out one of each. He couldn't read it out here on the street. People would look at him from every window in the development, wonder why he was buying all these papers, wonder what he was doing, wonder where he went in his lovely van. He walked sedately back into his house, wanting to run, not daring to. In the living room, he unfolded the paper, turned on the lamp beside the couch, and forced himself to look at the front page again.

"Have You Seen This Man?" the banner screamed in red above a sketch of someone intended to be him.

> Police sources revealed today that they are seeking a man in his twenties, about six feet tall, with light brown curly hair, for questioning in relation to a series of vicious attacks on women in the Metro area in recent months. The sketch shown was supplied by police artist John MacVey, working from descriptions given by an unidentified young woman who was attacked on Friday. Thanks to the rapid intervention of three bystanders, she was unharmed. It is possible that he has scratch marks on his face. The fourth victim in this series of brutal murders died this morning (see story, p. 5).

He got up and trudged up the stairs to the bathroom and stared once again into the mirror. Then at the sketch. Then at the mirror. They had made his face too long and too thin, he thought, and his eyes too small and narrow. He splashed water in his burning eyes, then turned and walked back down to the living room.

Two miles away Ginny stood perplexed in her mother's living room. After a minute or two, she walked over to the front hall and called upstairs. "Rob! Come down here a minute, will you?" A large, amiable-looking young man lounged down the steps, two at a time, and sat down at the bottom.

"What can I do for you, eh, lady?" he said, yawning.

"Are you busy right now?" Worried lines creased her face.

"Just studying. But it'll keep. What's the matter?"

Her eyes swam with tears. She always seemed to be on the verge of tears these days. "It's Glenn," she said. "Come up to my room. I don't want Mom to hear." He nodded and followed her up. He had long since ceased to expect his big sister to make sense. He sprawled on her bed and looked lazily at her perched on a hard-backed chair. "I'm not going back there," she said, grimly, as if he had just told her that she must, on pain of death. "I don't care what anybody says."

"I don't blame you," said her brother. "He's a jerk. And I don't think you have to worry about Mom, either. She never liked him. But what can I do for you right now?"

"All my clothes and stuff are there, and I should tell him that I'm not coming back, but I can't get through to him. I've phoned every time of day; I've let the phone ring twenty times. I just called Donna next door, and she said that he's home. She's seen him go out to get the papers and take the van out. But I don't want to go over there and see him." She shivered.

"Do you want me to go?" asked Rob. "I'm not scared of the son of a bitch. Just tell me what you want, and I'll go over right now. I need some exercise. I can take Kevin with me and we'll beat the shit out of him." He yawned again as he sat upright.

Ginny laughed. "No, that's okay. Just get my clothes — and my shoes, so I can go back to work. Here, I'll make a list for you. You can stuff it all in my old duffle bag." She pulled out a piece of paper from her little desk, and started making a list, looking animated and full of purpose for the first time in weeks. At that moment, the afternoon paper came flying across their front lawn, skidded over the porch, and landed, for the third time that month, in a wet and soggy corner of the front garden.

Rob had reflected briefly on his brother-in-law's uncertain temper, and therefore when he pulled up in front of the townhouse his formidable friend Kevin was with him. "Just in case the guy pulls a knife or something," he had said.

"Sure," said Kevin. They played on the same hockey team, worked out in the same gym, and he was just as happy to be mixing it up here as on the ice, as far as that went. Anything to help out a buddy and a teammate. As they were getting out of their car, however, reinforcements in the shape of a police car pulled up behind them. A uniformed constable climbed out and walked over to them.

"You Mr. Glenn Morrison?" he asked, reading from a list in his hand.

"Nope," said Rob. "He lives in there, and we're just going to pay him a little visit." The constable followed the two up to the minute front porch.

Rob leaned on the doorbell for about thirty seconds. No response. He looked at the police officer and shrugged. "Did you want to see him about something important?"

"Are you a friend?"

Rob shook his head. "Just a brother-in-law. What's going on?"

The constable raised his large fist and pounded on the door. All three of them listened for answering footsteps. "Does he own a light brown van?" was the response.

"Yeah," said Rob, "does he ever! It's like his baby. Did he have an accident?" he asked curiously.

"Is there a back door?" asked the constable.

"I have something better than that," said Rob. "I have the front-door key." He pulled it out of his pocket. "My sister asked me to go in and get some clothes for her. You want to look around, be my guest." He turned the key and threw open the door with a flourish.

The three men stopped dead at the front hall, assailed by the unmistakable stench of decay. "Jeez," said Kevin. "What died in here? It stinks."

"You better let me go first," said the constable, looking distinctly unhappy. "Just in case."

Rob walked up the steps into the kitchen and looked in. The afternoon sun played over the piles of filthy dishes and food that oozed with slime. He gagged at the smell, went purposefully up the steps into the living room, threw open the drapes and pushed the French windows open. There was a merciful blast of cool clean air. They glanced quickly at the chaos of the living room and solemnly followed the constable up the winding stairs to the bedrooms and bathroom. No rotting corpses, no surprises. Just filth and unmade beds. "Well," said Rob, "since we're up here, I think I'll throw my sister's stuff into a bag." He pulled out the list, looked at it carefully, and then started with the top dresser drawer.

"Where would Mr. Morrison keep the van?" asked the constable.

"It's probably in the garage, unless he has taken it out. Ginny's car sat out all winter in the snow so the damned van could stay safe in the garage — and she was the one who had to take her car to work all the time." He turned and started to stuff shoes into a big duffle bag he had taken from the closet. "Just let me finish this and I'll show you where it is. Kevin, grab those things off the hangers and let's get going. This place gives me the creeps."

The three men wound their way down the ever-turning stairway as far as it went. Rob opened the door at the very bottom and felt around for a light switch. "There it is," he said, as the lights clicked on. "I guess he didn't take it with him when he went out." The constable looked carefully all around the van. He peered in the side windows, rattled all the door handles, gave it one last look and walked out.

"Is that what you were looking for?" asked Rob.

"I couldn't say, sir," said the constable. "I suppose it could be. Anyway, thanks for your assistance."

"Think nothing of it," said Rob, cheerfully. "Anything to get that bastard in trouble, I always say. I hope he loses his bloody license. Here, Kevin," he said, throwing him the duffle bag. "I'd better shut that door up there." And the three of them closed up the house again.

Down in the garage, a trembling bundle of terrified humanity crawled out from underneath the shiny new van and listened for the cars to drive away.

The bar in the Manufacturer's Life building was almost deserted. Tuesday's sparse after-work crowd had given up and gone home. Paul Wilcox stood at the door looking about, until a subdued wave from across the room brought him over.

"Hello, Grant. How are things?"

"Hi, Paul. Thanks for coming." He ordered two scotches from the lazy-looking waitress who padded over. "Things don't look very good right now."

"Really," said Wilcox. "What do you mean?"

"Those goddamn cops were back at my door this afternoon, asking me the same stuff about Jane. Wanting to know exactly where I've been. Telling me everyone knows I had a fight with her the night before she was killed. Asking me about some guy I never even heard of — some cop. And asking me about some guys I'd just as soon not talk about when there are cops around."

"Who's that?"

"Never mind. Just some guys, okay?" He smiled automatically at the waitress and swallowed half his drink in one gulp. "Anyway, I can't afford this, you know. I have possibilities of big contracts turning up in the U.S. I don't like these guys breathing down my neck. They could screw me up."

"Look, Keswick, I don't know what you're mixed up in ——"

"The fuck you don't. You were at enough of those parties. Stop trying to look so goddamn pure. Just because you've decided to have a shot at the Cabinet, and maybe the leadership — I have friends, I hear things, let me tell you — doesn't mean that you weren't there along with the rest of us, your tongue hanging out over all the broads, and trying every kind of shit that was going. You forget that? Because if you do, I'm here to remind you of it." Grant's anger was palpable. Wilcox pushed his chair back a bit.

"Okay. Don't get so sore. Look, as far as I know, poor Jane was killed by that rapist — though, if they're asking you questions, I suppose they're not taking it for granted. But I can't horn in on a murder investigation. Now, come on. That's asking a bit much." He laughed uneasily, ready to duck if Keswick exploded. He had been known to do that often enough. "But they're not looking for drugs, you know — just trying to find out who killed her. So if you didn't kill her, you haven't got anything to worry about, do you? They don't have time to mess around with small stuff like that."

"What in hell do you mean by that? 'If I didn't kill her.' Of course I didn't kill her. Christ! It was probably that animal from Cobourg. The one who followed her around all the time. I don't know why they don't persecute him, instead of me. Or her husband. Being married to that slut would make anyone want to kill her. But I couldn't have cared less if she lived or died."

"The one from Cobourg's dead. Didn't you hear? So they can't persecute him. He blew his brains out. Anyway, you don't have to tell me. It doesn't matter whether I think you did it or not."

Keswick stood up, knocking the heavy chair over. "Christ almighty, I've had enough of you. And your fucking insinuations. I should paste you across the table, but I'd hate to damage the furniture. Good-bye."

Wilcox watched him thoughtfully for a moment as he stormed out of the bar, then dropped some bills down on the table and strolled out after him.

Chapter Fourteen

The offices of Van Loon and McHenry were in a pretty red-brick building with a tree and an attempt at a lawn on the tiny patch of dirt between building and sidewalk. A brass plate on the door proclaimed that a film company also did business there, and a dentist. A sign directed them up the stairs to the second floor. A young, vapid and gum-chewing blonde was typing rather inexpertly as they walked in the door. She abandoned her work in relief at the sight of them, and tried on a smile. "Yes?" she squeaked. "Did you have an appointment?"

Sanders nodded briskly. "Yes, we did." The news seemed to strike her as singularly amusing. She tittered in response. "With Mr. McHenry, I believe." That convulsed her in another burst of giggles.

The inner door opened, and a head stuck out. "Are these the gentlemen from the police, Stacey? Or have you bothered to ask?" She sobered up and cast him a reproachful glance. "Come in please. I'm Mark McHenry.

Sorry about that girl," he said, closing the office door. "She's new, and not long for this firm, I'm afraid. What can I do for you?"

"You might be able to give us some information on one of your clients — a Mrs. Jane Conway. We're investigating her case, and in the course of looking through her apartment, found some file folders marked with your firm's name. We were hoping that you could shed some light on the background to the correspondence. Or on anything that might help us."

He gave them the longish look of a man who is balancing conflicting ethical considerations. "I gather she was murdered," he said finally.

"That's right," said Sanders. "There's no question about that."

"But wasn't she killed by the same man who killed those other women? My impression was that she had been."

Sanders shook his head. "Probably not. Although someone has gone to a certain amount of trouble to try to convince us of that."

"Well, in that case, I suppose it's more clearly my duty to seek redress for the crime, in a sense, than to preserve confidentiality." He smiled and pushed a buzzer on the phone, then picked it up. "Stacey, bring me the Conway file. Jane Conway. Right now, please." He looked up. "If I don't say that, she'll wait until after lunch," he said sourly. The door flung open and Stacey dropped a file on the desk.

"All right?" she asked sullenly.

"Thank you, Stacey. You may go now." Conversation ceased as they watched her parade out. "Here it is. She wanted, in the first instance, to know how she could block divorce action on her husband's part in spite of the fact that she had left him." He grinned. "I told her it would be difficult, but she was very determined. Then she made a will, leaving everything to her Uncle Matt Jameson in

Cobourg; then she came in to find out how quickly she could get a divorce and to ask me how she could invest around twenty thousand dollars without getting it too tied up in red tape. By that I got the impression she meant without having the tax people find out about it, so I steered clear of that one. And that was where we were as of March 27th. Oh, except that she called to ask about an action for unlawful dismissal, but since her position was only temporary, I told her she didn't have a hope. She was, I would say, a very litigious lady." He produced that little gem with a satisfied smirk. "Oh, and she left something to be kept for her in the safe. Said that she needed it later in the summer. There's a note here about it. Do you want to look at it?" They both nodded. Sanders' eyes brightened slightly. McHenry moved over to an old-fashioned safe in the corner and pulled it open. "It's not all that secure," he said. "But it makes a handy place to store things. I inherited the office and all its appurtenances — except for Stacey — from my father and his partner, old Van Loon." As he spoke, he sorted quickly through the contents of one of the shelves. "Here it is. I'm afraid I'll have to have a receipt for it if you want to take it away."

It was a small white envelope with "Mrs. Jane Conway, February 24, 1984" written on the outside. It contained something small but bulky. Sanders accepted a proffered paper knife and carefully ripped it open. Inside was a black container, cylindrical in shape, with a gray top. Inside the container was a roll of film. Sanders dumped it out on his palm and looked at it.

"I'd be careful with that," said McHenry. "It isn't developed."

Sanders quickly returned it to its container, and then to its envelope, wrote out a receipt and handed it to the lawyer. "Thank you very much. This looks interesting. You wouldn't have any idea where the twenty thousand came from, would you? That's even more interesting." McHenry shook his head rather sadly.

"Ah well. Back to headquarters, Dubinsky, and get the lab on to this."

Not far from the legal office of Van Loon and McHenry, Eleanor was back at her desk at Webb and MacLeod, staring glassily at a pile of papers. Real estate seemed to be suffering from a mid-week slump, and she was having difficulty staying awake. It was warm and sunny out her window, and just as she was sleepily deciding to abandon all efforts at earning a living in favor of a walk, the harsh buzz of her phone sent her crashing back into the real world. It was a business call. A Mr. Jones, who had heard about her, and what a wonderful agent she was, from a friend of his, wanted to look at a house for sale in his neighborhood.

"Certainly," said Eleanor. Then, curious, "Who recommended me to you?"

"Al," said the voice of Mr. Jones laconically.

"Oh," said Eleanor, trying to remember an Al among her recent clients. Not that it mattered. "When would you like to look at this house? I could probably arrange something quite soon, if you wish." Strike while the iron is hot, she thought. "And which of our houses is it?"

He gave her an address on the Kingsway, far in the west end of the city. Good fellowship and ethics struggled for a brief moment in her breast against the thought of commissions — prices were generally very high on the Kingsway — and she muttered weakly, "Our west-end office usually handles houses on that side of the Humber. They know the area better. But if you wish to deal with me, I'd be glad to show it to you." That dealt with her conscience.

"Good," said Mr. Jones. "Maybe I'll look at houses downtown later. So you meet us there in an hour, me and my wife, right?"

"I could pick you up if you like. Then you and your wife wouldn't have to worry about driving there." Eleanor preferred to keep her clients under her nose between houses.

"No. It's better if we meet there. In an hour. Okay?"

Well, well, thought Eleanor. You never know when business is just going to fall into your lap, like manna from heaven. She put down the receiver and went for her book to look up the house she was supposed to be showing.

The west-end office had been a trifle sulky about the property. She had apologized for poaching; her client had seen the house and insisted on her showing it to him. "You know how they are," she'd said guiltily.

"Yeah," said the girl on the desk. "I know. Anyway, the house is empty now. They moved out last weekend, and it doesn't show very well now. But they might be a bit soft on the price." Eleanor's heart sank. That meant everywhere there had been furniture, there would be great stains or dirt marks. It might even be one of those houses where the paint job didn't extend to behind the big pieces, and a green room would have big pink patches where there had been chests and sideboards. She hoped they weren't a fussy couple, after she had driven out all this way to show them the damn place. She was beginning to wish she had insisted that they deal with the west-end office. O greed.

The house was very large and rambling, with half-timbers, diamond-paned-windows — the Tudor look. The grounds, she noted happily, seemed to be in good shape — neat grass, nice shrubs, a pretty tree. Good. A large tan Lincoln was parked out in front, and so she pulled into the empty driveway. Mr. Jones' voice might be a bit rough, but his credit was apparently sound. Two men, expensively dressed in dark suits, got out of the car and walked over to her. "Mr. Jones?" she asked, holding out her hand. One of them responded with his. "Mrs. Jones didn't come with you after all?" Damn. That meant they had changed their mind.

"She don't really like looking at a lot of houses," he said. "So her brother came instead. He knows what she likes."

"Fine," she said. Clients came in all shades of peculiarity. And even the strangest often bought houses. She pulled out the key with its big red tag on it — with the white slash across it to show that it came from the west end — and opened the door. Her heart sank even further. Huge curls of dust mingled with indescribable winter grime in the foyer and front hall.

"Nice house," grunted Mr. Jones. "Nice and roomy." Eleanor wondered if he had trouble with his eyes. If so, he might like this place. She conjured up the floor plan in her mind and headed confidently for the living room, trying to ignore the newspapers, torn and dirty, scattered on the floor, as she pointed out the working fireplace and the charming bay windows. Mr. Jones didn't seem to be paying much attention to her. He opened a door at the back of the living room and said, "What's this here?"

"That's a study, Mr. Jones, although it could be used as a breakfast room or even a spare bedroom, since it's close to the ground-floor washroom." Eleanor had done her homework in that hour. She walked in past the two men toward the rear windows. "And you can see from here what a nice garden there is. Isn't it a lovely ——" Her sentence was cut off abruptly as Mr. Jones' brother-in-law flipped her arm tightly up behind her back and clapped his other hand over her mouth.

Mr. Jones walked around in front of her and smiled. "Don't worry, Miss Scott. Nobody's gonna hurt you. Not now, anyways." He looked at her appraisingly. "Nice hair." She glared back. "I bet your boyfriend likes your hair, don't he? No, don't answer, I can tell he does." He slowly pulled a smallish knife out of his pocket, held up a huge chunk of hair from the side of Eleanor's head, and then, in one smooth gesture, hacked it off. Tears of pain started up in her eyes. "And because we're nice guys, we're gonna send your boyfriend some hair — like a memento, you know." He smiled and shoved his face close to hers. "I got a piece of advice for you. You shouldn't ought to go out with cops. Not with cops that tread on people's toes.

You tell your boyfriend. 'Bye now. Vito here will make you nice and comfortable for the time being.'' He started to walk out of the room. "Stick her in the corner over there, Vito.''

Sanders looked up as Dubinsky came in from lunch. In front of him was a file folder stuffed with sheets of paper. "This just came up,'' he said. "It's the first crop of sightings from the sketch. It would have helped if bloody MacVey hadn't been off for the weekend, though. By now this guy and his van are probably in Vancouver.'' He picked up half the pile and dropped it on Dubinsky's desk. "Might as well go through them and see if there's anything worthwhile. Then grab Collins and get him to start sifting.''

"Anything come in this morning on the license number?''

"Are you kidding? There are hundreds of light brown vans out there, most of them have a number in them that looks like a nine, and none of them so far is owned by someone who says he likes to go out to attack women in one.'' He picked up another set of reports. "When you finish those, you can look at these. Every van not more than five years old owned by a male, or a family in which there is a male between the ages of sixteen and forty-five. Have fun.'' He yawned. "Did you drop the film off at the lab?''

"Yeah,'' said Dubinsky. "They said it was exposed all right, and they'd develop it and get some prints over in an hour or two if it was that urgent.''

"I didn't need them to tell me it was exposed. She'd hardly be keeping extra rolls of film in her lawyer's safe, would she? But why didn't she take it off and get it developed like anyone else?'' He looked up again. "Yeah. They might have been that kind of picture. Funny thing for a girl to have around.''

"Depends on who's in the picture,'' said Dubinsky.

"Mm," muttered Sanders. "Before you get started on that, I want to see if we can make any sense of this stuff." He picked up a small slip of paper. " 'M. — 3 — Tues.' and 'G. — 5 — Tu.' We found that on Friday; it was sitting by her phone and she was a very neat person, wouldn't you say?" Dubinsky nodded. She was even neater than Sally. "So that must have been the Tuesday of the party at Marny's or she would have thrown that out. If these numbers aren't times, then what are they? What do you write down when you're on the phone to someone?"

"Amounts," said Dubinsky. "So you won't forget them."

"Three what? Five what?"

"Kilos?"

"That's a hell of a lot, if we're talking about coke. How about three grams? That's hardly enough to worry about. Three hundred bucks worth?"

"In that case, the three could just as well stand for thirty or three hundred grams. Who's M.? Mike?"

"Marny Huber, obviously. And G., of course, is Grant Keswick. It makes sense. Why else would Jimmy Fielding be hanging around? So that would have made her a distributor. Which explains the large amounts of cash in her bank account and the extra twenty thousand she wanted to squirrel away somewhere." He sighed. "Seems funny that she would be so upset at losing her job."

"I don't know about that. It was a good cover. Maybe she figured she'd just stay in the business until she made her pile, and wanted to have something respectable to fall back on. She should have stayed away from places like the After Hours, in that case."

"I wonder where Mike fitted in with all this," said Sanders, picking up the sad little note sent down by the Cobourg police. Dubinsky's reply was interrupted by someone sticking his head in the door and throwing a letter on Sanders' desk. It clunked as it landed.

"Mail for you," he said. "Just arrived by special

messenger. Since it was marked 'urgent' I thought I'd be a sweet guy and bring it up here." He waved and disappeared.

Sanders picked it up. His name was neatly typed on the envelope along with the word "urgent", underlined in red. It was very thickly stuffed with something that felt like cloth. Inside it was something hard and lumpy as well. "Jesus," said Dubinsky, "it's probably a bomb."

"Don't be stupid," said Sanders. "It's too small an envelope." He turned it over. "But I'm going to be goddamn mad if it blows up in my face." He slowly eased up the flap and peered gingerly inside. His face suddenly went gray. "God almighty," he breathed, and pulled out a long thick bundle of curly red hair and dropped it on his desk. Dubinsky leaned over to look at the envelope. Next he pulled out a door key, with a red Webb and MacLeod label on it, and an address on the label. Then he unfolded a piece of paper. His hands were trembling as he smoothed it down on his desk to look at it.

"Sanders," it said briefly, "You can rescue the lady at the address on the label. And if you don't want her to lose more than her hair, I suggest you stop meddling with Jimmy and his friends. You might hurry out there. She's anxious to see you." The message was typed and unsigned.

"Dubinsky," he whispered, his voice shaking, "get the dispatcher. Send out an emergency unit to that address." He pointed at the key. "Get someone working on where this came from. And get the car. We're going out there now." He took a deep breath, and then held up the key tag so Dubinsky could read the address. He dropped it in his pocket, looked back and picked up the hair, put it carefully into a clean envelope in his desk drawer, then headed for the door.

Eleanor felt as if she had been lying on the cold, dirty wood floor for at least a day. Her arms ached from being tied behind her back in an abnormal position. Her ankles were tied tightly together and then lashed to her wrists, preventing her from straightening out her legs and from attracting attention by kicking a wall. Her mouth was taped shut. The neighborhood seemed to be absolutely deserted. Surely someone must think it odd that her car had been sitting in the driveway all this time? But then, she thought, why should they? Strangers had probably been going in and out of here for days, doing all sorts of things. In the distance she heard the rising and falling hoot of a passing ambulance. Much good that does me, she thought. It was joined, however, by the shrill scream of a police siren, which suddenly got so loud it sounded like two police sirens inside the house. The ambulance stopped hooting. The police sirens stopped screaming. She heard the pounding of fists on the door, then more pounding closer to her. There was a confused babbling of voices, then a crash of broken glass. "We're in," called a voice loudly, then footsteps began to move very slowly and faintly in a room behind her. She tried to make a noise, but Vito had done his job very well.

"There she is." Above her loomed a uniformed figure, then two. "Miss Scott?" Hands quickly yanked off the tape before she could think about what they were doing, then untied the ropes on her hands and feet.

"Yes," she said. "That's me." Running footsteps rang through the empty house. Sanders, following the sound of voices, came into the study and was instantly on his knees beside her.

"Are you all right?" he asked, rubbing her wrists, scarlet with rope burns, then pulling her up to her feet.

"Ouch," she said. "Yes, I'm fine."

Sanders drove back in grim silence with Eleanor beside him. Dubinsky was driving her car. Still thinking of bombs, Sanders had inspected the Rabbit carefully for signs of tampering. The lady next door, however, assured him the two gentlemen in the Lincoln had left the house at a brisk pace and had promptly driven away in their lovely car. "How in hell did you get yourself in that situation," he said finally. "You went out all alone to meet someone you'd never even heard of to look at a house that isn't even in your district. Christ! You're lucky that's all that happened to you."

"I'm a real estate agent," she snapped back. "If I only showed houses to people I knew, I'd starve. That's the way we operate. On faith. I must say, you're not very sympathetic." Tears filled her eyes. "I didn't have a very pleasant time in there."

"I was too sick with worry to be sympathetic. I didn't know what they had chopped off besides your hair."

"Is that why all those cars and ambulances came? There seemed to be an awful lot of them."

"Well — they sent out the works."

"Where are you taking me, by the way?" she asked in a small voice as he turned off University Avenue onto Dundas.

"Where I can keep an eye on you, that's where."

"And my car?"

"That's going where no one is likely to tamper with it for the time being. I don't want to have to worry about you all the time." He turned and glared at her for a second, then pulled the car into the garage.

Eleanor sat in his office, moving slowly from fury to starvation. "Is it too much to ask for something to eat?" she said finally. "I haven't had any lunch, and it's past two."

Sanders looked up, then smiled. "Sure. I'll send out for sandwiches."

"Oh gee, thanks," she replied, with heavy sarcasm. "And I have a friendly message for you from Mr. Jones and Vito."

"Oh," he said warily. "What's that?"

"He told me to tell you that I shouldn't go out with peo-ple who tread on other people's toes. Who were those guys, anyway?"

"The whole thing had the nice clean touch of the profes-sional. Somewhere we're getting very close to the mob, and they're reacting predictably." He ruffled her hair. "But I'd rather they hadn't got on to you."

"Oh well," said Eleanor. "I always wanted to know what I looked like with really short hair."

Chapter Fifteen

As Eleanor bit voraciously into the second half of her pastrami on rye, wondering if it was really going to tide her over until John agreed to release her and she could get a proper meal, a tech wafted in from the lab. "I hope you realize what service this is," she said. "That 'urgent' had better be legit. They don't look very urgent to me."

"Was there anything on the film?" asked Sanders impatiently.

"Oh sure. Lots. Three shots out of a possible thirty-six were exposed, and you can almost see people in a couple of them. We did what we could. It's Tri-X — we pushed it a little and it's a bit grainy. You can't get what isn't there, you know. Whoever took them didn't know much about light levels, I guess. So long." She dropped the large manila envelope on the desk with a wink at Eleanor and left.

Sanders opened the envelope with great care and pulled three eight-by-ten glossy black and white prints out of it. Eleanor wiped the mustard off her fingers and pulled her chair over to get a look. The film had obviously been greatly underexposed, but it was possible to make out the faces of several people on each print. At first glance there was no apparent reason for the film to have been hidden away so carefully, but as Sanders pulled his desk light closer to look at the first enlargement, he whistled in triumph. In it they could see the smiling face of Jane Conway, dressed in something dark and hard to distinguish; leaning over her in a relaxed and affectionate way, was a tall man who looked vaguely familiar. Eleanor pointed at his face in astonishment. "It's that politician. The one who was talking to Grant at the party. Well, well. He seems to be a good friend, doesn't he?"

"Are you sure?" said Sanders. "Really sure?"

"Positive. Is he in the other picture?" Sanders picked up the next print and held it up to the light. "There they are again. See? She's half turned, but you can tell from the dress and hair, sort of, that it's her, and it's an even better picture of — what was his name?"

"Wilcox. Paul Wilcox."

"That's right. But I don't recognize the guy he's talking to — the little guy beside him." She pointed to someone who was apparently in earnest conversation with Mr. Wilcox.

"Ah," said Sanders. "He's a very interesting man to find in that group. The famous Jimmy Fielding. You know — the gray Honda."

"No wonder she hung onto these pictures," said Eleanor. "They're very suggestive, aren't they? Who's in the third one?" Sanders picked up a dark, badly focused shot in which it was just possible to make out the figures and faces of Conway and Wilcox, talking to a third man. Eleanor took the print and peered closely at it. "That's Grant," she said flatly. "I'm sure it is. Although you'd have a hard time proving it from this."

"So it is," murmured Sanders. "Isn't that interesting. Conway, Wilcox, Fielding, and Keswick, all in cosy conversation. The Government, the Mob, and the Arts, all together with one girl. I'm glad the head of the police commission isn't in one of those pictures. That's all we need."

"What do you suppose they were all mixed up in?"

"Who knows? Contracts, government jobs, drugs — Fielding's in drugs, but that's not all he's in. Maybe even murder. We'll find out soon enough." He paused for a second, and then, dismayed, looked at Eleanor. "My God, we have to do something about you. When does that child of yours get out of school?"

Her somach contracted ominously. "Three-thirty. Why?"

"You are to call the school. Get someone you know — Roz Johnson — on the line. Tell her that you, and you alone, will pick up Heather, and you will be arriving soon in a patrol car. On no account are they to release her to anyone — whatever the reason — but you. Even if you call and ask them to change the arrangements. Have you got that?"

Eleanor shuddered. "Yes. Do you really think they'd ——"

"They got you, didn't they? And they're going to get even unhappier once they figure out I'm not sitting on my ass doing nothing. Telephone."

Sanders saw Eleanor off to pick up Heather in a patrol car, with instructions to go straight home and stay put until he called. The car and its occupants would stay with her. As soon as that was done, he turned his mind to more urgent problems. "Well," he said to Dubinsky, "who do we pick up first?"

"I dunno," said Dubinsky, looking blank. "I'm out of practice arresting MPPs. Why don't you go get him and I'll pick up Keswick. He's more my type."

"Coward," said Sanders. "Let's send Collins and Wilson out to get Keswick — he's easy. All he's likely to do is paste them, and they can handle that." He twirled his pen in his fingers for a moment, watching the effect with admiring eyes. "Jesus." He let the pen drop. "There's no way we can get Wilcox without clearing it upstairs, though. Here, give us that stuff — and send Collins and Wilson off while I'm gone." He picked up the file folder, slipped the prints into it, and headed off upstairs.

"So that's it," said Sanders to the smoothly elegant man on the other side of the desk. "I don't know whether one of them killed her, or why. As far as we can tell now her death may be completely unrelated, but these prints show a connection between Wilcox and Jane Conway, and between Wilcox and Jimmy Fielding. And Fielding certainly has links with organized crime. I don't know where Keswick comes into this, but he does come into it. Anyway, he's being picked up right now. He should be able to fill in a few gaps."

His interlocutor folded his fingers together and rested his chin lightly on them. He seemed to focus on the middle distance as he contemplated. He was paid to be smooth, and clever, and to juggle all the possible strands and interconnections and pitfalls of any action taken by government, the attorney general's office, or the police. "I had better talk to the A.G.," he said finally. "This is too hot for me to stick my neck out alone on."

Sanders nodded. "What I need is to get into his office in the Parliament Buildings. We've got to have evidence, and it might be there."

"That's tricky," he said in a distant voice. "You, of course, have no shadow of a right to do that. But then, he knows that as well, and is likely to have left anything of a — uh — sensitive nature there for just that reason. If we go through regulation channels, we are likely to lose the element of surprise, I imagine. It's complicated."

Sanders nodded again. "Maybe we should bring the Chief in on this in case questions are asked. He's going to be mad as hell when he finds out."

"Good God, no! The fewer people who know about

this, the better." He reached for his telephone and spent the next few minutes in muttered conversation. Finally he hung up and spoke to Sanders. "At six o'clock tonight," he said, looking somewhere past Sanders' left ear, "everyone in whom you are interested will be at a small reception. It will last at least until seven. This will get you past the small east door" — he handed Sanders a card marked "Press/Special Occasion" — "and the regular patrolling of the halls doesn't start until after the House rises. It is sitting right now, so there are lots of people around and a certain amount of confusion." He stood up. "You're on your own in this. Don't get caught. You'd find it unpleasant, and we'd find it counter-productive."

It was four o'clock by the time Sanders got back to the office. "We're on," he said. "How are you at B and E, Dubinsky?"

"How complicated?" Dubinsky leaned back and yawned. Dinner looked to be a long way off tonight.

"Not very — an office door, some desk drawers, a few filing cabinets, maybe a small safe. Probably wouldn't be a difficult one, you know. Just one of those home-security types."

"Not a chance," he said, shaking his head. "I'm okay on doors, not too happy about filing cabinets, but no safes. That's not my line." He looked pensive for a moment. "I know a couple of guys who could do a safe without too much trouble — but I never acquired the skill. And I don't want to."

"Who's that?"

"A pal of mine from the RCMP is pretty good with small safes."

"Would he do it?"

"Naw. It really wouldn't be worth his while. I mean, they'd crucify him if he got caught." He shook his head. "And it's not even his bust. Eddy might, though. Eddy owes me. He's pretty good — doors, safes, anything at all. We went to school together.''

"Do you think you could get hold of him — soon? Before six?''

"I could try. Might take a few minutes, though. He travels around a bit." Dubinsky reached for the phone, and began dialing a number culled from his elephantine memory. Sanders wandered tactfully out of earshot. After twenty minutes of telephone calls and earnest quiet conversations Dubinsky finally put his hand over the receiver, and said, "Eddy wants to know how he's supposed to get in there.'' Sanders picked up the press pass. On it was neatly written the date and the number two, circled in red. No matter how sleepy the guy on the door was, he'd be able to count to two. "I told him about the reception. He asked would it be okay if he comes as a waiter. Then he can blend in if all hell breaks loose.''

"Sure. Anything. He can come as a duck if he wants.''

At six o'clock Dubinsky, Sanders, and a small man in a dinner jacket pulled into the University of Toronto parking lot across the street from Queen's Park. By the time they were out of the car, Eddy had disappeared. "Jesus,'' said Sanders, impressed. "Where did he go?''

"Don't ask," said Dubinsky. "I never met a guy who could vanish the way he does.'' They walked boldly over to the east entrance with the arrogance of reporters with a perfect right to be there. As they were showing the bored Ontario Provincial Police constable their press pass, a small figure nipped by them, squeaking, "Extra catering staff. Which way?'' The constable pointed to the left, and Eddy disappeared again. Sanders shook his head in admiration.

They walked confidently through the high-ceilinged corridors to the area in which important members of the current government had their offices — they hoped. Those few people who passed by them paid no attention to them at all; they turned a corner, and there they were, in front of the office of Paul Wilcox, MPP. "How does he rate such a classy corridor?" whispered Dubinsky. "The rest of these guys all seem to be Cabinet ministers."

"Yeah. And potential Cabinet ministers. Our boy is — was — on his way up. Now where's Eddy?" And then they heard a soft shuffle of fast-moving feet, and Eddy appeared behind them, a tray under his arm.

"Camouflage," he said. "Is this the door?" Without waiting for a reply, he loosened his jacket and extracted from a series of pockets inside the front a couple of odd-looking tools. "Simple locks," he said, fiddled, held his breath, slipped the second tool between the door and the frame, and opened the door. "Get in and close it," he said, flipping on the light. "Before someone comes along. Jeez, you guys are slow." They were in a small, well-furnished reception room, with a desk, filing cabinets, and a couple of comfortable chairs, coffee table, and expensive magazines. There was another door behind the desk, also locked. Eddy approached it, looked, murmured "piece of cake", and slipped open the bolt in a few seconds. In this room, also small, but pleasant, were a window letting in soft evening light; a bare desk, dark, reddish, and opulent; a couch, chair, and a large plant; and, in the wood panel-ing of the wall, something that was unmistakably a safe of ancient vintage.

Eddy walked over to it, sized it up, and opened his jacket again. He selected a couple of instruments, laid them down on the floor, and then crouched in front of the safe. Meanwhile Dubinsky took a flat tool from his pocket and set to work on the desk drawer. It took him a while, and a few breathy curses, to get that lock snapped back and the first drawer opened. Sanders began to flip rapidly through its contents, while Dubinsky, working on top of him, scrambled through the second one. Finally Eddy spoke. "Do you think you guys could crash around the outer office for a while? I can't hear anything — I'll never get this bitch open with all that noise. Besides, you make me nervous.'' Abashed, they fled.

"Might as well try the filing cabinet,'' said Sanders. "Can you manage that lock?''

"Only if someone has a paper clip,'' said Dubinsky in scorn. "I hope they don't keep important stuff in here. Security is terrible.''

"I don't suppose they do,'' said Sanders. "Come on, let's go.''

The metallic screech of the top drawer of the filing cabinet opening covered the quiet click of a key in the door. Sanders was already flipping through the contents when his hand stopped at the sound of Wilcox's pleasantly cultured voice.

"Well, well, gentlemen, isn't this a surprise! From the press, I assume? I assure you that whatever you might find in there would be very dull from your point of view.'' He walked over to the secretary's desk. "But I don't think that the police will find someone breaking into my office boring. Not at all.''

Sanders straightened up and looked at Wilcox with casual amusement on his face. "Ah,'' he said, "but we are the police. And we don't mind being bored, not at all. We're used to it.''

"The police?'' Wilcox paused a moment. "Then no doubt you have a warrant of some sort. May I see it?'' He looked steadily at them. "Or are you on some sort of fishing expedition here? And just what kind of police are you?'' His voice acquired a nasty edge. "Either you produce identification or God help me you'll never get out of here in one piece. And shut that filing cabinet. There's nothing in there anyway.''

Dubinsky automatically drew out his warrant card: "Metro Police — Sergeant'' — before Sanders could kick him hard enough to shut him up.

"Isn't that nice?'' purred Wilcox. "You gentlemen have

made a grave mistake, Sergeant. You have no jurisdiction in this building. You need permission just to set foot in the hallway." He reached for the telephone on the desk. "I hope you two weren't set on a career in the department, because you won't have one." Then he snarled, "You picked the wrong man to harass this time. I'm not some insignificant backbencher who's afraid of cops. The police commissioner can deal with this. I'll be seeing him on Thursday, and that's about as long as you'll be on the force."

Dubinsky looked appalled. An expression of detached amusement settled itself on Sanders' face. As Wilcox picked up the receiver and began to dial, the door to the inner office opened gently. "There wasn't much in there — is this what you guys were looking for?" asked Eddy, and held up a small green notebook and a black leather briefcase in front of Paul Wilcox's horrified eyes. A sound came out of his throat, part scream and part sob, and he flung himself out the door, slamming it in their faces.

"Well I'll be damned," said Sanders. "It worked."

"Aren't we going after him?" asked Dubinsky.

"Naw. Didn't you hear the gentleman? We don't have any jurisdiction in this building. If he's in the House, no one can get him for now, and if he headed out the door, someone else can pick him up." He dialed a number. After some rapid instructions, he looked around and said, "Hey. Where's Eddy?" The office was deserted.

"Long gone," said Dubinsky. "He's probably picking up his pay as an extra waiter by now — and helping himself to dinner and someone's diamonds at the same time." He picked up the notebook and briefcase. "Let's get out of here," he said. "This place makes me nervous."

Chapter Sixteen

Sanders swept aside all the accumulated memos, reports, coffee cups, and general debris on his desk with his elbow and carefully set down the notebook and the slim black leather briefcase. Gently, he sprung open its two silver fastenings and raised the top. Inside lay a modest pile of photocopied legal-size documents. Dubinsky peered over his shoulder as he lifted out the first one. It was on letterhead of the Pag-Jan Construction Company, and was headed "Tender no. 107593, Ontario Central Detention Centre". Sanders' eyes glittered as he leafed through the pages of figures and handed it to Dubinsky. He picked up the next one. Satisfaction twitched at the corners of his mouth — Beck Construction, same project. The next was from Jamieson Construction; below that, from Del-Fram Construction. Seven in all, from some of the largest and most solidly based firms in the area. "If you owned a construction company, Dubinsky, wouldn't you be happy if someone gave you all this material? I wonder when the deadline for tendering is. In two days, I'll bet; just enough time for someone to adjust a few of his figures after looking at these." Sanders put them all carefully back in the briefcase. "This will have to go to Fraud. My God." He sounded awestruck. "That detention center is a huge project. No wonder he was a little disturbed to see us with the briefcase. Let's have a look at the book."

His train of thought was interrupted by Collins bursting through the door, his normally stolid features pink with excitement. "We got him," he announced. "There's enough coke in that apartment to make trafficking stick tighter than . . . ." Comparisons failed him.

"Where is he?"

"Downstairs, with Wilson, keeping his mouth shut." Sanders started for the door. "But that's not all we found," said Collins following after him. "I found a" — he pulled his notebook out — "pair of women's lounging pyjamas, silk, purple in color, size five. Could have belonged to the Conway woman." He looked like a bird dog with a fat pheasant in his mouth. "They'd been worn, too. Smelled of perfume and were kind of wrinkled a bit."

Grant Keswick was sitting on a straight-backed chair looking coldly angry when the two men were let in to the interview room. He gave no sign of recognition or acknowledgement, but said in clear and clipped tones, "I would like to speak to my lawyer. Until then, I have nothing to say."

"Come off it, Keswick. You lawyer isn't going to be able to talk away four or five thousand bucks worth of coke. Not very bright of you to leave it lying around like that. Besides, that's not what we want to talk to you about, is it? Whose purple silk whatevers are those? Size five. Not many women around that small."

"Maybe not in your circles, pal, but there are in mine. I know a lot of very classy-looking ladies." He smirked in an irritating way, and Sanders stifled a flash of anger as he recollected that Keswick probably considered Eleanor to be one of them. His voice became silky and confidential.

"You have quite a temper, don't you, Keswick? Probably you'd think nothing at all of bashing someone's head in if you discovered she'd been sleeping around. You don't look like someone who'd appreciate that sort of thing from your women. Those silk things were Jane Conway's, weren't they? Someone will be able to identify them, you know. She had friends."

"So what you if they were? We used to see a lot of each other, back before we split up. Last October. That's a long time ago." Keswick laughed casually, but the sweat stood out on his forehead and darkened his shirt in patches; his clothes seemed tight, barely able to contain his stocky frame.

"Then why in hell did you get so mad at her the night before she was killed if you were all through with her? And why hang onto stuff of hers all that time? You don't strike me as the sentimental type, Keswick. What did you do when she told you she was pregnant? Was she trying to make trouble for you? That must have upset you." He drawled out the words.

Keswick froze into silence. "Pregnant?" he said cautiously. "What in hell are you talking about?" Then he pulled his indignation around him again. "I have friends who might have something to say about evidence being planted in my apartment, and about harassment of people in the arts, constant harassment." He attempted to drape his arm carelessly along the back of the chair. "You can't hang this on me, Sanders."

"If you're talking about your pal Wilcox — we've got him too. There are at least fifty men out there looking for him. I wouldn't count on his support right now. He has enough troubles of his own."

Keswick abandoned his efforts to appear casual. "I'm

not saying a word until I see my lawyer." His mouth closed in a thin line, then he spat out, suddenly and spitefully, "and if you're looking for someone to hang Jane's murder on, try her husband. He had a reason."

Sanders shook his head gently. "I don't think we need go that far, Mr. Keswick. Her husband was working in a lab with ten other people while you were smashing Jane's skull in. You should learn to control that temper of yours." He smiled and turned to the other men in the room. "For now, you can book Mr. Keswick for trafficking, Wilson. But be sure you let him call his lawyer."

"Do you think we can get him for the Conway woman?" asked Dubinsky as they walked briskly back to their own corner of the building.

"I don't know," said Sanders, looking gloomily at the squalor they had left behind them. "Probably not. I'm not even sure he did it." He shook his head and reached for the briefcase, still sitting in the middle of his desk. "Has anyone checked Wilcox's house?" he said suddenly. "We're going to look pretty goddamn stupid if he's at home, all quiet and cosy."

Dubinsky reached for the phone, and carried on a hasty muttered conversation. "Not yet. They've established that he's left Queen's Park — they think, although they're a little worried he's found himself a hole there somewhere. They've got Avenue Road pretty well covered, with all the adjacent streets, and there's someone out at the airport by now — and the bus depot and Union Station, just in case. I said we'd send Collins over to his law office and that we'd check out his house."

"Did you put some one else on the sightings and reports coming in on the van?" asked Sanders suddenly.

"Yeah," said Dubinsky. "McNeil. It's going to need more than one guy, though."

Glenn Morrison twitched back the floor-length curtains in

his living room and looked carefully out at the sky. The everlasting spring twilight had finally given way to dark, or at least as much dark as one was likely to get in a fifty-mile radius of the city. Now he would be safe. There was no one to ask him where he was going. The brand on his face would disappear in the darkness. The only problem was that they were always on their guard at night. He sat and thought, drew up plans, rejected them, considered, reconsidered. It was the only way. One last successful raid and he would stop for now.

He stepped out of the shower and scrubbed himself dry. Sitting in the drawer were one last clean shirt, one last clean set of underwear, saved for this particular occasion. He shaved with particular care, avoiding the wounds on his face, and then gently patted some beige liquid from an old bottle that Ginny had left behind over the scratches. The odd scent of the make-up stirred him with excitement. Not bad, he thought. It would look all right under street lights. His hair was getting a little long, but still looked respectable enough. With new jeans and a matching jacket he looked believable enough as an emergency trouble-shooter — maybe from Hydro or the phone company. Confidence surged back through his veins. Those last three misses were just temporary set-backs. That was it. Every good campaigner has to expect set-backs: the great ones don't let them distract them from their larger plans of action. It was time to get started. He straightened his back, squared his shoulders; and started down the stairs to the garage.

Adrienne Wilcox looked at her watch and frowned. If Paul wanted her to give up her evening to look after his hush-hush business for the riding, he could damn well keep up his end of things. She loathed making plausible excuses for him to agitated constituents and back-room boys, and the only reason he was so casual about appointments, she

knew, was because he could trust her to be good at it. She
sat back in the pale green velvet chesterfield, a languorous
French doll in exquisite harmony with her surroundings.
Every piece of furniture in this room had been selected and
arranged with the same rigor as her simple silk dress and
perfect make-up. From eleven in the morning until the last
guest left the last rally or reception at night she was
prepared to be flawless. And Paul appreciated that. She
knew he did, as much as he appreciated her money and her
connections. So where in hell was he now? Out with some
cheap, messy whore. This was the first time he had not
turned up at all when there were documents to be handed
over — but it didn't surprise her. He had been getting
more and more careless lately. It was time to terrify him a
little again. She hadn't had to do that for years — not
since just after Sarah was born. Poor shy, awkward Sarah,
upstairs studying furiously for some test or other. How
had she managed to produce an inept little swat with a lot
of shy, bookish friends? Time for a drink. No — better
save it until she had placated the people coming for that
material. Probably something for a speech that had to be
delivered at noon tomorrow; they would be absolutely
furious. She stood up, wavering between the drinks cabinet
and the telephone, when the discreet front-door chime
dragged her out of the room. She muttered a brief string of
surprisingly forceful crudities as she went. Her daughter
was already half-way down the stairs. "I'll get it, dear.
These people are here to see Daddy on business, and you
aren't going to make much of an impression in that
outfit." Her smile failed to take the sting out of her words.
Sarah turned abruptly and fled.

"Do come in, gentlemen, please," she said gaily, propel-
ing them in the direction of the small room she had just
left. "Do let me get you a drink, please. I was just about to
get one for myself. And let me explain. Poor Paul has been
held up again. There was a reception tonight, as you probably know, but one of his staffers took terribly ill and he

had to go with him to the hospital. He called me from there and said that he should be along soon — he just has to return to Queen's Park and pick up that material for you. It's ready." Her smile and air of calmness masked the frenetic quality of her chatter. "Now — scotch? Or there is wine, of course, and anything else you care to mention, I hope. We're always pretty well stocked here." Her smile became conspiratorial, inviting them into her little private world of political privilege.

Sanders nodded amiably at the suggestion of scotch, shook his head at water, and accepted his drink. He settled into a comfortable chair and looked at his admirable hostess. There was no doubt that she took them for the mob, here to collect their copies of the tenders, and it obviously didn't disturb her at all to be entertaining such men in her pretty sitting room.

"Your husband must have to be out late a great deal," he essayed, to keep up the conversational flow.

"It's not as bad as it might sound," she said, smiling a sweet Pollyanna smile. "Most of the evening engagements are social as well as business, and I can usually find the time to go with him. It's hard on the children, though. Some weeks they only see him on Sunday." She laughed, a sweet, tinkling laugh, as she turned her head to catch sounds from the driveway.

"Not even at breakfast?" asked Sanders. "Isn't that when kids see their fathers?"

"Sometimes," she said, beginning to look distracted. "Half the time, though, he's off for a run, and they just get a glimpse of him coming in, covered with sweat, on his way to the shower. I think that's him now," she said, walking quickly to the window. "Good heavens." She drew back abruptly. "There's a policeman out there, standing by your car. I hope that you — that they haven't . . . ." Her voice trailed away in alarm.

"Don't worry about him," said Sanders. "He's with us. We should have introduced ourselves when we first came in, but you really didn't give us a chance." He flashed his identification under her nose. "We would like to speak to your husband. He isn't home?" She shook her head dully. "When exactly did he telephone you?"

She shrugged her shoulders. "He didn't," she said in a flat voice. "I thought you were here for some stuff he promised one of his constituents. He's just late, that's all. It's not unusual. He gets sidetracked. If it's important I'll have him call you.".

"Don't bother," said Sanders. "We may see you later, Mrs. Wilcox. Good evening." He picked up his coat.

Sanders walked into the office with weary deliberation. The bored constable discreetly parked around the corner from Wilcox's house could do as much as Sanders could out there. This day had already gone on for a very long time and there didn't seem to be any end in sight. "Anything come in yet on Wilcox?" he asked Dubinsky while he picked up the new messages from his desk.

Dubinsky gave him that how-the-hell-should-I-know look but only muttered, "Just a minute. I'll check," as he picked up the phone. His "Nothing so far," however, had minimal impact. Sanders was standing with a slip of paper in his hand and a curious expression on his face.

"Listen to this," he said. "It's a message from a Mr. Smith. 'If you receive delivery of the consignment we were discussing earlier, you are welcome to it. We have withdrawn our claim since the goods no longer fulfil our requirements.' Those bastards have their nerve, don't they? And so much for Wilcox. I suppose he called them from somewhere and told them what happened, and they're dumping him as fast as possible."

"And that means he doesn't know anything of any interest to anybody," grunted Dubinsky. "Or they wouldn't let him go so easily."

"Probably. I suppose his contact was Fielding — he

won't know anyone else. Anyway, I can call the guard dogs off Eleanor now," he said, and made the call. As he hung up, he decided that Eleanor had probably been too groggy to be reassured; but her mother, at least, had been relieved to hear that the siege was over. The thought of Eleanor sleeping peacefully distracted him powerfully; his foggy brain and aching body wanted nothing more than to sink into oblivion beside her.

He was running down a long dark path that was arched with overgrown bushes. Each one that he passed turned into a running man, and then dissolved into a shadow behind another bush. As he grabbed out, an irritating voice penetrated his dream. "Excuse me, sir, but ——" He shook himself awake again. "Sir? I think we may have something here."

McNeil was standing over him, clutching a sheet of paper in his hand, waiting patiently for Sanders to wake up. "Yes? What is it? Don't just stand there."

"A woman called in about noon, apparently. Her baby's been sick and she only just looked at the paper. She said she thought the picture looked a little like her neighbor. She's not sure about the van, though. She said they had a blue Chevy but he sometimes drove a van. She thinks maybe he borrows the van sometimes." Sanders looked up at him with weary lack of interest. "But when I checked out the reports on light brown vans there is one registered to a Glenn Morrison on the same street."

"What did the report say?" asked Sanders irritably. "I thought all those local registrations had been checked out."

"No one home," said McNeil. "And nothing suspicious-looking about the van." He put the report down in front of Sanders. "Morrison's brother-in-law was home and let him in, showed him the van. Do you want me to check it out?"

"Yes, I do. Of course, you'd better check it out. Send

someone back there. And put out that license number just in case." Sanders yawned and reached over to pick up the little green notebook still sitting where he had left it on his desk.

The first page had been ruled off to accommodate a week and was covered with familiar neat handwriting; it was headed "January 1984", and there was a date sitting precisely in the upper left-hand corner of each segment. It had all been done by hand. Sunday the first had one entry; "20 degrees, cloudy, 4-1/2 miles". January 2, in addition to weather and mileage, had a note: "Paul, 4:30". Each page followed that pattern. Some appointments were identified merely by initials; many were with Paul, although those became less frequent as February progressed into March. Once or twice a week there would be a "J." and a time. In the back of the book were pages of names and addresses, two letters of the alphabet per page. "It looks like Conway's missing address book," said Sanders. "Why would Wilcox be hanging on to it?"

"So we wouldn't, I suppose," said Dubinsky sleepily.

"And when did he get it? And how?" As he talked, Sanders pulled a folded note from a pocket in the back cover. A small silver key dropped out with a clatter on the desk. "What does that look like to you, Ed?" he said, staring down at it.

Dubinsky yawned. "A safety deposit box key. Can't do much about it until tomorrow morning when the banks open, though. Unless you want to start dragging bankers out of bed." There was a slightly plaintive note in his last remark. "What's on the paper?"

"It's from Betty, thanking her for the lovely towels."

A harsh jangle interrupted them. Dubinsky leaned over and plucked the ringing phone off its cradle. He made a few indecipherable noises into the receiver and turned to Sanders with the ghost of a smile on his face. "They got Wilcox at the airport with a suitcase full of cash. They're bringing him right down. Does this mean we can get some sleep tonight?''

Constables Joe Williams and Andy Pelletier were sitting morosely in their car, guarding the approach to Highway 401. They were parked in Hogg's Hollow, just to the south of York Mills Road, within smelling distance of a cheerful roadhouse. Pelletier sneezed for the fifth time and blew his streaming nose pathetically. "Christ, but I'll be glad," he was saying, when news suddenly came through that the search was over.

"Great," said Williams. "I could use some coffee right now." He started the engine and pulled out onto Yonge Street, heading north.

"Hey," said Pelletier. "Whereya' going? Let's go down to the Northern." Andy was currently in pursuit of a girl who was temporarily employed at that place. Williams patiently turned right onto York Mills in order to turn around.

"It's okay with me," he said, "but I hope she's working tonight. Their coffee is lousy and the doughnuts are stale."

Pelletier was raising his head gratefully from his handkerchief to answer when he noticed it. "Whaddya know?" he said. "Another brown van. I've been seeing those goddamn things in my sleep." He looked more closely. Even dulled by a cold, Pelletier's eyesight and memory were enviable. "Wait a second," he breathed to Williams. "That's the license number that just came through." The van was parked half-way up the hill, facing the main street, between the subway exit and the first large houses, beside a park. Its engine was running, its parking lights were on, and it looked quite unremarkable. The police car was a couple of hundred yards away, about to make a U-turn. Pelletier nodded at Williams, and began to report their find as he accelerated into a sweep up the hill and in front of the van. The ensuing events were a trifle confused. As

Williams started to brake, the van slipped into gear and surged forward. They met on an angle, demonstrating an interesting problem in physics for those who enjoy such things. The accelerating van spun the police car around and sent it limping up on the sidewalk facing the way it came, but the effort required flipped the van over on its side, where it lay, wheels spinning helplessly. Pelletier and Williams were out and running before their car came to a halt. The distant wail of sirens mingled with the sound of the van's blaring horn.

Fifteen minutes later, the partners stood in meditative silence and watched the ambulance driver and his mate carefully deposit the unconscious Glenn Morrison into the back of their vehicle and speed off. "So that's that," said Williams. "I wonder if he's the right guy?" Pelletier shrugged. Right now he didn't care. "Did someone call for the tow truck for this thing?"

"Yeah," said Pelletier, and sneezed. "One of the guys over there." He pointed at a patrol car that was preparing to leave.

"We'd better have a look inside, you know," said Williams, who had been visited by an unpleasant thought. "There could be something — or somebody — in there."

Pelletier scowled, walked over to the toppled van, leaned over the roof, reached in with a martyred sigh and took the keys out of the ignition. "Come on," he said. "The truck'll be here in a minute." He walked around, tried one key in the back door, then another. The second one turned smoothly. "Come on, Joe," he complained. "Give me a hand to hold this door up." Williams lifted up the top door as Pelletier reached down and freed the latch on the bottom one, then shone his flashlight inside.

"Jesus," said Williams. "Look at that! The whole goddamn thing is lined with broadloom, even the ceiling. Gold, with brown patterns." Then he looked again.

"That's not a pattern," said Pelletier, turning even

paler. The floor and sides of the insulated, padded, carpeted interior were soaked in dark splashes of dried blood.

Sanders' head had scarcely hit his pillow when something jerked him back to consciousness again. He groaned as the light of real morning stabbed his tentatively opened eyes. To hell with it. He wasn't getting up yet. But his tired muscles twitched and quivered as he tried to compose them for sleep again. It was hopeless. Until he took care of whatever was keeping him awake, he could kiss sleep good-bye. It was the good old Puritan mentality he had inherited from a long line of conscientious forebears. What in hell was bothering him? He dragged himself out of bed and into the shower, hoping for inspiration from the pounding of water on his head.

At 7:15 he was opening the door to Grant Keswick's apartment. He had already been into the file and stared at Cassidy and Rheaume's neat list, but couldn't decide whether it was comprehensive or merely contained items they had considered interesting. More likely the latter, since it would have taken them days and reams of paper to do an inventory of the possessions of a well-heeled cocky bastard like that. There was everything in the living room that he would have expected — flashy audio equipment, white and beige furniture and rugs, plants, paintings and wall hangings lending splashes of discreet and irritatingly trendy color. The kitchen was the same. Plants, blond wood, copper and red enamel pots. It had a static and unused quality; if anyone had done more than fry an egg in here he'd be very surprised. The bedroom had almost as much closet space as floor space — king-sized bed, every-thing else modular or built-in, a cosy chocolate rug with a vaguely South-East Asian pattern. He went carefully through the drawers, the closets, the bathroom cabinets, the contents of the clothes hamper. Somehow the pattern of Grant Keswick as anything but a small-time operator didn't add up to anything he was happy with.

He brooded over his coffee and raisin roll at the small French café on the edges of Rosedale while he waited until it would be a reasonable hour to ring the expensive doorbell at Wilcox's solidly impressive house. Nothing trendy there — just old money, well spent. At least now he knew what he was looking for. He glanced impatiently at his watch for the fifth time, put the morning paper back on the rack unread, and tried to inject a note of cordiality into his good-bye to the girl behind the cash.

Adrienne Wilcox had been dragged reluctantly from her bed by her daughter, and if she was surprised by Sanders' desire to inspect her husband's clothes, she concealed the emotion expertly. Sanders concluded that it was more likely that her apathy came with the hour. This was probably the earliest she had been out of bed in years. She left him alone to plow through closets, drawers, and laundry hampers once again. This time he emerged with his eyes glittering in satisfaction. Mrs. Wilcox had disappeared, no doubt back to her bed, apparently unperturbed by her husband's predicament. He said his farewells to the maid who was vacuuming the front hall, the only sign of life in the dark, cold house.

By the time he got downtown again, the working day had begun in earnest. Dubinsky had surfaced, looking repellently undisturbed by lack of sleep. "I located the safety deposit box," he said. "It's in the Bank of Nova Scotia on Adelaide. The manager said he'd open up as soon as we got there. Where in hell have you been? No point in coming in until the banks opened, eh?"

Sanders glowered. "I've been working. Since 6:30 this morning. So cut the crap and drive us to the bank."

Opening up a safety deposit box obviously caused the bank manager something akin to physical pain. Their possession of the key, their identification, and a hastily ac-

235

quired court order were not enough to stem the flow of
muttering. "Most unusual — we don't do this sort of
thing you know — absolute privacy — our customers
don't like to think — " He was clearly intent on getting rid
of them as quickly as possible before anyone figured out
that the police could get into someone's box. Sanders
wrote out and signed the receipt as slowly as he could, en-
joying the man's agonized dance of despair. He was damned if he was going to slink about because some bank
manager didn't like the look of him. Still, eventually they
did depart, carrying a plastic bag which contained a small
bundle of letters. Extravagant girl — hiring a safety
deposit box to hold such a modest cache.

Less than an hour later Sanders walked into the room
where he had spent so much time the night before getting
so little out of a stony-faced Paul Wilcox. The intervening
time had not served to wipe the stubborn glare from his
eyes or the taut control from his jaw. Sanders smiled
pleasantly at him and sat down. "I'm not going to bore
you any more about that little matter of the tenders, Mr.
Wilcox. We'll leave our people in Fraud to deal with that.
It's not in my line of competence anyway. But I do have
something here that I'd like to discuss with you." And
from his pocket he withdrew a small bundle of letters and
spread them on the table in front of him. "They're not all
here, of course. I thought we could just go over some of
the more interesting ones." Wilcox stared incredulously at
the paper laid out in front of him. His face whitened and
then turned gray with shock; the smooth tight muscles
under his cheeks and jaw spread and sagged, making his
stern profile puffy and aged.

"Oh my God," he whispered. "She told me she'd burned them — all of them. She promised." His face fell forward into his hands and he began to cry, with deep racking
sobs of exhaustion and despair.

"Paul McInnes Wilcox," said Sanders, his voice almost

lost in the tumultuous hysterical weeping of the man he addressed, "I charge you with the murder of Jane Annette
Conway."

Eleanor walked into the Indonesian restaurant and looked
around. There he was, sitting over by the wall, his back to
her, reading a paperback. "Hi," she said nervously, and
sat down. "How do you like it?" She gave her head a funny little shake. "He said it was the best he could do
without shaving my head. I don't think he believed my
story." She grinned. "He seemed to think I had a very
kinky boyfriend."

Sanders looked at her critically. Her inch-long hair curl-
ed tightly all over her head. "I like it," he said. "It looks
good on you. Which is a damned good thing, because I'd
be in real trouble if it didn't."

"You said you talked to the guys who did it?"

"Oh no. The guys who did it are back in Detroit or
Montreal or wherever by now, I imagine. They were probably here to look after something else, and came in useful
picking you up. I got a message from the guy who ordered
it done."

"Who is he?"

"How should I know?" Sanders laughed. "If I knew
who he was, I'd be a hell of a lot more famous, or at least
richer, than I am." He stopped to order two bottles of German beer. "No. His communications are anonymous."

"What did he say?"

"Not much. Just that he was getting out of my life
again — actually, our life. He's lost interest in Wilcox and
friends. That's one more thing we don't have to worry
about right now."

"Oh, sure," complained Eleanor. "You weren't lying
on that cold hard floor for hours. And you don't look like
a French collaborator after the war right now, either."

"Come on," said Sanders. "Where's your adventurous

spirit? Besides, it's cute and fluffy-looking. And anyway, when I saw that envelope full of hair, I was expecting much worse.''

"Where is my hair, anyway?"

"Tucked away safely. It's evidence."

"Sure. A trophy, you mean."

"That too. Let's order. Can you work your way through a Rijstaffel?"

Eleanor finally put down her knife and fork with a contented sigh, and then looked at the scraps remaining on the dishes arranged on the hot plate in front of them. "No," she said, "I couldn't eat another green bean right now. Although I could choke down another beer if one were put in front of me." She pushed her plate to one side and leaned comfortably on the table. "You know, I find it hard to believe that Grant Keswick would kill a woman in cold blood like that. People really surprise you sometimes."

"He didn't."

"Didn't what?"

"Kill Jane Conway in cold blood — or even in hot blood, as far as that goes. His vices don't seem to run to murder."

"Then why do you have him locked up for it?" Eleanor shook her head impatiently. "And if he didn't do it, then who did?"

"Well, actually, at the moment he's locked up for trafficking, but he'll probably be out on bail by tomorrow. And once we got into Jane Conway's safety deposit box, it wasn't too difficult to work out. Paul Wilcox had been her lover for some time, and he's one of those guys who have a compulsion to commit themselves to paper when they're in love. Surprising how many people are like that. Anyway, we have a small bundle of tender little notes that she carefully kept together. He tells his 'darling Jane' several times that his life would be perfect if only they could get married, but that he knows she understands that his career would be ruined if he tried to divorce his wife — who isn't an understanding sort of woman, apparently. In one he explains to her that she will definitely have to get rid of the baby, and if she doesn't feel like having it done here, he'll pay for a fancy clinic somewhere else. Obviously nothing was too good for her."

"Except marriage."

"Exactly. But you can tell from her correspondence with her lawyer that she was hell-bent on divorce because she was planning on marrying again. It looks as if she kept those pictures and letters to blackmail Wilcox into marrying her." He gazed deeply into the newly arrived beer for a moment. "It was obviously a mistake on her part."

"It's a damn good thing for Grant that she kept those letters and that you found them. My God, imagine if they still hanged them here!"

"I was never entirely happy about Keswick as anything but a pusher. I just couldn't come up with a mental picture of him actually doing it. I mean, here's a girl, in top physical condition — granted that she's pregnant, of course — who runs miles every week and gets killed in daylight on a public running path, potentially in full view of anyone coming along. How does an actor who boozes and God-knows-what-else catch her?"

"Easy. He waits for her and grabs her. He's maybe in lousy shape, but he's very strong." Eleanor shivered. She remembered that rock-hard arm steering her across the floor at the party.

"Uh uh. How does he know where she runs, when she's coming along, and that someone else isn't going to be running by at just the moment she appears? It was sitting at the back of my mind, ever since I decided the rapist didn't get her, that it had to be someone she went running with. And her husband had one hell of an unshakable alibi. And then Mrs. Wilcox talks about her husband coming in at breakfast time all sweaty from his run — although how she knew is beyond me, since she hasn't been up before ten in years. When I woke up the next morning it clicked. Keswick's apartment doesn't even have a pair of sneakers or sweaty shorts in it — but Wilcox's laundry smells like a locker room after a soccer game. He admitted it; I don't know if he'll keep on admitting it once he discusses it all with his lawyer, but I don't think he's the type that stands up well when he feels guilty.''

"What's going to happen to the others? The ones who kidnapped Amanda?''

"Not all that much — it's going to be almost impossible to make kidnaping stick under the circumstances, and all her injuries were caused by her falling over the edge of the ravine when she ran away. Gruber's going on fast and furious about drug dealing to get himself out of the soup, so that's what the Crown is going for. I'm sorry,'' he said, looking at the expression on her face, "but really you don't want to put Amanda through a court case as well. They'll get a few years.''

"And what's going to happen to the guy that killed all those girls? After all those months of being terrified of him, it seems impossible that he's actually been caught. Where is he?''

"In the hospital. He's suffering from a concussion and a few broken bones, I guess, but he's babbling away about his mission, and failed tactics, and that sort of thing. He seems to think he's in some sort of commando unit. He'll never even see a courtroom. He's really out of it.'' Sanders picked up his glass. He had been profoundly shaken by those honest blue eyes and his earnest explanations. "They'll put him away somewhere until he pulls out of it or is just too old to do any more damage.''

"Horrible,'' said Eleanor. "Was he married?''

"Yes. And his wife is pregnant.'' Sanders shook his head dubiously. "She doesn't seem very unhappy, though, according to Dubinsky. Once she realized she would never have to see him again, that is. She has a good job, and she's clever. Ed liked her. He figures maybe she already has someone else in mind — but he has a very suspicious mind. She said when we were through with the van we could give it back to the dealer or drive it off a cliff — as long as she never had to look at it again. She sounds like a gutsy sort of girl. But he said he never wants to look at anything as disgusting as that van again.''

"So all these people get off practically scot-free — with deals and pleas of insanity. I don't like it.''

"Not really. Morrison will be locked away for years, and who are the others? A two-bit hood, a coked-up actor, and a stupid little cop. We got Wilcox, and I've got ten days off coming to me. Life looks pretty good really.'' He stood up and pulled out her chair. "Come on, let's start my vacation right now," he said, dropping a kiss on her short, tangled curls.